JUST THE WAY THE STORY GOES

Geonn Cannon

Supposed Crimes LLC • Matthews, North Carolina

Published in the United States.

ISBN: 978-1-952150-47-0

www.supposedcrimes.com

This book is typeset in Goudy Old Style.

JUST THE WAY THE STORY GOES

I. TWO BIRDS

Brooklyn, New York
1991

Chapter One

IT WASN'T Miriam Balfour's job to make the coffee. It also wasn't her job to type up and file everyone else's reports, just like cleaning the squad room's only bathroom was supposed to be the janitor's job. Her job, like every other detective in the 2-1 precinct, was to investigate crimes and bring the perpetrator to justice. There was only one difference between her and the detectives who actually got to do their real jobs. It wasn't very hard for a trained detective to figure out what that was. Hell, a civilian off the street could do it.

So it was with more than a little dread that she turned toward the sergeant when he called her named across the bullpen. She didn't dare hope he was about to hand her a case. She would've taken a purse snatcher, a break-and-enter, hell, even vandalism. But in the six months she'd been assigned to the squad, the sergeant and captain both had treated her like a secretary and a maid rolled into one. She was starting to regret the promotion from patrol. She'd spent long frustrated nights lying awake and wondering if it wouldn't be better to go back to the uniform just to get out from behind this damned desk.

When she brushed past the sergeant into the captain's office, Miriam was surprised to see a woman seated in front of him. Mousy hair, large round-rimmed glasses perched on a mousy nose, and doll-like hands folded in her lap. The flowered blouse underneath her maroon vest was buttoned to her throat. Her long brown skirt reached almost to the floor, but stopped just high enough to reveal a pair of two-tone pumps. Even her socks had frills on them.

Maybe someone had broken into a nunnery. Maybe this woman had insisted on a female detective. Despite her cynicism, Miriam allowed herself to hope as she looked away from the guest and met the captain's eye. Captain Jonathan Webster would have looked more at home on the deck of a fishing trawler. He was a short man, barely topping five feet, and most days he acted like everyone in the world owed him a debt and they were months overdue on paying.

The sergeant, a stick insect without a chin named Peter Babbitt, closed the door and stood next to it like a sentry.

"You wanted to see me, sir?"

"Detective Miriam Balfour," Webster said in his deep baritone, "this is Jane Ross. She's a reporter for the *Sentinel*."

She nodded, still not understanding. Jane Ross looked confused as well.

Webster held his hand out to Miriam, then at Jane, and then back again. Neither woman budged. "There you go, Miss Ross," he finally said, as if he'd explained everything they needed to know.

"I don't understand," the reporter said.

"You wanted access." Webster sounded like he was talking to a child. "Here you go. Balfour is one of my newest detectives and she's all yours for the ten days."

Miriam said, "I'm sorry, 'ten days'?"

"*One* of your detectives?" Jane said at the same time. "Captain, I asked for permission to observe your entire squad."

"And this is what's called a compromise." Webster had already opened the file in front of him. "You can have full access to Detective Balfour~"

"I didn't agree~"

He cut her off. "~or you can turn around and leave right now. Honestly? I don't care which it is, because either way you're out of this office and out of my hair."

Jane looked at Miriam, then back to Webster. "It's my intention to write a thorough, complete story about~"

"I don't give a damn what your intentions are," he snapped, his eyes locking onto her with such intensity it had to have felt like a slap. "I'm not letting you lurk in the corner and second guess my detectives. We've got enough people playing armchair quarterback out there on the street without letting you snoop and sneak around. But I know you'll never shut up, so you can follow Balfour. Take it or fucking leave it."

Miriam squared her jaw and looked down at her shoes. The shoes she'd bought as a reward for her new position. Shoes she'd intended to get scuffed and worn down following leads, interviewing witnesses, chasing suspects. Shoes that still looked as pristine as the day she took them out of the box. She knew exactly what Webster was doing. She got saddled with a reporter, who in turn didn't get access to anything worth writing about, and they both kept each other busy for a few days.

Two birds with one stone.

"I don't suppose I get a say in this," Miriam said.

"You wanted better assignments, Balfour," he said. "This one is gonna make you famous. And you, Ross. These men are rough and tumble. They're drunks. They smoke cigars. They swear. Do you really want to hang around with them the next few days? Really get to know them, figure out what's in their male heads? Or do you want to write about the first female detective in this precinct? That's a hook right there. You can talk about hair and makeup tips."

Miriam was glad she'd already put her hands behind her back so Webster wouldn't see her ball them into fists. Jane looked down at her lap and twisted her lips to one side.

"I suppose if I don't have a choice, I'll take what I'm given."

Webster nodded and turned his attention back to the file. Babbitt opened the office door. Miriam understood she'd been dismissed, and Jane seemed to get the message as well. She picked up her bag and rose from her chair. Since the captain had no intention of ending the meeting politely, Miriam simply walked out and went back to her desk. She could sense the reporter following her but didn't look back. It was already after lunch. Most days she was able to leave by five o'clock when the night squad came in. She could cope with a shadow until then, and she'd spend the night figuring out ways to get rid of her permanently.

Jane stopped next to the desk and looked around for an empty chair. She finally found one and pulled it over.

"What paper did he say you worked for?" Miriam said as Jane sat down. "*Sentinel?*"

"That's right."

"That's a rag."

Jane flinched and twisted her lips again. "Well," she said, keeping her voice steady, "they can't all be the *Times*. Some might say that a more modest paper, with a smaller circulation, has the freedom to be more honest in its reporting since it's less beholden to shareholders and advertisers who–"

"Jesus Christ, did you have that rehearsed?"

Jane swallowed the rest of what she had been planning to say. "There's nothing wrong with working for a smaller paper."

Miriam shook her head. "Don't expect anything worth your time here. You're going to spend ten days sitting in that chair watching me type up everyone else's reports and maybe doing a coffee run if the machine craps out again."

"But you're–"

"A detective?" Miriam picked up the name plate from the front of her desk. She turned it around and examined it as if for the first time. "So it would seem. I have a badge and a gun, the whole thing. But watch. Keep a record in that little notebook I see poking out of your bag. Whenever a case comes in, he's going to call one of these fuckers–" She gestured at the other detectives around the bullpen. "And if they're all occupied, he'll give it to Peter Rabbit or take it himself. Because someone has to be here to answer the phones and take the lunch orders from everyone else."

Jane sighed. "I wonder what that's like. Because I've never had a huge story yanked out from under me. But I've gotten a lot of free detergent so I could review it for the Happy Housewife column. Oh, and I get to read all the depressing relationship letters that get sent in to Dear Donna. That will make you want to take a long walk off a short pier, let me tell you. Some of these men out here..." She shook her head. "The only reason my editor agreed to let me write this story is because it got me out of *our* office for ten whole days. They probably think it's Christmas over there."

Miriam said, "Well, one person's Christmas is another person's..." She trailed off.

"What's the opposite of Christmas?" Jane asked.

"You tell me. You're the writer."

Miriam took the top report off the pile in the corner of her desk. Bill Dooling, with his horrible penmanship and pencil scratches so smudged by the fact he was left-handed. Typing up his reports was like transcribing a foreign language, and she was actually grateful for something that would take up all her focus. Maybe if she ignored the reporter she would just go away. She clipped the page to her lampshade and positioned her fingers over the typewriter keys.

"You still use typewriters?" Jane looked around the room, apparently surprised by the lack of any desktop monitors. "Wouldn't it be easier to get computers?"

"Easier?" Miriam said. "Hell yes. Expensive, too. The upgrade has been a few months away since I was in uniform. I don't expect it to happen here any time soon."

"That's frustrating."

"Not for me. I hate the things." She patted the side of her typewriter. "I trust this. I know this. I don't need to learn some stupid new system."

"Hm."

She was halfway through the report when Jane uncrossed her legs and stood up. "You mentioned there was coffee?"

"Over there." Miriam nodded without looking away from her work. "Use a paper cup. People get pissed if you use their mugs."

Jane made a noise of understanding and headed away. She was gone longer than Miriam would have imagined necessary for the task of getting coffee, but she didn't intend to question the silence. She finished the report and started on the next one. She was nearly finished when Jane finally returned and placed a cup of fresh, steaming coffee down next to the typewriter.

Miriam looked at the mug. It was her mug, kitschy tourist bait with the Statue of Liberty on it. More importantly, the smell coming from it was not the usual odor of the department's coffee.

Jane had taken her seat again and took a sip from her paper cup. "I asked one of the detectives which mug was yours."

"What did you put in it?" Miriam picked up the mug and brought it closer to her face.

"Coffee."

"Our coffee doesn't smell like this."

"Yeah, about that. You guys know those machines are supposed to be cleaned, right? And new filters? And there are bags of fresh grounds in the cupboard."

Miriam took a sip. It was actually very, very good. She kept her face neutral and put the mug back down.

"You clean the coffee machine once, you become the coffee machine cleaner. I've got enough janitorial work around here without adding to the list."

"How do you think I became such an expert on making a decent pot? You're looking at the dedicated coffeemaker of the New York *Sentinel*."

Miriam said, "Ah, so they're going to miss you after all."

Jane chuckled. "Yeah, maybe so. Maybe they'll actually appreciate me when I get back."

"Well, they just have to say the word and they can have you back early."

While Miriam typed, Jane sipped her coffee and scanned the room. She occasionally opened her notebook and wrote something down. Miriam wanted to know what the hell she was writing, but she didn't care enough to ask. Whatever kept her busy and quiet.

At one point, an hour after Jane arrived, Webster came out of his office. "Abbamonte? Anyone know where Eric's gone off to?"

Dominic Clark, across the room, didn't look up from his typewriter. "Taking a statement from the pizzeria owner."

"Shit." Webster scanned the room. Miriam was sitting with her back to the captain, but she could feel his eyes linger on her briefly before continuing on. "What about Dooling? Where's he?"

"Got a lead on that prowler," Clark said. "Doing a stakeout."

"You're not busy," Jane said to Miriam under her breath. "Volunteer."

Miriam said, "It doesn't work that way."

"Babbitt," the captain finally said. "You take this one. Couple got held up at gunpoint."

Jane stood up. "Excuse me."

"Sit your ass *down*," Miriam said through clenched teeth.

Everyone in the room looked at Jane as if she had appeared out of thin air. She didn't seem to notice the attention, gesturing at Miriam.

"You have a detective right here. I'm sure the sergeant has better things to do than take a statement. Send Detective Balfour."

"It was an armed suspect," Webster said. "I'm not sending a lady into a situation like that."

"The suspect is long gone," Jane said. "Surely there's no--"

"Babbitt is going," Webster said, then jabbed a finger at Jane.

"And if *you* think you're in any position to dictate how this squad is run, you can just go ahead and not come back tomorrow. *Capisce?*"

Jane lowered her head slightly but didn't say anything.

"And you, *Detective Balfour...* if you can't even keep a girl reporter under control any better than this, maybe you should think twice about coming in tomorrow, too."

Miriam was glaring down at her desktop. "Won't happen again, sir."

"See that it doesn't." He handed Babbitt a paper with the victims' address on it, then went back into his office.

As soon as his door closed, Miriam shot to her feet. She pointed at Jane the same way Webster had a moment earlier.

"*You.* Stairs. *Now.*"

She turned and stormed to the access door, slamming it open and stepping out onto the landing. The door swung shut behind her, almost hitting Jane in the face. She closed the door behind her.

"I was just trying to--"

"Well, *stop*," Miriam interrupted. "What do you think would happen if I walked into the office of your rag and demanded the editor gave you an interview with the President? Or insisted you get to write the front page headline for the week? Maybe if I said it real nice and asked with sugar on top."

Jane's face was slowly turning pink. "I get it."

"Do you?" Miriam moved closer until their noses were almost touching. "Because if you ever fucking do *anything* like that again, I will gladly walk you out of this precinct myself. And I will make sure that no one from the two-one ever speaks to anyone at the *Sentinel* ever again. Do I make myself clear, Miss Ross?"

"Yes, ma'am," Jane said.

Miriam looked at her watch. "Shift ends at five. I think it's abundantly clear that nothing of any interest is going to happen here today. Right?"

Jane nodded, her eyes still on the floor.

"Come back tomorrow. Eight AM." She opened the door to go back to her desk. "Webster said you're here for ten days, right?"

"That's right."

"Today counted as one," Miriam said. "Tomorrow, try to keep your mouth shut. And be prepared to make coffee again. You might really have found your calling with that." She looked down at Jane's dress. "Do you own slacks?"

Jane looked down as well. "Yes..."

"Wear them tomorrow. If I *do* end up getting assigned something, I don't want to worry about you hobbling along behind me."

She went into the bullpen and let the door shut behind her. It was only when she got back to her desk that she realized Jane had taken her bag with her. Apparently she'd anticipated the day being cut short and hadn't intended to come back from the stairwell.

Good. It meant she was capable of learning and reading a room.

There was a chance the next nine days wouldn't be complete torture.

Jeremy and Samantha were at the dinner table when Miriam got home. There was an open coloring book and a collection of toys which, at first glance, seemed unrelated. She hung up her coat and went to get a closer look. "What's going on over here?"

"Helping her with homework," he said.

Miriam put a hand on top of their daughter's head. "What kind of homework does a four year old get from pre-school?"

"The kind I can actually help with," Jeremy said, raising a crayon and waggling it like a cigarette. "Coloring shapes and finishing patterns. When she gets to math more complicated than addition, I'm doomed."

"You and me both," Miriam said. "I'll get started on dinner."

She went into the kitchen. Jeremy followed her. "Ah. Yeah, about dinner..."

"I think we have some ground beef. We can do spaghetti..."

"It will just be you and Sammy tonight."

She turned to look at him. "Did you already eat?"

He put his hands in his pockets and looked at the counter to avoid eye contact. "No." That was the only word he got out before his ability to speak seemed to fail him. "I'm... I've actually got... I'm going to meet..."

Miriam figured it out. "You have a date."

"Not a date," he said quickly. He lowered his voice so Sam wouldn't overhear. "It's... just dinner. Having a meal with a, um, a friend from work."

Miriam said, "A guy friend?"

He didn't answer.

She smiled. "So. A date."

Jeremy sighed. "I don't know. I didn't want to spring it on you like this. It-it was just a last minute thing."

"You don't have to explain. More spaghetti for me and Sam." She opened the cabinet and took out the noodles. "Do you know how late you'll be coming home?"

"Probably not too late. If it's past Sammy's bedtime, I'll keep quiet. But it shouldn't go that long. It really is just grabbing a bite to eat."

Miriam was focusing more on dinner than anything he was saying. "It's fine with me if it's a date. I just don't want you coming in and waking her up."

"I won't." He leaned against the counter. "She knows about you, by the way. About us, and Sammy, and this whole..." He jerked his head to indicate the apartment. "The separation and everything. She thinks it's weird. But she understands. I think she wants to meet you before anything actually happens, just to be sure I'm not lying."

"Why would someone lie about this?" She snapped her fingers, pretending an epiphany. "Oh right. Men, trying to get laid."

He smiled awkwardly. "I'd like to think she knows I'm not that kind of asshole. But I can't blame her for being suspicious. The odds aren't on my side with that sort of thing."

"I'll write a note and pin it to your jacket. I have no interest in meeting her or giving my blessing for anything."

"That's fair." He checked his watch. "If you've got things covered here, I should..."

"Go. I can handle spaghetti and meatballs." She pointed at the dining room. "And you said it was shapes and patterns?"

"And coloring inside the lines."

"I think I can fake it well enough to take over."

He smiled. "Well. Okay, then. I'll, um, I'll see you in a bit."

"Have fun."

He left the kitchen and went to get ready. A few minutes later, after Miriam got the food started, she went back into the dining room and took Jeremy's seat. Sammy had continued on her worksheet during their conversation and seemed to be almost done.

"Hey, baby," Miriam said. "How are you doing on these?"

Sammy pointed at one of the entries she'd left blank. "That

one's too hard."

"Hm. Okay. Let's see if we can figure it out together."

"Did Daddy go?"

"Yeah, he's having dinner with someone tonight. A friend of his from work."

Sammy nodded solemnly. She picked up a purple crayon, examined it, then colored in a square. Miriam hated their arrangement, even though it had been her idea. It was just the only solution that made any sense for them. She'd realized about a year earlier that she'd lost any romantic feelings she'd once had for Jeremy, and that lack was starting to curdle into resentment and anger. Ending things had been the only way to preserve their relationship so they could continue raising Sammy together.

And to that end, it had worked. She could suddenly tolerate his presence now that he was sleeping in another room. Now that she didn't feel obligated to play the doting wife, she was much more willing to support him whenever it was required. He couldn't afford his own apartment on a teacher's salary, not unless he left Brooklyn, so he stayed in the apartment to be close to Sammy. And if the oafs at work thought she was taken, they were much more tolerable in their harassment and innuendos. As far as they were concerned, she and Jeremy were still a perfectly happy couple.

Dating was a new thing, though. He'd been on three that she knew about, and every time it was an awkward dance where she had to grant him permission. It was more annoying than anything else, and she was starting to wonder if she should start saying no just to see what he'd do. Maybe he would start keeping nights like this secret. That would have been fine with her. It was more preferable than going through the whole song and dance.

She was mostly annoyed because she hadn't had the inclination to follow his lead. She never met eligible men, not that she was particularly interested in finding another Jeremy. He was a perfectly fine man, she couldn't imagine anyone being a better choice, and her feelings for him hadn't even lasted a decade before they faded away. If she couldn't maintain a relationship with him then it didn't seem like it was possible.

Maybe she was just one of those people who was all about her job and her kid. There were worse fates, and far worse lives she could have ended up living.

CHAPTER TWO

JANE WAS waiting outside the bullpen at a quarter to eight the next morning. She wore her only pair of slacks, as directed, but they were a size too big and had to be cinched to her waist by a thick belt. She self-consciously tried to cover it with a sweater but, as she waited for Miriam to arrive, she worried the day would be too warm to justify it. She could take it off, the thin t-shirt underneath clearly showed the outline of her bra, and she had no intention of spending all day with the male cops ogling her.

Those same male cops ignored her as they passed by into the bullpen. She checked her watch to confirm the time, then followed the one she thought was Bill Dooling inside. He sensed he had picked up a tail and twisted to look back at her without slowing down.

"I ain't gonna feed you, kitten. I thought you got adopted by Balfour."

"She's not here yet, so I thought I'd--"

"No one is gonna talk to you." He groaned as he lowered himself into his chair, which let out its own sound of complaint. "Balfour really was your best shot, and we all saw her giving you the cold shoulder yesterday. So if I was you, I'd cut my losses and go find another story. There's got to be a bake sale somewhere in Brooklyn that needs to be covered."

Jane sat down in the empty chair next to his desk. "Or you could get me *and* Detective Balfour out of your hair for the day." She looked at the folders on his desk. "There's got to be some case here that isn't worth your time and effort to investigate. Some open-and-shut thing you want to get rid of. Let Balfour take it and everyone will be happy."

He grunted and looked at the files. Finally he leaned forward and began searching them until he found something specific. He tossed it in her direction and she caught it before the papers could slide out.

"This came in a couple days ago. Hooker. Suicide by OD."

"You've already confirmed it was suicide? Why is it still open?"

"Because you have to go through the motions. But that's what it is. That's what it always is. The chick spent everything on drugs, couldn't afford her rent anymore, decided she didn't want to be homeless. I was going to wait until tomorrow and file it, but hey, if Balfour wants a shot... Maybe she can find the guy who provided the drugs, I dunno, but odds are she's just going to put on a show and then sign the papers to close it."

"You weren't going to investigate this at all?"

"It's not like her family is going to pound down the door demanding answers, kid. Lady made her choices and she ended up right where those choices always lead. Maybe you can figure out a way to fill out some newsprint with it."

Miriam finally arrived and headed straight for her desk, either ignoring or not aware of Jane's presence in the room. Her dark hair was down today, and she was wearing a blue turtleneck with what looked like dried milk on the sleeve. She tossed her jacket over the back of her chair and opened the bottom drawer of her desk to toss her purse inside. It was only then that she acknowledged Jane was standing nearby watching her.

"Coffee," Miriam said.

"Sure. But..." Jane stepped forward and held out the file. "You have a case."

"I have a..." She frowned at it, then looked past Jane at Dooling. He smiled and lifted his coffee in a 'you're welcome' gesture. She clenched her jaw and glared at the reporter. "You went begging for scraps?"

Jane was suddenly afraid she'd made a horrible mistake. "I thought... th-there are plenty of cases to go around, and I thought that-"

Miriam snatched the file from Jane's hands so quickly that it made her yelp in surprise. She flipped it open and scanned the report.

"For fuck's sake, Bill," she said. "Dead hooker? Seriously?"

Dooling laughed and held his hands out to either side. "You're always saying they're as important as any other victim, right?"

Miriam swore under her breath and glared at Jane, then grabbed her coat again. She pivoted and marched back the way she had just come. She was already through the stairwell door before she called back to Jane.

"I'm not waiting for you!"

"Shit," Jane muttered.

She hurried to catch up, ignoring the snickers of the detectives in the bullpen. She closed the distance quickly, but Miriam didn't acknowledge her until they reached her car. She put the file on the roof and slid it across to the passenger side.

"Address."

"Uh... it's, uh..." She skimmed the report as she got into the car. "Red Hook."

"Of course it is."

Miriam started the car and Ernie from *Sesame Street* started singing 'Rubber Duckie.' Miriam swore under her breath and ejected the cassette. She opened the glove compartment, put the tape in a plastic case, and put it back in. Jane watched the whole procedure and then looked at Miriam.

"You listen to--"

"I have a daughter. I was taking her to preschool." She backed out of the slot. "She likes Ernie."

"Oh. That makes sense." She struggled for something else to say. "I like the song about living on the Moon."

Miriam grumbled something under her breath. Then, after almost a minute, said, "Yeah, that one is pretty good."

Jane stopped herself from smiling. It wasn't much, but it was the smallest crack in the shell. She didn't intend to throw in the towel before her ten days were up, and it would be a lot easier if Miriam was on her side.

They stayed quiet for the rest of the ride, save for Miriam asking for the exact address and Jane reading it off the report. Jane kept her hands in her lap and her eyes out the window, trying her best to be a non-entity in the car. Miriam broke the silence when she parked in front of the building.

"You don't go into the apartment, you don't touch anything, you don't talk to anyone. If there's anything I think you need to know, I will tell you. Is that understood?"

"It's understood, yes."

The address was across the street from a playground that looked more like a torture chamber for any children brave or stupid enough to venture into it. A trio of bicycles, one with a broken seat, were piled on the front steps near a pile of smashed cigarette butts. Jane followed Miriam into the building and tried to ignore the smell. She didn't want to come off as precious or fragile, but it was a trial not to cover her nose with her sleeve.

Miriam led the way upstairs. Their destination was apartment 2C, marked by a single strip of yellow crime scene tape across the door. The apartment key had been included in a small baggie clipped to the file. Miriam unlocked the door and turned to Jane.

"Stay in the hall. Keep your mouth shut."

Jane nodded, and Miriam ducked under the yellow tape. She shut the door behind herself, cutting off any attempts Jane might have made at snooping.

Left alone in the hall, she wasn't entirely sure how to fill the time. First she leaned against the wall across from the crime scene, then she paced ten steps left, ten steps right, and then back again. She could hear TVs playing in most of the apartments, music, raised voices. She smelled food being cooked, even though it was a weird time of day where neither breakfast nor lunch seemed likely.

A door down the hall opened. A Black woman around Jane's age stepped out, narrowed her eyes at the person lurking in the hallway, then disappeared back inside. She returned a few seconds later with a Polaroid camera. Jane was so surprised by it that she only had time to widen her eyes before the woman snapped a picture of her.

"Now," the woman said, "you want me to give the police a name to go with the face?"

"I'm... I..." Jane couldn't say 'I'm not allowed to talk,' because that was ridiculous. "I'm with the police. I mean I'm not police. But..." She pointed at the apartment. "There's police in there. Detective Miriam Balfour. She's investigating the death at this address. I came with her."

The woman was shaking the photo as it developed. "Investigating? Kimmy didn't even get a write-up in the newspaper, and you expect me to believe a *detective* is here digging for clues?"

"It's the truth." Jane remembered the name from the file was

Kimberly Bremer, and she remembered what Dooling had said back at the precinct. "Kimmy is as important as any other victim."

The neighbor sniffed and shook her head. "You think she was just a dumb hooker who shot up too much, either on purpose or because she was too dumb to know better. They're not going to waste time on this. You said the detective's name was *Miriam?*" She laughed harshly and looked down at the picture, then held it out to Jane. "You look like a deer in headlights. Now I know why."

Jane took the photo, pinching it between two fingers. "The death may have been accidental, or suicide. But everyone deserves to-"

"Who are you talking to?" Miriam ducked back under the tape and joined them in the hall. "I told you to keep your mouth shut." To the neighbor, she said, "Who are you?"

"Bess Forester."

"Go back into your apartment, Bess Forester."

Bess brought her camera up to her face again.

"Don't-"

She snapped a photo. "Just so we know if you come around to 'investigate' any other deaths 'round here, Miss Police. It'll be helpful to know who to look for."

"This isn't just lip service, Miss Forester," Miriam said. "I want answers. And part of that is talking to people who knew Miss Bremer. I'm assuming that would be you?"

Bess said, "I knew Kimmy, sure. Talked at the mailboxes all the time. Passed in the hallway. Borrowed shit from each other sometimes. I knew her well enough to know she didn't touch anything stronger than marijuana, and that piece of shit in a uniform who was here the night she died was talking out his ass if he expected anyone to believe she died of an OD. Girl cried through her flu shots, she's not using the needle for fun. No way. But you hear dead hooker-"

Miriam interrupted, "She had a sober apartment."

Bess looked at her. "Say what?"

"No syringes, no kits, nothing that even hinted at the fact she used regularly. Or at all. The person who lived *there*," she pointed at the apartment, "wouldn't have died of a drug overdose."

Bess looked completely shocked. Jane was sure her face looked similar, with the deer in the headlights gawp all over again.

"You talked to the uniformed officer the night Kimmy died?" Bess nodded. "Do you remember his name?"

Bess shook her head no, but Jane said, "It was in the file."

"Good." Miriam kept her attention on Bess. "So you were here on the night. Did you see anyone or hear anything suspicious? Maybe she brought home a date, or a customer?"

"Oh I don't know, I kind of learned not to pay attention to that sort of thing." Bess's voice was small now. She sounded like someone who had just realized she was on the wrong side of an argument. "I can't say for sure either way if I heard anything. I-I just didn't pay attention anymore."

"That's all right." Miriam reached into her coat pocket and brought out a business card. She held it out between two fingers. "If you remember anything else that might be useful."

Bess took the card. Miriam closed the apartment door and locked it again. She motioned for Jane to follow her and headed for the stairs.

"Detective." Bess caught up with them. She held out the photo she'd taken of Miriam and Jane. "I'm sorry for jumping to conclusions about you."

Miriam looked down at the picture. Finally, she took it and handed it to Jane. "Considering how the people here have been treated in the past, those conclusions were probably justified. No apologies necessary. Have a nice afternoon."

Jane watched Bess go back into her apartment with her camera, then hurried to catch up with Miriam again.

"Were you just being nice back there?"

"When?"

"When you implied Kimmy's death was a cover-up."

Miriam stopped and looked at her. "What part of implying her neighbor had been murdered would be *nice*? That woman is probably terrified now. She might have suspected foul play but now that a cop has told her it's plausible, she's not going to sleep well for a week. Maybe never again. So. No, Miss Ross. I wasn't being *nice*."

"I didn't mean—"

"I know what you meant." Miriam continued toward the car. "Nothing is gained by lying to people. Giving false hope or placating someone who is screaming in your face. You end up screwed either way. The only real option is to stay calm and tell them the truth."

"I guess that makes sense." She opened the passenger side door and got in. "So where are we going now?"

Miriam checked the file. "Now we're going to find Billy Callahan and find out why he decided to lie about solving a case while the body was still warm."

Jane familiarized herself with the details of the case while Miriam drove back to the precinct. The victim was Kimberly "Kimmy" Bremer, twenty-six, known to local patrol cops as a prostitute. She'd been picked up for soliciting seven times in the past year. Jane thought that sounded like a lot, but Miriam didn't have any reaction when she read it aloud.

Her body was found when a neighbor - not Bess Forester - called the landlord to complain about loud music coming from the apartment. When there was no answer to his calls or knocking, he let himself in and found her on the bathroom floor propped up against the tub. The syringe was still in her arm, which was still tied off with a length of rubber hose. She had been dressed for a night in: pajama pants with cartoon characters on them, pink T-shirt, no makeup, feet in fuzzy slippers.

"This is awful," Jane said. "You really think someone killed her?"

"I think if she regularly used, I would have seen *some* sign of it. If not physically, the apartment would have given it away. Junkies aren't known for being neat and tidy with their trash."

"It could have been her first time. That happens, right? Someone decides to try the hard stuff, and they get unlucky." She looked down at the list of clothes Kimmy had been wearing. "She could have just been planning to have a relaxing night at home and wanted something to take the edge off."

Miriam shrugged. "Sure. It's possible. And when we meet Billy Callahan, we'll know if he seems like the kind of cop who would have connected those dots in the time it took the medical examiner to arrive."

From the tone of her voice, Jane doubted she thought that was a plausible answer.

It was easy to find Billy Callahan. Miriam asked the desk sergeant, who pointed her in the right direction, and they found him at a desk on the second floor. Jane trailed behind and tried to do her best impression of a shadow. Callahan looked like he had been hijacked from a farm and put in a police costume. He had ruddy skin, a pale blonde flat top, and just seeing Miriam approach was enough to put him on the edge of a nervous breakdown.

"Why did you call this an OD?" She slapped the folder down on his desk.

"What?"

She flipped the folder open and jabbed the report. "You officially declared Kimberly Bremer's death as an overdose. She hasn't even had an autopsy yet. So why were you so confident?"

He frowned and skimmed the file. "Uh. Uh, I... I don't... um... Wasn't she? I mean, the place where she was living? A-and she, she had a record. She was a hooker, right? She literally had a needle in her arm, ma'am. If I'd wasted time on an autopsy, my sergeant would've smacked me for wasted time and resources on it."

Jane could read Miriam's face well enough to know she agreed with what Callahan was saying, but she didn't want to admit it.

"Look, if I'm wrong, I'm-I'll go over it again, it's just-"

"Don't bother," Miriam said. "It got thrown upstairs despite your best efforts to close it. Next time, do better."

He nodded rapidly.

Miriam gathered the report and left him looking shell-shocked. Jane hurried after her.

"Now what do we do?"

"Now *I* go to the medical examiner and pray the body is still available to do an autopsy. They might still be trying to find next of kin before they cremate her."

Jane said, "Wouldn't they do an autopsy anyway? Just to confirm cause of death?"

Miriam sighed. They were in the hallway now, but she lowered her voice. "Callahan was right. They don't have the time or resources to do that with such an apparently obvious case. The same thing probably would have happened if she'd been found with a bullet hole in her temple and a gun in her hand. Digging deeper based on one witness and a hunch isn't much better than Callahan jumping to conclusions based on the scene he walked into."

"So what's next with the case?"

"We wait," Miriam said. "And if there's anything worth investigating, we'll follow the trail."

Jane said, "I guess it's pretty good that I got this case from Dooling, huh?"

Miriam glared at her. "What, are you looking for an apology? A pat on the head? I'm still pissed off you did that. You're here for a week. One damn week. And then you get to fuck off back where you came from. But I'll still be here. I'll still have to work with these assholes. Chances are they're already loading up jokes about how I need you to get cases for me, or planning to load me up with every dead hooker that comes across their desk. And yes, they deserve as much attention as anyone else, but honestly, tragically, nine times out of ten, it *will* be exactly what it looks like. And that gets fucking depressing in a job that's already top tier depressing on a good day. Whatever happened to Kimberly Bremer, you're not getting Brownie points for crossing that line."

Jane had shrunk under the force of Miriam's monologue. It took her a second to gather her wits and follow her back upstairs.

Chapter Three

THE GOOD news turned out to be that the medical examiner had already done a tox screen on Kimberly Bremer. The bad news, at least from an investigation standpoint, was that it proved Miriam's hunch that the victim hadn't been a drug user. She did have heroin in her veins, but her heart had already stopped by the time the drug was injected. There was still no definitive answer as to her actual cause of death, so manner of death had been upgraded from accidental to suspicious.

According to Kimberly's file, four of her most recent arrests occurred at or in the vicinity of a bar called The Cellar. Miriam determined there was a good chance either she'd been there the night she was killed, or someone there might be able to offer a lead.

Jane spent the drive to the bar trying to sort out her conflicting emotions. She felt victorious and shitty in equal measure. She'd uncovered a murder, yes, and she'd saved Kimmy Bremer from vanishing into a cabinet somewhere, but the girl was still dead. There wasn't a happy ending waiting for her when this was all said and done. The only thing they could hope for was justice, and she didn't know if that would be enough.

The bartender spoke to them through the diamond-shaped glass in the door. "We don't open until five o'clock."

Miriam held up her badge. "I have some questions."

The man behind the glass groaned, shook his head, and

disappeared from sight. A moment later the door swung open.

"Nothing happened here last night."

"What about a few nights ago? Do you know this woman?"

Miriam took out the photo of Kimberly Bremer. It had been in her file, the picture from her driver's license. Jane had thought the girl had the saddest smile she'd ever seen, but she didn't know if she was projecting her knowledge of Kimberly's fate onto the picture. Or maybe it was just the shitty DMV lighting. Either way, she looked like she'd just woken up, with her lips were pressed together in a tight almost-smile and center-parted hair descending into tangles where it framed her face.

He looked at the picture, squinted, then pinched the bottom edge to angle it toward the light. "Is that Kimmy?" Miriam confirmed it was. "She's in here all the time. She's usually made up better than this, though. I read about what happened in the paper. Shame."

"So you believe that she died of an overdose?"

He shrugged. "Wouldn't be the first hooker who stopped hanging out here because of that. I try running those guys off, but they're like cockroaches. If I get rid of one, there's two more around the corner. It's not worth the effort trying to keep them out. And those girls are going to get their fix no matter where it comes from. I figured it's better happening in a relatively safe place with witnesses around, you know what I mean?"

Jane was shocked that he was being so open with a cop about drugs being sold in his place of business. Miriam seemed unphased, however, and just wrote down a note.

"Was she in here the night she died? This would've been two nights ago."

"Last time I saw her..." He lifted his head like the answer was on a billboard posted above their heads. "Yeah, it was probably two, three nights ago. She usually set up station at the end of the bar near the jukebox. She nursed a drink for an hour or two while she waited for someone to take the bait. It didn't take that long most nights. But that night, no, I don't think she picked anyone up. I remember she was here for a long time, maybe two and a half hours? Then she finally settled her tab and left."

Jane was stunned. "You remember all that about one random customer?"

Miriam glared at her for speaking, but the bartender was already answering.

"They show up often enough, you start to build up a relationship. You get to talking some nights, get to know each other. I can't swear to everything I just told you, like under oath or something, but to the best of my recollection, yeah, that's how it went down."

"So she was a regular?" Miriam asked.

He shrugged. "Regular enough. I knew her name and what she liked to drink. If things were slow, we would talk about baseball or music or whatever."

"Did *she* have any regulars? Guys who maybe got a little possessive?"

"We didn't talk about her work. I never saw anyone like that, but I don't know either way."

Miriam took out her card and handed it to him. "If you think of anything else, give me a call."

He nodded and glanced at the card before slipping it into his pocket. "You really think she was killed?"

"It's looking that way."

He sighed and looked down the street. "I mean. I never saw her buy from anyone. And she never seemed like a junkie. But when I read that, it just sort of made sense, you know?"

Miriam shrugged, but it was clear she had more she was holding back. "Have a nice day."

He nodded and went back inside.

On the way back to the car, Jane said, "What did you stop yourself from saying back there?"

Miriam sighed and shook her head. "It just sort of made sense. Oh, dead hooker? Needle in her arm? Sure. This guy *knew her*, and she was sitting in a drug grocery store, and he never saw her high or buying anything, but he *still* just accepted it. Because of her job."

"A lot of prostitutes are hooked," Jane said. "He might've thought she was better at hiding it or something."

"Maybe." Miriam looked at her watch. "We'll stop somewhere for lunch. What do you eat? I didn't see you eat anything yesterday."

Jane couldn't help but laugh. "What do I eat...? I *am* human, you know."

"You might be vegetarian for all I know. You look like you'd be vegetarian."

"Why does that sound like an insult?"

Miriam just grunted.

Jane chuckled and shook her head. "I'm not a vegetarian. I'm good with anything, really."

They got back into the car and Miriam drove a few blocks east to a pizzeria that, from the awning, seemed to just be called PIZZA. The man behind the counter was dressed all in white - shirt, pants, apron, hat - and flashed a smile at Miriam as she came inside.

"Mimi! And you got a new friend! They finally give you a babysitter, keep you in line?"

Miriam looked at the pizzas on display under the curved glass. "You have any fresh meatball and pepperoni, Massimo?"

"I make it every day 'round lunchtime just in case you come in." He moved down the counter. The requested pizza had four slices left. "How many you want?"

"Two." Miriam turned to face Jane. "You?"

Jane quickly scanned the offerings. "Ah... d-do you have any, um, Hawaiian?"

Massimo's smile faded. He put a hand over his heart and gave Miriam an offended look. "Who do you bring into my store, Mimi?"

"She'll take the other two slices," Miriam said, glaring back at Jane.

"Right," Jane said. "Meatball and... mm-hmm. Sounds good."

Massimo plated the slices and moved to the cash register. Jane looked at the menu board for the price and reached for her wallet. Miriam saw her take it out and shook her head, holding up a ten.

"You can get the next one."

"Thanks."

Miriam paid for the slices and two drinks, leaving the change in a jar next to the register. Jane took her plate and a bottle of water, thanked Massimo in a meek voice, and followed Miriam to a table in the corner. There were five tables crammed into the narrow shop, leaving very little room to move around. If anyone sat at the table next to them, Jane's chair would definitely get hit by theirs. A tall cooler of soda bottles hummed against the back wall, almost drowning out the sounds from the street. The wall was covered with a cartoonish mural of Italy that was almost half-decent.

"Pineapple on pizza?" Miriam said. "Are you serious?"

"It's good," Jane said. "Have you tried it?"

Miriam said, "There are a lot of things I've never tried that I can take on faith as bad."

"You'll miss out on a lot of great stuff with that attitude."

Miriam made a face and took a bite of her pizza. She looked past Jane, watching people pass by on the street for a while. Jane assumed the time for talk was done and focused on her food. The pizza was really good, and she could understand how someone could get on a nickname basis with the owner. Even if he was biased against pineapples.

"You must be happy," Miriam said. "It looks like you got your excitement after all."

"Trust me, I'm regretting the wish for excitement. Thinking about that poor girl. To be murdered and have everyone just assume the worst about her. Even people who knew her." She shook her head. "I don't know how you deal with that every day."

Miriam shrugged and used a napkin to blot the grease from her fingers. "You learn how to cope. It's either that or go crazy. Crimes like this take their toll. I've seen a lot of good detectives get crushed by it. I can compartmentalize. I can empathize without letting it overwhelm me. It's tough sometimes. But someone has to do it. And if it's not me, it's going to be someone like Bill Dooling or Dom Clark."

"Yikes," Jane said.

"Exactly." She lifted her pizza, then lowered it without taking a bite. "Why would you want to follow any of these bastards anyway? Bunch of hard drinking, chain-smoking bullies who would just spend the whole time talking shit about their wives. And when they actually deign to do some police work, they're just as likely to plant evidence and beat a confession out of someone than anything else. Off the record, of course."

Jane was startled by the monologue. "Uh. Well, yeah, I figured. The original plan was to observe *everyone*, the whole squad, as a unit. Tying me to just one detective was, I think, the captain's way of putting me in a cage. Also, I honestly didn't know you were an option. It didn't occur to me there would be a female detective. If I had, I'd absolutely have requested you."

"I suppose that's fair." She took a sip of her water. "I guess you're not as big a headache as I thought you'd be. And I'm glad you don't have to suffer with the guys."

"We're both grateful for that. I think we can make the best out of the next week." She realized how that might sound, given the circumstances. "Not that... this girl's death..."

Miriam waved off her spluttering. "I know what you meant. You don't have to twist yourself in knots every time you open your mouth."

They finished eating and Miriam waved goodbye to Massimo as they left.

"How long do you have to come here before he gives you a nickname?"

"I don't know," she said. "He just called me that once and I didn't punch him in the face, so I guess he'd already grown on me. But if one person back at the station starts~"

Jane raised her hands. "They won't hear a word from me. Honest."

"Good girl. You can learn. It's a good sign you'll survive this week."

Jane grinned and got in the car.

When they got back to the bullpen, a male detective was sitting at Miriam's desk. Judging from his posture and the way he was jogging his knee up and down, he'd been waiting for a while. When he saw Miriam enter, he shot to his feet and grabbed a folder off the corner of the desk. He held it out and shook it in Miriam's face.

"Are you Balfour?"

"No, she's the *other* female detective in this squad."

He ignored the sarcasm. "Why are you sniping my case?"

"I beg your pardon?"

He slowed his speech. "You *are* Detective Balfour? So *you're* the one investigating *my* case."

"I'm doing no such thing. Who even *are* you?"

"Kenneth Patterson, with the six-two." He held the paper up again. "The medical examiner updated me on the fact she's looking deeper into one of my murders. She said it was because *you* were asking questions."

Miriam took the paper from him, frowning as she scanned the information. "The victim here is Leigh Hunter. In Gowanus."

"That's right."

"My case is Kimberly Bremer in Red Hook." She slapped the paper against his chest. "The M.E. fucked up the case numbers. I'm nowhere near your territory, so back off."

Patterson's angry mask slipped into confusion. "The details were right... hooker, overdose in her apartment."

"Right," Miriam said. "Dressed in pajamas and~"

"Fuzzy slippers?" Patterson said.

Miriam tensed. "Yeah."

"Needle still in her arm."

Miriam took the report back from him, reading more closely this time. "Any sign of previous drug abuse?"

"No." Patterson's anger was all gone now. "You're really not stepping on my case?"

"This is a completely different woman. Different address, responding officer, date, everything. But the details. Pajama pants with cartoon characters on them. But yours is two weeks old." She looked at Patterson. "You've been sitting on this for two weeks?"

"Waiting for lab results, looking for next of kin. She didn't have anybody. Single."

Jane looked between the two detectives, both of which seemed lost in thought. "Um, sorry. What exactly are you saying happened here?"

"Two dead bodies found in the exact same position," Miriam said. "Same job, same cover-up. There's a very good chance we're looking for a serial killer."

Jane felt a chill and a hush fell over the room. Even though Miriam hadn't spoken loudly, it seemed like everyone had heard her say a magic word. She ignored the staring faces and went to the captain's office, knocking on the glass and letting herself in before Webster could have possibly replied. Jane moved to follow, but the door slammed in her face. She didn't have the confidence to open it and invite herself in.

Instead, she turned and looked back at the room. Everyone was now staring at her. She felt like the only cast member left on stage during a play that had gone horribly, horribly awry.

"It... uh, it's..." She wet her lips. "I don't..."

Dooling was the first to look away from her, turning his attention to Patterson. "You actually think it's a serial killer?"

Patterson grimaced and crossed his arms over his chest. "If what she's saying is right, the bodies were staged similarly enough that the medical examiner got the two cases confused. Called me with an update instead of Balfour. I guess... it *could* be a coincidence." He looked at Jane. "Your girl. What else do you know about her?"

"She wasn't a junkie? Uh... she worked out of a bar most nights..."

"She was invisible."

They both turned to look at Miriam, who had just come out of Webster's office. "That's what they had in common. That's the part that matters." She worked her jaw as she looked down at her file. "And that's going to make it next to fucking impossible to find the others that are sure to be out there."

Jane stayed at the station an extra two hours, going through recent unsolved cases to find any others that matched the two they'd already uncovered. Patterson went to the medical examiner to see if she knew of any other cases, and then returned to his squad to call other detectives around the city and ask if the details sounded familiar to any of them.

She made it through half a dozen files before she had to stop to rest her eyes. She took off her glasses and pressed her fingers against the closed lids.

"A computerized database would be a miracle right now," she said.

"Don't be so sure." Miriam leaned back, stretching her arms out to either side with a groan. "We're all territorial assholes. You saw how Patterson came at me when he thought I'd trespassed on a case. Odds are, the files we want would be locked behind passwords and firewalls and all kinds of computer crap I don't even want to think about." She put her hands in her hair and scratched, then checked her watch. "You can get out of here if you want."

Jane looked at what was left of her stack of folders. "I think I'll stick around and finish these."

"Suit yourself."

In the end, she'd stayed another hour. Patterson had just returned with a new report from the medical examiner that stated Kimberly Bremer officially died from asphyxiation. She'd retrieved fibers that she expected would match a towel or pillow or some other item at the crime scene. Jane had left Miriam dealing with that new information and finally dragged herself out of the building to the bus stop. She was proud of herself for it, but she also regretted the eye strain and the exposure to so many horrible moments for so many people. Every report was written in cold, clinical language, but that almost made it worse. Real human people became "the victim." Their final moments were detailed with less emotion than stage directions in a play. She didn't want them to be lurid, she didn't want details of every wound, but it made her sad to imagine someone's death could be reduced to so little.

She almost fell asleep on the bus but managed to stay awake so she wouldn't miss her stop. She dragged herself home and managed to turn on one light before she collapsed on the couch. She didn't even have the strength to reach down and untie her shoes, even though she knew it would feel like heaven to take them off. Dinner still needed to be sorted out as well. The only food she'd had all day was the pizza, which meant hunger was starting to win the battle against exhaustion for priority.

It was times like these she regretted being single. Moments of regret were few and far between, but she couldn't deny it would be helpful if there was someone in the apartment she could just ask to prepare the food for her and bring it into the living room. Maybe even feed it to her like she was an invalid. Men did that sort of thing, right? They were happy to cook and serve and—

"Yeah, right," she muttered.

Jane pushed herself up and dragged herself into the kitchen. She could always have something delivered. Pay someone to provide her with sustenance. There was a Chinese place on the corner. She could call, and a delivery person would go out on the street, and maybe they'd pass a dark alley, and maybe someone would be waiting at just the wrong time, and oh lord, what if the delivery person was a woman, and—

She choked and gasped, realized she had stopped breathing while she pictured the horrible scenario. She'd been reaching for the phone when her imagination ran away with her, and she withdrew her hand to press it against her chest. Her fingers were trembling. She turned and rested her hip against the counter.

"Another week of this?" she whispered to the empty kitchen. And it was only likely to get worse, if they really were dealing with a serial killer. More victims. More staged deaths with disturbingly cozy pajamas. She shivered and hugged herself. Her appetite was shrinking more with every thought that passed.

She went to the fridge and found turkey, cheese, and mayonnaise. She had some fortunately unmolded bread on the counter. She made herself the weakest sandwich imaginable and ate it over the sink to catch any crumbs. The food didn't taste like anything, but she knew it would carry her through until morning. Maybe then she would feel up for breakfast, and when she got to the station she could ask Miriam how she shut off the bad thoughts when she got home.

When the sandwich was done, Jane drank a glass of water, turned off the light, and finally took off her shoes. She undressed next to the bed and crawled under the blankets, eager for sleep but fearing that her brain might provide her with some horribly nasty nightmares after what she'd read. She folded her pillow in half and pressed her face into its curve.

She wanted to see the case to the end, wanted to know what really happened to Kimberly Bremer and Leigh Hunter and any others waiting to be uncovered.

She just didn't know if she would survive any more horrible discoveries.

Chapter Four

JANE LOOKED like death the next morning. Miriam saw her as soon as she came in from the street, leaning against the wall outside the squad room again like someone had hung her there on a hook. The reporter's skin was pale, her hair unwashed, and Miriam was certain she couldn't have gotten more than a few hours of sleep since she'd last seen her. Part of her wanted to make some snide comment, but she couldn't bring herself to be that cruel. Jane had actually been a good help yesterday, more asset than hindrance, and she'd spent a very long time going through some very depressing files. Miriam felt that earned her a little leeway.

Jane stood up when she saw Miriam approach, but Miriam stopped her from going inside.

"Are you okay?"

"Mm-hmm." There were dark smudges under Jane's eyes, mostly obscured by the glasses. "Just didn't get a lot of sleep last night."

Miriam said, "The files?"

Jane pressed her lips together.

"I should have warned you." She noticed the top button of Jane's shirt was done in the wrong hole. She reached out and undid it, which made Jane jump and look down to see what she was doing. Miriam ignored her and slipped the button into the proper hole. It had been instinct, the mother part of her spilling over from the fact she'd just helped Sammy get put together for school. "It gets to all of us. Even those guys in there. So if any of them give you a hard time, let me know. I'll make them regret it."

"Okay. Thank you." Jane self-consciously touched her collar.

"You're welcome. Go to the bathroom and get fixed up. You don't have to be beautiful but right now you look like you slept in a bus station. I don't give a shit about looking pretty, but it'll be one less thing for those jackals to pounce on."

"Right."

Jane went to the ladies' room and Miriam continued into the squad room. Webster came out of his office before she had reached her desk.

"Balfour. We've got three more."

She stopped. "You're kidding me."

"Word got out and guys started looking at their files. They came in overnight. Files are on your desk."

She walked over and found the reports. She read each name and took note of each neighborhood. Rosario Walker, Red Hook. Sadie Wolf, Red Hook. Kathy Drake, Carroll Gardens. Kimmy was the most recent, while the oldest was eleven weeks old. She didn't immediately see a pattern. Two had happened in the same week, while the rest seemed spaced out at random. All the women had been found in their own apartment, all dressed the same as the first two. Pajamas. Fuzzy slippers. Evidence of an overdose. She was marking the addresses on a map when Jane appeared. She definitely looked more put-together and professional now. She eyed the map, then the files spread out next to Miriam's typewriter.

"More?"

"Afraid so."

Miriam stepped back to look at the map. Most of the crime scenes were clustered in Red Hook, but not tightly enough to indicate a hunting ground. Oddly, the killer had ventured into other neighborhoods for Kathy Drake and Leigh Hunter before coming back to Red Hook for the rest. Kathy Drake lived right at the edge of Carroll Gardens and, theoretically, could have frequented the same Red Hook bar as Kimmy Bremer. But Miriam thought it was highly unlikely she would have gone there when she had so many other seedy bars closer to home to choose from. It was the same for all five women. They were just far enough apart that it didn't make sense their paths would overlap except on rare occasions.

"Can I ask you a question? And please don't give me some cliché or boilerplate answer, I sincerely want to know."

"Okay," Miriam said.

"What did you do last night?"

Miriam frowned and looked at her. "What?"

"We spent yesterday looking at all those reports. All those women... victims... we put aside because they didn't fit the formula, they were still people. People who died in horrible, sometimes terrifying ways. How did you just go home after that? To your husband and your kid?"

Miriam crossed her arms. She had to fight the urge to break her promise. *You either learn how to do it or you quit* was a standard response to this kind of question. But she decided to give Jane a break and actually try to answer her honestly.

"Last night, I went home, and my... husband was washing the dishes with my daughter. They'd had dinner without me. Wasn't the first time, or the last. Then I gave Sammy a bath, got her ready for bed, and I read her a story. Then I had a beer. I watched something stupid on TV. Then I went to bed. Why, what did you do?"

Jane was shaking her head. "I barely made it home, I was so exhausted. And then... I could barely even think of food, even though I was starving. So I made a sandwich, ate it over the sink, and I spent the whole night tossing and turning because I was afraid to fall asleep in case I had any dreams." She touched her hair. "I have very vivid dreams usually. I-I didn't... I was terrified of what might happen, given everything I'd seen and read about yesterday."

Miriam said, "Yeah. That's a valid concern. I did mention alcohol was involved in my night."

"I don't drink."

"You might want to pick up the habit if you're going to be sticking around." Miriam looked at the map again. "I don't know if we're going to find any others, but just these are going to be bad enough."

"Thanks for the warning." Jane cleared her throat. "I'll do my best to power through."

"Good luck." She looked at the files, already dreading them. "To both of us."

Jane grunted. "So what do we do first?"

"First," she picked up one of the files at random. "We go back and talk to the witnesses. See if any of them recognize any of the other victims."

"Oh."

Miriam looked at Jane and tried reading her face. "Look. I know this isn't what you signed up for. It's a lot. And I've decided you're... not... the worst person in the world to have hanging around. If you want to take a step back and put a pin in this, come back when the dust has settled, I wouldn't blame you."

Jane looked tempted. She looked at the files on the desk. "It's never going to be a quiet week, though. Right?"

"Right."

Jane took a deep breath. "I want to see this through. I owe it to Kimmy."

Miriam felt her last vestige of irritation at the reporter crumble away somewhat reluctantly. She nodded.

"Okay then. Let's get to work."

"I have to confess something."

Miriam kept her eyes on the road. They were on the way to re-interview witnesses in the Rosario Walker case, since she was the first known victim. "I'm all ears."

Jane took a breath and let it out slowly. "I... went... back to the newspaper this morning. Before I came into the station. I wasn't sleeping anyway, so I thought I'd type up some notes of what we had so far. And at the time, I thought I could justify holding the story. Not saying anything until you gave the go-ahead. But now there are *five* women out there. And~"

"You are not printing anything about this case."

She had to stop and process the interruption, taking a moment to adjust. "Whoever is doing this is still out there. He could be targeting other women. If we can warn them~"

"We alert the asshole to the fact we're onto him."

"So then maybe he stops!"

"How does that help get justice for the women who have already died?" From the corner of her eye, Miriam could see Jane staring at her. "I'm not saying I want more women to die. The women he's targeting are already more cautious than anyone else on the street. They watch out for each other. They don't need us telling them to watch out for creeps, because there are a hundred creeps out there every night. Sometimes one of them falls through the cracks. It happens. But putting a big flashing light on the fact we've connected these dots doesn't help anyone but the killer."

Jane was silent for two blocks before she spoke again. "How long am I supposed to sit on this?"

"Give me the ten days. If your little ride-along ends without making progress, you can print your story. Does that sound fair?"

Jane took a deep breath and looked out the window. Finally she nodded. "I think that's reasonable."

Miriam said, "Good."

According to the original officer's report, Rosario Walker had a day job working as a waitress at a burger place called New Jerrk. According to the sign on the glass door, the name was a blending of "Jersey" and "York", and she wondered if anyone but the owner had ever actually found that funny or clever.

Inside, the store was separated into Manhattan and Jersey sections. Sinatra and Bon Jovi on one side, Patrick Ewing and the Beastie Boys opposite them. Blondie was playing quietly from the speakers. A man came out of the kitchen and moved to a station behind the cash register as they came in. He gestured at the empty tables.

"Have a seat anywhere."

Miriam showed him her badge. "Actually we need to talk to you about one of your waitresses."

He slumped against the counter, hanging his head. "Damn it. Another one? What the hell. Who is it this time?"

"I'm here about Rosario Walker again."

He frowned. "What? Why? I already told the detective that I didn't even know she was whoring after hours. That didn't have anything to do with me or what she was doing here."

Miriam said, "And her murder might not have had anything to do with her other job."

"What murder?" he said. "I thought it was an OD. She was a junkie."

"Did you ever see evidence of drug use in her work?"

"I..." He hesitated. "Well, no. She did her job well enough. Showed up on time. Didn't beg for advances on her paycheck or anything like that. But they literally found a needle in her arm, right? And don't people like that...? They...?" He shrugged. "It's not exactly strange for people like her to end up like that, right?"

"We have reason to believe the scene was staged. Did you ever see anyone hanging around when Rosario was working? Maybe a customer who gave her extra attention?"

He scratched his temple. "Not really. The customers liked her. But I don't remember anyone specific being creepy. She would've asked to have someone else cover her table if that was the case. Uh." He turned and looked into the kitchen. "Phoebe! C'mere!"

"Yeah, DJ?" A girl who looked fresh out of high school appeared. Her polo shirt had NEW JERRK embroidered on the chest. She was taking a pad and pencil from her apron as she approached, clearing expecting customers. Her hair had been hastily pulled back into a sloppy ponytail. She froze when she saw Miriam and Jane, but continued cautiously forward after the recovered from the initial surprise.

DJ gestured. "These are cops." Miriam didn't bother to correct him about Jane. "They want to know if anyone was bugging Rosario. Was there anybody she didn't tell me about?"

Phoebe furrowed her brow and shook her head. "No. Just the normal creeps telling her to smile more or checking out her ass or whatever. Nothing she mentioned. Why, what's going on?"

"They think she was murdered," the boss said.

Her eyes widened. "What? No. She died from drugs."

Miriam said, "Can you confirm she was a user?"

"Well." She tilted her head to the side. "I guess not. Wait, she didn't die from OD'ing? That's what the newspaper said."

"We're still looking into it," Miriam said.

Jane cleared her throat. "Sorry, I have a question. Um, Phoebe, right?" Miriam glared at her, but Jane kept her eyes on the waitress. "There's a school bus depot across the street. Those places are usually very well-lit at night, and it would be a good place for a drug dealer to set up shop. Would you mind walking over there with me so I could take a look."

Phoebe looked at DJ, confused. "Um. Why?"

"Strength in numbers?"

Miriam realized what Jane was doing. "Dealers tend to leave signs of their presence. They're like raccoons. Trash, broken syringes, all kinds of things. If she finds evidence someone was lurking there to sell, it could support the theory that Rosario was using without your knowledge."

DJ shrugged and gave Phoebe a nod. She shrugged and stepped around the counter, leading Jane out the door.

As soon as they were gone, Miriam said, "DJ. What's that stand for?"

He looked like he didn't want to answer but couldn't think of a good reason to refuse. "Dennis Jones."

"Okay, Dennis Jones. Is Phoebe the only employee working right now?"

"It's not a very busy time."

"Must get kind of boring around here. Just the two of you. Alone."

DJ twisted his lips. "She's nineteen, if that's what you're getting at."

"Gotta love guys who use that number as a starting line." She crossed her arms. "Is Phoebe the only employee you have a 'special relationship' with?"

"I never forced myself on~"

"That's not what I asked you, sir. Did you sleep with Rosario Walker?"

His face was red. "No. But even if I did, what the hell would it matter? She was a whore. She was out there just giving it to whoever has a few bucks to throw away."

Miriam raised her eyebrows. "Whoa. Sorry. I didn't mean to touch a nerve. Did Rosario reject you?" He looked away. "That must have stung. Turned down by a whore. Did you think providing her with a paycheck earned you a freebie?"

"I'm not talking to you anymore."

"That's fine. I need some fresh air anyway."

She turned and left the restaurant. Jane was already coming back with Phoebe. Miriam blocked the door, waiting for them to cross the parking lot.

"Do you need a ride anywhere?" Miriam asked when they were close enough.

Phoebe looked at Jane, then gestured at the restaurant. "I'm still in the middle of my shift."

"That wasn't my question."

"I..." She looked at Jane again, then squared her shoulders. "No. Thanks, though."

Miriam nodded and took a card from her wallet. "If you think of anything else about Rosario or any customers that might help us, give me a call."

Phoebe took the card. "Okay. Thanks."

Miriam stepped aside and let Phoebe go back into the restaurant. Jane's mouth was open in an expression of shock, but Miriam ignored it and walked back to the car.

"You're just going to let her walk back in there?"

"To her job? Why wouldn't I?"

Jane said, "That man is taking advantage of her. I thought you picked up on that! It's why I got her out of there. You confirmed it, right? You talked to him?"

"I did. And he is. But she's an adult. I gave her the option and she said no. I'm not going to drag her out of there against her will." She opened the car door. "Get in. We've got a lot more people to talk to before the day is out."

Jane looked back at the restaurant. For a second, Miriam thought *she* was going to go back inside and drag Phoebe out. But after a moment, she shook her head and got into the car.

Once they were back on the road, Miriam could tell the situation was still weighing on Jane's mind. She went a block before she gave in.

"So what is it? A boss grabbed your ass at your first job?"

She could see Jane tense from the corner of her eye. "Don't make light of that kind of thing."

"Fair enough," Miriam said. "But obviously there's some kind of history there. And most women have at least one story of a boss who crossed the line."

Jane sighed. "A teacher, actually."

Miriam nodded. "Second most popular suspect. Working after school for extra credit?"

"Finishing a project." Jane's voice had gotten small. "Came up behind me, put a hand on my shoulder. Told me what a..." She swallowed a lump in her throat. "...smart and dedicated student I was. And then kissed my neck and tried to grope me."

"God. I'm sorry."

Jane waved off the apology. "Don't be. Like you said, who doesn't have a story like that?" She looked at Miriam again. "Phoebe might have said no to your offer, and she might have even meant it.

But she might have only said it because she didn't think she could say yes. That's her job. Her income. Walking away from that isn't as easy as just getting in a car and letting someone drive her off."

"I know that," Miriam said. "Doing this job, you think I don't know that? But you can't force someone to take your help. All you can do is make the offer and hope she gets out before anything too traumatic happens."

Jane slumped back in her seat and put her hand over her eyes. "I don't care what you told me earlier. I still don't know how you do this job without going crazy."

Miriam shook her head. "I'm not sure anyone does."

Chapter Five

THE NEXT five days were indistinguishable from each other, at least as far as Jane could tell. She felt herself forming memories and adding them all to a single horrific stew of interviews with witnesses and coworkers. No one was suspicious of the official report. No one questioned the original assessment of an overdose even though none of the victims showed signs of using. "I didn't know she was a hooker, either," most of them said. "Who knew what else she was hiding?"

The medical examiner confirmed all five victims were killed by being smothered with something from their apartment. Three with pillows, two with blankets. Jane tried not to picture them struggling under the killer, but it was impossible. She'd gotten maybe two hours of sleep every night since she started following Miriam, and her body was starting to rebel at the stress.

Miriam was the only bright side of the week. She'd thawed out, just a bit. Enough that they were having actual conversations over lunch. Jane never felt like they'd been forced to share a table, and it was less awkward in the car. Miriam still insisted on controlling the radio, but that was fine. Jane didn't mind her music, which was mostly classic rock. Beatles and the Stones, the occasional Bowie. She checked in regularly to make sure Jane was okay, and Jane didn't feel like she'd be judged if she said she needed to take a break and step away for a few minutes.

The worst part, other than the horrors of each case, was the fact that after a week they were still no closer to an actual, viable suspect. No one had seen anything. None of the victims had been seen with anyone suspicious, or worth noting. Jane thought there were plenty of potential killers lurking in every woman's periphery - lecherous bosses, anonymous bartenders, aggressive johns - but any further investigation into them led to quick dead ends.

Jane was lying in bed on her stomach, her face buried in a blissfully soft pocket of a folded pillow, awake but trying desperately not to be. She was on the verge of finally succeeding when her phone rang. The sound was so jarring that she shot up onto her hands and knees, back arched like a startled cat. It took her a few seconds to realize what the sound was, and almost two full minutes before she untangled her legs from the bedding and made it to the living room to answer.

"Hello?"

"Do you know where Bay Street is?"

Jane closed her eyes and pushed her hair out of her face. "Is this Miriam?"

"Can you get there within the next half hour?"

She looked down at her underwear and T-shirt. She tried to picture a map of Brooklyn, but all the grids kept twisting and turning around and blending into each other.

"Jane!"

She jumped. "Yes! Yeah, I can be there. What's going on?" She looked at her alarm clock. "It's four in the morning."

"I know," Miriam said. "We have another body."

"Another..." She shivered. "Oh no. Oh, no, is it a crime scene?"

Miriam lowered her voice. "Can you handle that?"

Jane swallowed the lump in her throat. "I can. I'll be there."

Miriam gave her the exact address. "There will be an officer on the door. Tell him you're with me and he'll let you in."

The call disconnected. Jane hung up and went back into her bedroom. An actual crime scene. Would the body still be there? The thought almost made her throw up, but she fought the urge and focused on getting dressed. She grabbed the first pair of pants she found and the first shirt, putting them on over the clothes she'd worn the bed. She was out the door before she realized she wasn't wearing socks, but she didn't think she had the strength to go back and start over. If she went back, she would never start forward again.

She had to catch a cab, and then had to repeat the address Miriam had given her because she mumbled it the first time. In the cruelest of ironies, the movement of the cab was enough to rock her back to the edge of sleep. Her head dropped, her lips slackened, and she told herself she was still awake because she was aware of the cabbie's radio crackle and traffic noises.

She realized she'd been lying to herself when the cabbie said, "Miss? Miss…" Jane lifted her head and snapped her mouth closed, and she knew they'd been stopped for longer than she wanted to think about. She wiped the back of her hand across her mouth and pulled out her wallet.

"Are you sure this is where you want to be?" the cabbie looked forward again.

Jane saw two police cars, lights still flashing, parked at the curb. "No," Jane said as she handed over her cash. "But it's where I have to be, I think."

"Good luck," the driver said.

Jane walked to the building where, as promised, a uniformed police officer was waiting. He was very blurry, as was everything else on the street, and she realized she also hadn't been able to read the cash in the cab. Maybe this was all just a bad dream. She'd once heard that it was impossible to read in dreams. She looked at the officer's badge and name tag, but neither of the marks on them sharpened into letters or words. The smudge man stepped into her path.

"Do you live in the building, ma'am?"

"I'm Detective Balfour." She shook her head. "No. Um, no I'm not. She's inside. I'm hers. With her. I'm… my name is--"

"Are you Jane Ross?"

She nodded. "Yessir."

He stepped aside. "You can go on inside. First floor, end of the hallway."

"Thank you."

She went into the building, where the world remained frustratingly soft. She couldn't make out any details, and the tension started to fade from her shoulders. It was a dream. It had to be a dream. She wasn't at a crime scene with a bunch of cops, and she wasn't about to walk into an apartment where someone had just died. She was going to wake up, she would cry, and then she would go back to the precinct and pretend she could handle two more days of following Miriam on this godawful job.

A shape stepped out of the apartment ahead of her, and even in the foggy dream world, she could tell that it was Miriam. She made her way over, wondering what the detective would think if she knew Jane was dreaming about her.

"Jane?" There was something strange in Miriam's voice.

"Hi," Jane said.

"Sorry," Miriam said after another second. "I've just never seen you without your glasses."

"My..."

Jane's hand went to her face. No glasses. That explained why she couldn't see anything. But that also meant this wasn't a dream. She had no idea how she could have forgotten them, or gone so long without realizing she wasn't wearing them. She dropped her hand to her throat and let it rest there.

"My glasses. Right." She blinked and squinted, which helped a little bit. She was going to have a hell of a headache all day now. "I-I left in such a hurry. And I was asleep when you called..."

"So you've been sleeping better?"

Jane was touched by the hopefulness she heard in Miriam's voice, so she lied. "Yeah, a little bit each night. Getting... getting better."

"I'm not sure that's a good thing," Miriam admitted, "but it'll help you get through today and tomorrow. Can you see well enough to come in?"

"Yeah, just don't let me trip over anything."

"Okay. Come on."

Miriam put her hand on Jane's elbow and guided her into the apartment.

"Here's what you need to know. Victim's name is Angeline DiFabio. Twenty-nine, works part-time as a file clerk at a law firm downtown, I forget the name soup. Dewey Cheatem and Howe or whatever. Anyway, when she's not working there, she's earning supplemental income the same way as our other victims. And the rest is the same story we've had five times already. Right down to the fuzzy slippers."

Jane swallowed hard, grateful she couldn't see the finer details of the apartment. But even while there was comfort in that, it was also frightening to think she was in the same place a killer might have stood and she was vulnerable. She was grateful that Miriam was still hanging onto her arm. Even though the lights in the apartment made it easier to see, and she was certain she would have been fine on her own, she made no move to free herself from the detective's grip.

"Is she still..."

"The medical examiner took the body before I called you," Miriam said. "Uniforms found a pillow that the killer might have used. That's going to the lab along with a couple of towels and a robe. Maybe we'll get lucky."

"Why did you call me to come here?" Jane said. "I feel like a reporter is the last person you want at an active scene."

Miriam said, "Well, usually. But I guess I've gotten to like you a little. This feels like it's our case. I wanted you to... well. See it."

Jane smiled. "Sorry."

"The important thing is that you know about the new death. I didn't want to drop the bombshell on you when you came into the station today."

"I appreciate it."

"I'm sorry I had you come all the way down here just to send you back, but if you can't see..."

Jane said, "That's my fault. I don't know what I'd even look for anyway. But I think it helps. To... to be in the place where it happened. Even if it feels creepy as hell."

Miriam nodded. "If there's anything you want a closer look at..."

"No. I kind of want to leave as quickly as possible, if that's all right."

"Yeah, that makes sense. Come on, I'll take you home."

Jane held up a hand to stop her. "Wait. Is there a picture of her somewhere that you can take? All the other files had such awful pictures. Driver's license photos and mug shots from when they were picked up for soliciting. Can you find something better?"

"Um." She looked to the left, scanned the walls, and then looked to the right. "Yeah." She let go of Jane's arm and went to a table next to the door. She picked up a framed photo and opened the back to take it out. "That was a good thought. Anything else?"

"No, we can go."

Miriam put her hand on Jane's shoulder and guided her out of the apartment. Jane wanted to say that she could see well enough to navigate the stairs and hallway. She wasn't blind. She could see everything around them, it was just foggy and not as detailed as it could've been. She couldn't see the picture Miriam had picked up but otherwise, unless she was asked to read something, she could have taken care of herself. She'd gotten herself to the scene easy enough, after all. But she knew if she said that, Miriam would move her hand. It was too early in the morning for her to think about why that would be so disappointing.

Miriam's car was parked at the far end of the block, past the parked cruisers. Jane gave her address, and Miriam nodded and said, "I know where that is."

It was almost five by that point, and the city was waking up. More people on the streets, more cars to contend with, but the sun still hadn't gotten high enough to crest the buildings of Brooklyn.

"Your husband probably wasn't too happy about you running out like this."

"He's used to it," Miriam said.

Jane nodded. "Sure. That makes sense." She looked out the side window, squinting to see if that put things into any more focus.

"I should've let you print the story."

Jane looked at her. "What?"

"I stopped you from writing something. And now another woman is dead."

"My story wouldn't have changed that."

"It might have." Miriam's eyes were straight ahead. Even without her glasses, Jane could tell she had a white-knuckle grip on the steering wheel. "Angeline might have decided not to go out tonight if she saw someone was targeting prostitutes."

Jane said, "So he would've gotten someone else."

"Or maybe not. Maybe she was the only one he had a chance to grab. It doesn't matter. We won't know. But I'm giving you permission to print the story. Whoever the next girl is needs to know he's out there."

Jane nodded. "Okay."

Miriam didn't say anything for the rest of the drive. She parked in front of Jane's building. Jane opened the door and started to get out. When she remained in her seat, Miriam looked over at her.

"Something wrong?"

"Are you going home from here?"

"I'm going into the station," Miriam said.

Jane settled back in her seat. "You're not even going home to shower or anything?"

"Are you saying I need to?"

Jane decided not to answer that. "You at least need breakfast. Come upstairs. I'll get my glasses, change into something more appropriate than this, and you can make some toast or cereal or something."

Miriam looked at the building. She drummed her fingers on the steering wheel, then sighed and turned off the engine.

"I am a little hungry."

They went upstairs together. Jane looked down and finally saw, to her horror, that she was wearing tartan pants and a Tom Petty concert T-shirt. She decided there was no point being ashamed of it now. She unlocked her apartment and ushered Jane inside.

"My humble abode."

"It's nice."

Jane nodded awkwardly. "Um, okay. Kitchen is there, obviously. Cereal. Toast. The usual stuff." She gestured to the bedroom. "I won't be too long."

Miriam nodded and crossed to the kitchen, while Jane closed herself in her bedroom. She peeled off the T-shirt and the pajama shirt she had under it - that was a plain tee, which was thin and almost see-through but would've been so much less embarrassing - and unbuckled her belt. She saw her glasses on the nightstand and swore at herself as she slipped it on. Focus came back to the world and she sighed with relief.

Once that was dealt with, she changed into an outfit that would be appropriate for work and went into the bathroom to splash some water on her face and apply her makeup. She wished she had time for a quick shower but the thought of Miriam wandering loose in her apartment made her antsy. She braided her hair as quickly as she could, not worrying about how neat or tidy it looked.

When she returned to the main room, she was surprised to smell fresh coffee and hear the crackling of something on the stove.

"Detective...?"

Miriam looked over her shoulder, brow furrowed. "What happened to calling me Miriam?"

"I don't know. It felt... weird." She rolled up her sleeves and looked at the pan on the stove. "Are you making eggs and bacon?"

Miriam pointed the spatula at the coffee maker. "And coffee."

"Could you not find the cereal?"

"Frosted Flakes? What are you, eleven?"

Jane blushed. "I normally get Cheerios."

"Sure." Miriam almost smiled as she turned back toward the stove. "I tried to imagine Sammy getting away with just sugary cereal and toast for breakfast, and Mom mode snapped in. So I decided we have time for a proper breakfast."

"Thank you."

"You're welcome." She pointed with her spatula again. "Sit. It's the least I can do after dragging you out of bed at four in the morning."

Jane sat down and folded her hands in front of her. "It's not like I was sleeping anyway."

"You said you were doing better."

"Yeah. That was a lie."

Miriam grunted. "Well, you definitely need the coffee, then. Don't lie to me, Jane. We've come a long way since I got stuck with you, and I'd hate to backtrack now."

"Understood," Jane said. "I'm sorry."

"It's okay. I understand. You didn't want to come off like you couldn't handle it. I was the same way when I started. I can handle anything you throw at me, I can cope with it, I'm totally fine with all the gory details. I ended up nearly having a breakdown because I was holding everything in." She brought a plate over and put it down in front of Jane. "If you need to take a breath, take a breath. It's okay."

"I appreciate that."

Miriam went back to the stove. "It's like on airplanes. When the masks drop down. Take care of yourself before you try to help other people."

Jane nodded. "That makes sense. I will try to be better about telling you when things are too much."

"Good girl."

Jane tried to ignore the thrill that went through her at those words, and what that thrill might mean. She poked at her breakfast.

"You're not going to catch him today, are you." It wasn't a question. "Unless he walks in the door and confesses, you're probably not going to find him today or tomorrow."

"It could happen," Miriam said. "We have a fresh scene. We

have new witnesses who haven't had time to forget. There's a chance he got sloppy this time, or he's getting cocky. The break we need~"

Jane interrupted her. "What are the odds? Honestly."

"There are no odds," Miriam said. "There's no timeline. There are myths about the first forty-eight hours being critical, and it's true that we have a better chance inside that window. So in that respect, any nonexistent odds are in our favor. But at the same time, this man has killed nine women, and we don't even have a hint about who he might be or how we'll catch him. The clock reset last night, but we're dealing with someone who is clearly good at covering his tracks. So I don't know, and I would be lying if I tried to put a number on it. It's just how the chips fall."

"So I probably have to walk away from this without knowing how the case is going until it's over."

Miriam nodded. "There's a chance. Yeah."

Jane put down her fork. "As bad as all this has been, I think that would make it worse. Not knowing. No closure. That's going to drive me crazy."

"Look... as far as I'm concerned, you're part of this case. There wouldn't even *be* a case if it wasn't for you. So if you want to stick around~"

Jane laughed harshly. "That wouldn't be any better. I'm counting the hours until I'm not around this shit anymore."

"Well." Miriam sighed. "You can't have it both ways, Ross. Either you stick around and keep following the case until it's over, or you walk away tomorrow even if we haven't caught the guy. You'll still find out the whole story when the arrest hits the papers. You'll probably be the first to know, so you have that advantage over anyone else."

"Yeah. I guess so."

Miriam took a sip of her coffee. When she put it down, she said, "I'll keep in touch. If we're still chasing the guy when your time is up, I'll... call. We can meet up for lunch meetings or whatever. I won't just leave you in the dark waiting for a bulletin."

"You would do that?"

"It's obviously weighing on you," Miriam said. "If you were a cop, I'd tell you to toughen up. Learn to cope, to deal with it. But this isn't your life. You're not going to deal with things like this on a daily basis. So. Yeah. If it will help, I'll let you know how the case is going."

"Thank you."

Miriam shrugged.

Jane watched her. "Do you have to do that? Do you just... I don't know, shut down part of yourself so you won't think about..." She shook her head. "You have a daughter. How can you *not* think about these bastards running around?"

"Because I'd go crazy if I did," Miriam said. "And staying focused is how I catch these guys so I don't have to worry about any of them finding Sammy and hurting her. That's how I deal with it."

Jane shook her head. It was a good method, and she could understand how it helped Miriam sleep through the night. But she couldn't imagine doing it herself, having such a big part of her emotional soul closed off to suffering and pain. She didn't think she could live that way.

She hoped she would never have to find out.

CHAPTER SIX

MIRIAM SPENT the morning fighting hope, desperately trying to keep her expectation low even as she was gifted multiple miracles. First, Angeline's friend knew that she'd spent the night before working at a bar called Broke. Second, when Miriam and Jane arrived to question the bartender, Jane spotted both interior and exterior security cameras. Both cameras were recording, and the tapes were handed over by the owner without an argument or any fuss. Thirdly, the medical examiner determined Angeline had been smothered by one of the pillows in her apartment, which had been immediately sent off to the crime lab to be thoroughly examined.

She refused to prematurely celebrate. She'd seen too many cases start promising only to fizzle out. So she didn't held off hope until she had something solid, something she could grab hold of. Jane found an empty desk and typed up her notes. When she was finished she left to drop it off at the paper so it could get in the early edition the next morning.

Miriam's wariness was proven correct that afternoon, when all their promising leads added up to a sum total of zero. The bartender on duty didn't remember seeing her talk to anyone in particular. The security footage showed Angeline arrive and talk to a man who, by some miracle, sat facing the camera. She left with him, and even Miriam's hopes spiked. But a half hour later, his car returned and Angeline returned to her stool. She finally left alone just after midnight and vanished out of the camera's range.

The day ended with a report that their last lead, the pillow, didn't have any workable fingerprints, DNA, hairs, or anything that might lead them to their man. Miriam tossed the report down on her desk and walked away, holding her breath until she got to the break room. She was afraid it would come out as a scream or a curse.

She managed to wrangle it down to an ursine growl, pulling her arm back to punch the vending machine. Luckily she managed to stop herself before she caused any damage to it or her hand. She paced to the far end of the room and looked out the window. Then she turned around to see Jane had returned from dropping off her story. She was lurking in the doorway and seemed to be torn between saying something and just running away.

"Did they tell you?" Miriam said. "Nothing. All that shit we had this morning? All those smoking fucking guns? They amounted to *zero*. We have the exact same amount we have on the other five, which is jack shit. So no, Jane. We're not going to catch this bastard. Not today, and probably not tomorrow. We're not going to fucking find him before he kills another girl."

"I was just going to ask if you're okay."

Miriam breathed in deeply through her nose. She put her hands on her hips. "No. I'm not fucking okay, Jane, thank you for asking."

Jane nodded. "Okay, then. Good."

"Good?"

"All that talk about closing yourself off this morning, shutting down, that whole thing. I was worried for you. Seeing you like this means you still care. It means you get angry about this shit. It makes me less worried for you."

"Don't waste your time worrying about me."

"I'm not like you, remember? I worry. I can't not. So worrying about you is on my way to worrying about everything else."

Miriam tried to scoff at that, but it turned into a laugh. "Fine. If you must."

Jane came into the breakroom. "My editor said the article will be in the paper tomorrow morning. So in about twelve hours, the city is going to know this monster is out there. Girls like Kimmy and Angeline will know to watch out for each other. Maybe Angeline will be the last one."

Miriam took a series of steadying breaths. She kept her eyes on the scuffed tile of the floor. "Yeah," she said. "Maybe."

"Your shift is almost over, right? So go home, get some fresh air. Play your daughter and kiss your husband. Let them, you know, show you the other side of humanity. I assume. Maybe your husband is an asshole."

Miriam laughed again. "He's not that bad." She looked at the vending machine she had almost punched. "He's also not my husband."

"What?"

"I mean... he is. Technically, we're... he's..." She pinched the bridge of her nose, then spread her finger and thumb across her forehead. "We're separated. We still live together. But separate rooms. It makes sense, financially."

"Oh." Jane looked confused but then nodded. "Well, okay. Uh. Your daughter. She can help take your mind off things."

Miriam nodded. "Yeah. She's good at that."

Jane said, "Well, there you have it. Tomorrow, we'll try to solve the puzzle again. This guy isn't magic. He made a mistake somewhere. You'll catch it. I know you will."

"One of us has to have faith in me, I guess," Miriam said.

Jane smiled sadly. "Yeah. Okay, then. I'll see you tomorrow."

Miriam watched her go. "Wait." She followed her into the hall. "What about you?"

"Me?"

"You're just going to go home to your sad apartment by yourself?"

"You said it was nice."

Miriam said, "It's fine. That's not what this is about. You need something to take your mind off the case as much as I do. More, even. Come home with me, have dinner with us. Get some of that, uh, what did you call it? Other side of humanity. It might help you get some sleep."

Jane smiled. "Really? It wouldn't be too much of an imposition?"

"I'm not making a four-course meal or anything. It'll be probably be leftover lasagna."

Jane laughed. "Then... yeah, of course. That sounds much better than the frozen dinner I was planning to warm up. I would love to meet your fam... your daughter."

Miriam nodded. "I'll wrap things up here and then we'll head out."

"Okay."

Miriam started to step around her, then stopped. "And thanks. For checking on me."

"Any time."

Miriam patted Jane's arm and walked away before she could say anything else.

"Tell me you didn't have the leftover lasagna for lunch."

Jeremy looked away from the television. "What? We have leftover lasagna?"

"Good." Miriam hung her coat up and went to check the fridge. She was almost positive they had enough to feed an extra person but, if not, she only had an hour to come up with a plan B.

Jeremy came into the kitchen. "Is everything okay?"

"Everything's fine." She closed the door. Plenty of lasagna. She always made too much. "I invited someone over for dinner and wanted to make sure we had enough before she got here."

"You invited someone over for leftovers?"

She shrugged. "It would go to waste otherwise."

He chuckled and shook his head. "Well, if it helps, I won't be around tonight so she can have my share."

"Another date?" She went to the cupboard to check for clean plates. "Is this getting serious? It would be really helpful to divide the rent three ways."

"You'd let her move in here?"

She shrugged. "Built-in babysitter, what's not to like?"

"As weird as that is, no, this is someone new. Long way from talk about cohabitating. But it's nice to know the option is there." He put his hands in his pockets and came further into the kitchen. "So who is this mysterious coworker who suddenly warrants a dinner invite? Did you actually make a friend?"

"God forbid," she said. "But she's been having a rough time on the case, and she lives alone, so I thought it might be nice to be around... you know, people. Sammy. Get some of that little kid brightness."

"Aw, that's sweet." He tilted his head to the side. "Wait, the case? I thought the only person working with you on that was whatshername, the reporter."

"Yeah, that's her."

He laughed. "The same reporter that, last week, you talked about abandoning on the Brooklyn Bridge at rush hour?"

"That was like the second day we worked together. I was bitter about being stuck with her. She's not so bad."

"You're getting soft, Miriam."

"Shut up," she said. "She went home to get ready, but she'll be here in about half an hour. Are you going to help me?"

He backed out of the room. "If I'm not eating, I don't have to help prep. Besides, you can just microwave it. How much prep is really needed?"

"Get out, you're useless. Go get ready for your date."

"I am ready."

She looked at his outfit, then turned away and shook her head. "God, I'm never getting you out of this apartment."

"You just said we could stay here if I~"

"*Leave*. Be elsewhere."

He left the kitchen. "I'll go tell Sammy there's going to be a guest tonight."

"Thanks, Jeremy."

She set the table, mainly to be sure she had enough of everything, and checked the fridge. She had most of a two-liter of soda, some tea, milk, orange juice, and a few beers. She had no idea what Jane drank. She tried to remember their lunches together. Sometimes Jane got a can of Sprite, but she usually just ordered ice water.

Sammy came into the kitchen. "Someone coming to dinner?"

"Mm-hmm. A friend of mine named Jane."

"Is she a police?"

"No, she works for the newspaper. She writes stories about the police."

"And she's writing a story about you?"

Miriam said, "More about how we solve crimes."

"Oh-h." Sammy folded her arms on the table and rested her chin on them. "Is she nice?"

"Yeah, she's nice. She's nicer than me."

Sammy said, "You're *very* nice."

"Not at work," Miriam said. "At work I'm a mean scary lady who growls a lot. And I look at people like this." She wrinkled her nose and crossed her eyes.

Sammy laughed. "That's not scary."

"Well, you haven't done anything wrong. If you were a criminal, you'd be shaking in your boots."

"I don't even *have* any boots!"

"That's another reason it doesn't work. Did Daddy tell you to wash up?"

Sammy lifted her head and showed off her hands.

"Do you want to help me fix dinner? It'll be real easy."

"Yes."

Sammy immediately marched into the kitchen, forcing Miriam to catch up. As Jeremy had said, there really wasn't much to do, but she found enough fixins so they could make a salad as an opening course. It ended up being more like playing with their food, but whatever distracted Sammy and kept Miriam occupied was good in her book.

Jane knocked at precisely eight o'clock, and Miriam silently made a note of her punctuality. Dinner was ready, Jeremy was gone, and the only thing she hadn't managed to do was change clothes. But that was fine, she had no need to impress Jane. So she didn't know why she felt the need to run a hand through her hair and tuck in the tail of her shirt before she opened the door.

"Right on time."

Jane was standing awkwardly, one hand behind her back. She twisted to look past Miriam into the apartment, then leaned close and lowered her voice.

"What's your policy on sugar?"

"My... what?"

Jane revealed her right arm and the plastic container with four cupcakes. "I thought I'd provide dessert, but on the way here, I realized I didn't know what your policy was when it came to sugar. For your daughter, I mean. Or for yourself, I guess. We can leave them in the hall if–"

"Sugar is fine," Miriam said. "Thank you. It's very thoughtful." She took in Jane's outfit, a pale yellow sweater and blue jeans. Her hair was pinned back, but the wet ends implied she'd managed to take a shower. "You look great."

"Thank you, you too."

"I look the same as I did at the station."

Jane said, "Well. Sure. But still."

Miriam nodded and closed the door. "Jeremy isn't here, so it's just going to be the girls tonight."

As if cued, Sammy marched in from the kitchen and stopped directly in front of Jane. She stared up at her, arms crossed over her chest.

"How old are you?"

"Uh." Jane smiled. "I'm twenty-nine."

"That's a lot," Sammy said. "I'm four."

Jane nodded. "It's a good age. I liked four."

"Mommy is thir—"

"Mommy is not involved in this interrogation." Miriam put her hands on Sammy's shoulders and guided her toward the table. "Go. Sit down."

Jane chuckled. "She's cute."

"We'll see if you still think that an hour from now."

As it turned out, the interrogation was only just beginning. Miriam tried to start a conversation, but found it strangely hard. She and Jane never had a hard time filling silences when they had lunch. Of course, those meals were usually in crowded restaurants, diners, the squad room. They were rushed and it was easier to tap into the energy of people around them. Now, it was just the two of them and a little girl, and the quiet of the apartment was almost overwhelming.

So they just ate, Miriam trying to ignore her discomfort, knowing Jane was waiting for her to step forward and be the host.

In the end, Miriam was saved by her daughter. They were halfway through the meal when Sammy decided enough time had passed to start her interrogation again.

"Do you write the whole paper?"

Jane shook her head. "No, I just write certain parts of it. There are a whole bunch of writers doing little pieces, and then an editor puts it all together."

"Do you have a daughter?"

"I haven't been that lucky, no."

"Brothers or sisters?"

"Nope."

"Where's your mom and dad?"

Miriam stepped in. "Hey, Sam, maybe we can cool it with the questions, hm?"

Jane laughed. "No, she's fine. My parents live in Vermont, where I grew up."

Sammy tilted her head to the side. "So who do you live with?"

"Just me."

"Wow," Sammy said. "I would be sad if I lived here by myself."

Jane said, "It works fine for me. But I don't think your mom and dad are going anywhere, so you shouldn't have to worry."

Sammy nodded. "Daddy said sometimes people move out, but that's fine and it doesn't mean they're gone forever. It just means they live somewhere else."

Miriam frowned. "Daddy said that? When?"

Sammy shrugged and took another too-big bite of her lasagna.

Jane cleared her throat, trying not to look at Miriam. "Well, um, sometimes it can be good to live alone. You never have to wait for the bathroom. No one eats your snacks. You can watch whatever you want on TV."

"That sounds fun."

The cop side of Miriam's brain wanted to chime in, but she smothered it before the words could reach her mouth. Living alone was also dangerous, as the women on her desk could…

She blinked at the thought.

Jane looked at her. She wondered what she'd done to draw the reporter's attention. She pushed her chair away from the table and gestured vaguely toward the kitchen.

"Jane, can you help me in there?"

"Sure…"

Miriam put a hand on Sammy's shoulder. "You stay here and finish your food, okay?"

"Mm-hmm."

The adults went into the kitchen. Miriam looked at the photos and menus and business cards stuck to the fridge with magnets shaped like fruits and letters of the alphabet. When she finally turned around, Jane was waiting patiently next to the stove. Her face betrayed the fact she was dying of curiosity but didn't want to risk breaking Miriam's thought process.

"They all lived alone," she said, her voice barely above a whisper.

"Who?"

"Kimmy and Leigh and Angeline and, and…" She waved her hand. "The others. The victims of this asshole. They were all hookers, and we assumed that was the connection. But what if we were wrong? Because all the women lived alone. No partner, no kids, none of them lived with their parents, no roommates."

Jane thought about it. "Maybe he got lucky."

"*Six times?*" Miriam hissed.

"Maybe he follows them, and he only attacks if he can tell there's nobody home. The reason there aren't any victims with roommates is because those are the ones he calls off."

Miriam was shaking her head. "If he did that, he would still show up on security cameras following them. He would be seen by witnesses. The only thing that makes sense is that he *already knows*. These aren't women he's picking at random. He targets them beforehand somehow."

"How?"

"I don't know." She was looking at the floor, trying to think of who would have access to that kind of information. "But I can feel it. However he's doing it, *that's* how he's hunting them. That's how he's finding them."

Jane said, "Okay. I'll trust your~"

"Mommy, I finished!"

Jane looked back at the table, then finished her thought. "I'll trust your gut on this. I'll try to think of ways he could be finding women who live alone."

Miriam got the cupcakes out and placed them on plates. "This is how we're going to find them."

"I have faith."

They took the cupcakes back to the table, much to Sammy's delight. Miriam insisted the girl had to use a knife and fork on it to minimize on the mess. She had no idea if her epiphany was going to lead anywhere, but she had a buzzing feeling in her fingers that told her she just might have found a golden thread. But there was nothing she could do about it tonight.

She put thoughts of the case out of her mind and focused on her little girl and the cupcake.

Chapter Seven

DESPITE THE sugar, Sammy started flagging almost immediately after the cupcake was gone. Miriam got up and started corralling the little girl out of her chair so she could go get ready for bed.

"It shouldn't take very long," Miriam said. "If you want to stick around and talk."

"Oh." Jane was surprised by the invitation, even more surprised by how grateful she was for it. "Y-yeah. Sure. Okay. It was nice to meet you, Sammy."

"Mm-hmm," the girl murmured.

Miriam nodded and patted Sammy's shoulders. "When she's this far gone, it's more about guiding her to a soft place than trying to put her down. I'll be right back."

Jane chuckled and watched them go down the hall. She stood up and gathered the plates, glasses, and silverware from the table. She took it all into the kitchen and filled the sink. She could hear water rushing in the pipes to fill the tub and, a few minutes later, the hum of Miriam and Sammy's voices as they talked to each other down the hall.

She didn't want to waste Miriam's soap, so she went ahead and washed all the dishes in the sink and transferred them all to the drying rack. She had just finished when Miriam reappeared. Her sleeves had been rolled up, and splatters of bathwater had dampened the untucked tail of her shirt.

"I basically had to hold her up to keep her from falling asleep in the tub. Have you ever tried to get a sleeping kid into pajamas?"

"Can't say I have, no."

"It's hard." She examined the counter and sink. A line appeared between her eyebrows. "Did you wash my dishes?"

Jane nodded. "Kind of, yeah. I mean, I wasn't doing anything else."

"Oh. Thank you. That was..." She nodded. "Thanks."

"Sure. Host cooks, guest does the cleanup. That's how it usually goes, right?"

Miriam shrugged. "I don't really have enough guests to know the etiquette. But I do appreciate it. One less chore for me to take care of." She opened the fridge and took out two beers. "C'mon."

Jane pulled the plug on the sink and followed Miriam to the couch. It was arranged in the center of the space, its back to the apartment door. She took her beer and popped it open as she sat down.

"Sammy's cute."

"Yeah, she's okay. Normally I'm not crazy about kids, but I got lucky."

"Well, you got the best one."

Miriam chuckled and nodded, head half-turned to look out the window. It wasn't much of a view, but it seemed like her attention was turned inward. The apartment was completely silent and still, but sounds of traffic still drifted up from the street. Every now and then, someone passed in the hall or a neighboring apartment door shut just a little too loudly. Jane watched her, tried to make this quiet, calm person blend with the serious, gruff woman she'd gotten to know over the past nine days.

"I don't want to be rude..."

"Oh." Miriam faced her again. She put her elbow on the back of the couch and rested her head on her hand. "That's always a great way to break a silence."

Jane grinned. "We've spent a week and a half together, and I never got a hint of this side of you."

"What side?"

"The domestic side. The..." She nodded her head toward the hallway. "The mommy side."

Miriam gave a short, sharp laugh. "Well, sure. There's no way

I'm letting this side show up while I'm out there. The guys would destroy me. I have to be brass and steel, all the time. If those guys saw me cutting a cupcake in half or wrestling with a pair of footie pajamas, they'd never trust me in the field again. They don't think you can be both things. Tenderness is weakness. So it's better if they just don't see it." She looked sharply at Jane. "None–"

"None of this goes in the article," Jane interrupted. "I knew that when you made the invitation. Don't worry. Your personal life isn't part of the story."

"Good. Thank you."

Jane nodded. "I'm sure it goes the other way, too. Detective Balfour never shows up here in the apartment."

"Well." Miriam waved her hand side-to-side. "I leave my work at work, sure. I have to. I'm not going to expose Sammy to any of that hell. But Detective Balfour *does* show up here from time to time. The Case of the Missing Cookies. The Case of the Mysteriously Dry Toothbrush."

"The Case of the Light On Under the Covers."

Miriam smiled. "I'd let that one slide. I like that she wants to read, and kids need to be sneaky sometimes."

"Seems fair."

They lapsed back into silence. Jane sipped her beer. She didn't know if it would be polite to offer to leave, or if she even really wanted to go home yet. She felt comfortable even in the silences. But she didn't want to linger if Miriam was just waiting for her to do the right thing and get the hell out. She realized she didn't even know what time it was and tried to subtly check her watch. She was surprised to see it was just after eight o'clock.

Miriam noticed the look. "One of the side effects of the kid. They go to bed and you still have a whole night ahead of you to fill somehow."

"Not to mention our day started at four. Oh, hell. Yours started even earlier." That was the opening she needed. She leaned forward to put her beer on the coffee table, moving to the edge of the cushion. "I should go and let you get to bed."

Miriam said, "No, don't be silly. I've had worse days than this. Trust me. You're fine."

"Are you sure?"

"Yes, I'm not rushing you out of here. Unless *you* want to go..."

Jane considered the question. Part of her felt like lying, but a bigger and easier to surrender to part demanded she tell the truth. To say that she actually wanted to stay. She split the difference. "Not really."

Miriam nodded. "Okay, then."

Jane scooted back and settled in again. "If we're just hanging out, can I ask a very stupid and cliché question?"

"Uh oh," Miriam said, but she smiled.

"Why~"

"Yeah." Miriam laughed. "Why did I become a cop?"

Jane shrugged. "It's a reasonable question. It just seems like an uphill battle to get people to notice you, let alone respect you or treat you like a colleague. And to do all that just so you can do a job that is so mentally damaging and hard..."

Miriam nodded. "Sure. That's fair, yeah." She rubbed her jaw with the back of her hand, stared at the coffee table, and then nodded again. "The downside is that it's a boring answer. I wanted to be a superhero. Like Wonder Woman or The Flash."

Jane laughed. "You read comic books?"

"When I was a kid, sure," Miriam said. "They were great. As far as I could tell, being a cop was the closest thing to that. Plus, honestly, I'm not suited to do anything else. So I applied to the police academy, got in. Discovered I was good at it. It didn't take me long to realize that cops don't prevent bad things from happening. We just catch whoever does it, maybe explain why it happened. It's not the same thing. It's not a *bad* thing. But it's really nothing like being a hero."

"Oh," Jane said, unsure what else she could say.

"And," Miriam said, changing her voice to be more spritely to get away from the valley she'd just plunged them into, "when people started telling me I *couldn't* be a detective just because I was a 'girl,' then I did it to spite them."

"People have done worse for less," Jane said.

"Damn straight."

Jane ran her thumb along the edge of her beer can, smearing away the lipstick stain she'd left there. She didn't know why she'd put on makeup for the dinner. She had only halfway dressed up, but on the way out of her apartment, she hurried back inside and did her face up like she was about to go on a date. She knew Miriam didn't see it that way, because it wasn't that way, but she couldn't bring herself to leave with a plain face.

"Thank you for letting me see this side of you," she said. "I'm sure it's not something you share with many people."

"There are people on the squad who don't even know I have a daughter."

Jane took another drink. "A couple of days ago, I told you about the teacher who took advantage of me. What I didn't tell you was that she was a woman." Miriam looked sideways at her. Jane looked away, already feeling a cold sweat building in the small of her back. "Mrs. Campbell. I was too young to really even understand what she was doing or what was happening, so I just let it happen.

"A few years later when I started having feelings for other girls, I thought it was because of what she'd done. Like a symptom or something. It took me a long time to figure out it had nothing to do with her or what happened."

Miriam finally looked fully at her. "You're gay?"

"Yeah." Despite feeling clammy with sweat, she also felt frozen as she waited for Miriam's reaction. "I figured you... you opened up to me, I wanted to level the playing field a little. Tell you something about me that no one else knows about."

"Huh." Miriam looked at the coffee table again.

The silence built until it was too much for Jane to bear. "I'm sorry. I should have told you before I came to your apartment and met your daughter and–"

"What?" Miriam looked at her, looking legitimately confused. "What are you talking about?"

Jane said, "Well. You know. Some people might have an issue with a gay person meeting their kid, being in their home..."

"Jesus. You think I give a shit about..." She shook her head firmly. "No. That's ignorant bullshit. I've seen plenty of shitty people in my line of work, and they come in all varieties. I'm not going to treat you like you're toxic just because you like women." She gave a small, sad laugh. "Actually that might make me more likely to keep you around. It means I don't have to worry about you getting together with some jackass."

Jane tried not to focus on the *keep you around* part. As far as she knew, their working relationship was in its final hours. If Miriam was thinking further in the future... She dismissed the thought and got herself back on track.

"There are plenty of female jackasses, you know."

"Oh, for sure. But they're a different beast, usually."

Jane said, "That's true."

"I'm sorry I zoned out after you told me. I was just thinking that you were trying to make us even. You tell someone I have a daughter, and I tell everyone you're gay and maybe get your fired or make you the victim of some hate crime or something. You really went to eleven there, Jane."

"Right. I tend to overshare, I guess."

"I guess," Miriam said. "You don't have to worry about me saying anything to anyone. Even if you pissed me off, that's not the kind of ammunition I would ever use on a person."

Jane said, "I appreciate that."

"No. Not 'appreciate that.' You want to make us even and you went way too hard. It means we're still not even. You've got to try again. Give me something I can actually use if you reveal my dark domestic secret."

"Oh!" Jane tried to think of a secret that would suffice. "Gosh. I don't think I really have anything else that I'd be embarrassed by if it came out."

Miriam said, "Did you just say 'gosh'?"

"Uh…"

Miriam laughed and shook her head. "The woman says gosh. Wow."

Jane smiled. "Maybe you can use that against me."

"Nah. Anyone who knows you wouldn't be surprised."

"True."

Miriam sighed and rested her head on the back of the couch, staring up at the ceiling. "I hope to god this living-alone thing goes somewhere. I'm sick of this guy. And, like, does he get the women to change into the outfits? Do they already have them or does he bring it along like some kind of uniform? Should we be calling stores asking them about men buying this sort of thing?"

"I suppose there are worse ideas."

"Not many." Miriam closed her eyes. "When we do catch him, it will be thanks to you."

Jane said, "I've barely done anything."

"You put the case on my desk," Miriam said. "Patterson and Dooling, those guys were ready to just toss those women in a file.

Same with the other three we dug up. If you hadn't shown up and been your obnoxious self, no one would even know this bastard was out there doing this. You're the one who kicked the wasp nest."

"Well. Any time I can help by being a pain in the ass..."

Miriam raised her can in a toast, then took a drink. "You're not that bad."

"That's one of the nicest things you've said about me."

"That's one of the nicest things I've said about anybody. You should feel special."

"I do. Trust me."

They sat in silence after that, until Miriam suddenly twisted around and looked at the stereo on the bookshelf, then stood up.

"We have records."

"What?" Jane was clearly thrown by the sudden movement, and confused by the statement. "What records?"

Miriam went to the stereo. "You know, albums. Musical... songs." She took one off the shelf and held it up so Jane could see the artwork. "U2. *Joshua Tree*." She searched the rest of the collection. "Kate Bush, Elvis Costello, The Smiths... between me and Jeremy, we have a wide selection. Who do you like?"

"Uh. I like the Eurythmics."

Miriam checked. "I think we actually have one of... yeah." She took it down and opened the record player to put it on.

"*You* like the Eurythmics?" Jane asked.

"Yeah. Why? Who am I supposed to like?"

"The Police."

Miriam couldn't stop herself from laughing at that. "Okay, fair. We do have them if you want to switch out later." She moved the needle and 'Love is a Stranger' started playing. She lowered the volume so it wouldn't wake Sammy. "I'm getting another beer. Do you...?"

"No, I'm good. Thanks."

She got another can and went back to the couch.

"I like this," Jane said.

Miriam looked around, trying to figure out what she meant. "It's just a quiet apartment. Your apartment is probably the same."

"Sure. But it's different when there was a lot of sound earlier, you know, conversation and a little kid running around. An apartment that has become silent is different than one that's *always* quiet. Thank you for inviting me over tonight."

"You're welcome. Not to give you any extra dirt on me, but I'm actually a little disappointed tomorrow is your last day." She held up a finger to stop Jane from getting too excited. "I do *not* want you hanging around all the damn time, don't get me wrong. But it's been nice having you there. Having another lady in the room makes a real difference."

"Maybe you could come hang out at my work for a few days. Although I'm not sure what we'd need a detective in the bullpen for."

"Oh I'm sure someone there is breaking some kind of law." Miriam winked at her. "I appreciate the thought."

There was a rattle at the door and Jeremy let himself inside. He looked at Jane, but managed to hide his 'you're still here?' expression before she turned around.

"Oh hi," he said, keeping his voice low. "Jeremy Balfour. You must be, um..."

Jane smiled and raised her hand in greeting. "Jane Ross. Hi."

"Nice to meet you." He held up both his hands and moved toward the hall. "Don't mind me. I'll just head on to bed."

"Did you have a good night?" Miriam asked.

"It was fine," he said. "You?"

Miriam said, "Well, I haven't kicked her out yet. So it's not the worst."

He smiled. "Glad to hear it. Have a nice talk." He lifted his hand again, this time in farewell, and disappeared down the hall.

Jane watched him go, then turned to Miriam. "You know that's strange, right?"

"Why? He's still Sammy's father. I still *like* him well enough. We're just better as friends than anything else. It makes sense for him to live here with us."

"And you both just go out on dates and, and see other people? What if his date had gone well and she came home with him?"

Miriam laughed. "Trust me, that's rarely an issue with Jeremy. Bless his heart. But if he *did* bring someone back, they would've had a conversation about it before he walked in the door."

"Do you still sleep together? Same bed?"

"No. We have the Rob and Laura Petrie special. Two twin beds with a nightstand between them."

Jane shook her head. "I don't understand that at all. I'm sorry.

But I'm glad it works for you. I'm glad Sammy has that kind of stability in her life."

Miriam shrugged. "That's all it comes down to. Sammy. There are times when it's weird and awkward, but I just remind myself it's for her. If a time comes when this arrangement is harder for her than some other alternative, we'll reassess."

"Good luck with it."

"Mm-hmm."

Jane checked her watch. "I think the adrenaline of the day is starting to wear off. I can feel myself lagging."

Miriam said, "We can call it a night."

Jane nodded, eyes closed. "I just hope it doesn't wear off before I get home."

"Just stay here."

Jane opened her eyes and looked at her. "What? Really?"

"If you feel like you might actually get some quality sleep, don't risk the bus. Just stretch out here and give in." She patted the cushion next to her. "It's not the most comfortable thing in the world. I mean, it'll always be a couch. But as couches go, it's not the worst. I'll get you a pillow and a blanket."

"Are you sure?"

Miriam nodded and stood up. "Wait here." She went to the hall and came back with a pillow and blanket. "Bathroom is down the hall if you need it. Feel free to take a shower if you want."

"I appreciate this, Miriam. Now that I'm considering the option I am feeling very, very tired all of a sudden."

"Then I'll go ahead and say goodnight. I'll see you in the morning."

Jane nodded, already putting the pillow against the arm of the couch.

Miriam turned off the record player and turned off the overhead light. She turned around, her hand still on the switch.

"Too dark?"

"No." Jane gestured to the window. "There's still a lot of light coming in from the window."

Miriam said, "Okay. See you in the morning. Sleep well."

"You too."

Miriam headed down the hall. Jeremy was sitting up in his bed, shoes off and shirt unbuttoned to reveal his undershirt. He was reading a novel that he closed on his thumb when she came into the bedroom.

"What the hell was *that?*"

She frowned at him as she crossed to her closet. "What? I told you she was coming over."

"You just spent a week bitching about this leech that's been foisted upon you, this pain in the ass you'll finally be free of this time tomorrow, this obnoxious reporter that you haven't had *one kind word* for, and I walk in on you just... hanging out with your buddy."

Miriam scoffed and rolled her eyes. "She's not my buddy."

"Let me list all the people I've seen you hanging out with by choice." He held up his hand. "There's me... let's see, uh, Sammy."

Miriam held up a finger. "Lisa."

He rolled his eyes but added a finger. "My *sister* Lisa..."

"Okay, so I'm picky. There's nothing wrong with that."

"Nope." He smirked and went back to his book. "Nothing wrong with that at all."

She sighed and unbuttoned her blouse to start getting ready for bed. She didn't know why she was fighting so hard. So she had a friend. Big deal.

It wasn't like she was feeling anything else for her.

It wasn't like she'd invited her to spend the night because the alternative, saying goodbye to her, was too much to bear when she knew they might be saying a permanent goodbye tomorrow.

"What's wrong?" Jeremy asked.

"What?"

"Your face just got weird."

"It's been a long day. I've been up since two this morning. Your face would be weird, too."

He let the matter drop, and she turned her back to avoid any more revelatory faces as she finished getting ready for bed.

Chapter Eight

JANE WAS tired enough that she did manage to fall asleep quickly, but being on a couch in a strange place meant that she kept waking up through the night. Every time she was shaken from sleep by an air conditioner clicking on, voices in the hall, or street sounds, she took a few minutes to process everything that had happened that night.

She'd come out to Miriam. She'd barely come out to *anyone*, and for Miriam Balfour to be one of the first people to know felt strange and wrong. But also... right. She was glad Miriam knew. And she was proud of herself for saying the words out loud. Her voice hadn't broken and she hadn't run out of the room in terror. Even better, the information didn't seem to have changed how Miriam saw her.

She was out, and her world hadn't come crashing down.

By morning, she had no idea how much she'd slept or how long she'd spent tossing and turning on the couch. She got up once to use the bathroom, being very careful not to barge into either of the bedrooms. She did know that she'd been woken up by movement in the kitchen at a little after five-thirty. She stayed still and listened as someone prepared something - it sounded like cereal being poured into a plastic container - and then quietly slipped out the front door.

Husband going to work, she deduced. Miriam had said he was a schoolteacher, so that made sense. It was only a couple of minutes more until she heard Miriam's voice drifting down the hall from

Sammy's bedroom, waking her up for breakfast.

Jane decided that was enough of a cue for her to get up as well. She sat up and stretched her arms over her head, twisted her head to the left and then the right, and rolled her shoulders. She had just stood up when Sammy appeared, marching ahead of Miriam like she was leading her on a chain. The little girl stopped when she saw Jane. She blinked, then waved, and kept going. Jane waved back, but Sammy was already back on-mission.

"Morning," Miriam said. "Hopefully the couch wasn't too terrible."

"It was fine. I slept~"

There was a thump against the door. Miriam held up a finger. She changed course and opened the door, stooping down to retrieve the newspaper. She peered down the hall and shook her head as she closed the door and came back.

"I've told that kid there's no need to actually wing it at the doors, but he doesn't listen."

Jane smiled, then turned her head to the side to read the portion of the masthead visible on the rolled-up paper. "Is that the *Sentinel?* You subscribe?"

"I wanted to make sure you weren't a tabloid rag or something." She zipped her hand down the length of the paper to remove the rubber band. "You passed muster. Barely."

"Good to know."

Jane followed Miriam into the kitchen. Sammy was already making herself a bowl of cereal, carefully pouring milk into the bowl without spilling. Miriam leaned against the counter and watched her, then turned her attention to the paper.

"The article I wrote about the... the case should be in there. It's not a full version, of course, but it gives a taste of what~"

Miriam said, "What the fuck is this?"

Jane blinked in surprise. All the softness from the night before had vanished from Miriam's voice. Even her face was different. This was the woman she'd met a week ago. A woman who resented her and didn't trust her. She held up the newspaper and then thrust it forward like she was trying to swat a fly that had just landed on Jane's face. Jane flinched and took a step back, taking the paper and skimming to find what could have changed Miriam's mood so completely.

"What the hell is *the Cozy Killer?*"

Jane's breath seemed to have turned into a solid block in her chest. She saw the article, a narrow inset on the front page. COZY KILLER TARGETS SIX PROSTITUTES IN BROOKLYN. Her heart thudded against her ribs as she read the story. Words, her words, but slaughtered and surgically repositioned, stripped of context until only the lurid parts remained. Six women, dressed in pajamas, killed in their homes.

"I didn't write this," Jane said. "I-I mean I did... I wrote... these sentences, most of them, but my editor cut out... I-I don't... I *never* wrote the words 'cozy killer.' You have to believe me."

Red had filled Miriam's cheeks as she grabbed the paper back. "I knew this would blow up in my face. I *knew* it. But I let you worm your way in..."

"Mommy?" Sammy said, looking fearfully up at Miriam.

"It's okay, sweetie." She didn't take her eyes off Jane, but she put a hand on her daughter's shoulder. "Mommy's just angry because she made a stupid mistake."

"No," Jane said. "Look, the story would've gotten out anyway, and maybe other women will take it as a warning. We might have saved lives~"

Miriam said, "Or we might have let this bastard know we're onto him. This is exactly what I was afraid of. If he wanted notoriety, he would've done the Zodiac bullshit, but he didn't. He liked flying under the radar. And now it doesn't matter if we find out how he was choosing his victims because you can be damn sure he'll stop now. We were sneaking up behind him and now you've lit off a flare gun."

Jane felt her own anger starting to build in response to Miriam's energy. "You were *completely* on board with doing this. You decided it was a good idea! You *told* me to print the story early!"

"Because I *liked you,*" Miriam snapped. "You made me forget *every* other fucking journalist I'd *ever* dealt with, and why I always regretted it, because you all do the same goddamn thing every time. You're the same. You're just like every other fucking one, but the difference is you're better at it. I *cannot believe* I fell for~"

"Mommy!" This time Sammy's voice was as loud as a snap. She had put down the milk carton and was leaning against the counter, both tiny hands clutched in front of her chin like she was praying. Her lower lip trembled and her eyelashes glistened with tears. "You're *yelling,*" she said in a small, terrified voice.

Miriam reached out and cupped her daughter's cheek. "I know, baby. I'm sorry."

"And saying bad words."

"I know. I'll stop when Jane leaves." She looked at Jane. "She's leaving right now."

Jane let go of the tension in her arms. She realized her whole body had been tensed, as if she and Miriam were about to have a physical fight.

"You're right. We'll talk about this at the station."

"Oh, you're not going to the station." Miriam seemed to be making an effort to keep her voice steady and calm for Sammy's sake.

Jane frowned. "I still have one more--"

"That's *done.* You've done enough damage. And you clearly have enough for whatever shit you're going to write."

Jane wanted to fight back, wanted to say something about how unfair it was, but she knew how pointless it would be arguing about fairness. They weren't kids, and nothing about the world was fair. Besides, she wasn't going to risk escalating things in front of Sammy. She nodded and held her hands up in surrender.

"Okay. Fine. But you have to believe that I had nothing to do with giving him a name."

Miriam shook her head. "It doesn't matter. Damage is done."

Jane nodded and turned away. She only stopped long enough to get her shoes from next to the couch and put them on.

She could hear Miriam talking softly to Sammy in the kitchen, comforting her after the angry outburst. She quietly closed the apartment door behind her, fighting back tears at what had just happened. She'd almost had a true friend, a confidant, and it was all gone in an instant.

By the time she reached the ground floor, her sadness had turned to anger. If she'd truly lost Miriam, it wasn't because of anything she'd done. It wasn't *her* story that had made Miriam so angry. It wasn't *her* words that had destroyed their promising connection right as it was starting to become something real. The rug had been pulled out from under her, and she knew exactly who was to blame. She stepped to the curb and raised her hand. It would be cheaper to take the subway or the bus, but both those options were far too slow.

She needed to have words with her editor.

Simon Ludwin looked up with a bright smile when Jane burst into his office, completely ignoring her energy as she slapped the paper down on the desk. She'd bought it at the newsstand downstairs with the expectations of hitting him with it, but she'd chickened out at the last second.

"Isn't it great?" he said, flashing his perfect white teeth. "We've been getting calls all morning. The *Times* called us! Can you believe that? They're so pissed off that we scooped them on a story like this. They wanted to know your sources and I said, look, she got it straight from the po-po themselves. I told them you'd been *at the crime scenes* and they almost shit themselves."

"This is not the story I wrote."

"Sure it is." He craned his neck to look at the paper. "We had to trim it down to fit the space, you know, cut the unnecessary stuff..."

"The 'unnecessary stuff' is the story of the cops who are actually investigating these murders. The story I wanted to tell in the first place. The human beings who have to go in there and expose themselves to this evil—"

He held up a hand. "Boring shit. No one buys papers for that sort of thing, Ross. No one buys baseball cards for the boring stats on the back. They buy them 'cause Wade Boggs and Roger Clemens." He tapped the paper. "And they buy newspapers for serial killer in the making. Lurking in the shadows. Hunting women. If it bleeds, it leads, right? You oughta be happy. This is so much better than the fluff you were planning to write. People are going to want to talk to you. And hey, once this story takes off, maybe we'll be able to find more room to tell your, uh, little stories."

"And who came up with the fucking name?"

He lifted his chin, proud. "That would be me. But you can go ahead and take credit if you want. It's catchy. It'll catch on, trust me."

"You're a monster."

"I'll try not to let it keep me up at night."

Someone knocked on the door and poked his head into the office. "Ross. You got a call."

"Take a message."

"I've taken, like, nine. He's been calling all morning."

She rolled her eyes and picked up the paper she'd dropped on

Simon's desk. "We're not done talking about this."

"Of course not," he raised his voice to be sure she'd hear him as she left his office. "You can still do a story on the cops! We've got a gap next to the Sunday crossword it can fill!"

Jane threw herself into her chair. Line 1 was blinking on her phone. She picked up the receiver and jabbed the button. She had to force the bare minimum of professionalism into her voice.

"Jane Ross."

"Tha-a-a-at *isn't* my *na-a-ame*."

Jane frowned. She was pretty sure it was a man's voice, but he was speaking just above a falsetto. Each word was drawn out and breathy as if he had just gotten back from a jog.

"No, it's my name," she said. "And what *is* your name?"

He laughed, and the sound made the hairs on the back of her neck stand up. "Do-o-o you really want to kno-o-ow?"

She looked around the bullpen. No one else was paying attention to her. Simon's door was standing open, but they couldn't see each other from her position.

"Sure," she said.

"Yo-o-ou wrote the story about me."

She slowly put her other hand on the desktop. She felt like she was suddenly sweating, but her whole body was cold at the same time. Her skin was overly sensitive, like even the collar of her shirt felt like sandpaper against her neck.

"You're claiming to be him."

"I *am* him." His voice hadn't changed. It was the same low, breathless hum that made her think of robots or those machines smokers with cancer pressed against their windpipe to produce sound. "You wrote a story about me-e-e. But you don't even know my na-a-ame."

Jane's mouth was dry. "If you'd like us to print a retraction, I could~"

"I know *your* name."

More chills, a shiver that ran deeper. "I~"

"Ja-a-a-a-a-ane... Ross-s-s-s-s."

She couldn't bring herself to respond to that. She looked down and saw that her hand was trembling. She curled it into a fist and desperately looked around the bullpen again.

"How do I know~"

"Fuzzy slippers," he interrupted, anticipating her question. "You just said pajamas. You didn't say they were all wearing fuzzy slippers. I bring them with me. Not everyone has a pair, you know. Can't take a chance."

Jane stood up so quickly that a few heads turned toward her. She snapped her fingers and pointed at the receiver. To her great relief, an intern realized what she needed and ran for Simon's office.

"Are you going to tell the world my name?"

"I'm ready," she said.

There was a buzz of silence on the other end of the line. She was terrified he'd hung up, that he was just trying to tease her. She pressed the receiver harder against her ear.

"Are you th~"

"*I AM THE GOODNIGHT MAN!*"

The voice was louder than it had ever been, almost barked into the phone. Jane jumped and pulled the receiver away from her ear. When she put it back, all she heard was the hum of a dead line.

The intern reappeared with Simon. The editor frowned. "What's going on? Jesus, you look like you just saw a damn ghost."

Jane was still holding the receiver, even though it felt like it weighed a hundred pounds now. The cradle was much too far away to hang it up.

"I think I just talked to the killer."

An hour later, Jane was back at the Twenty-First precinct. This time she had been escorted upstairs by a desk sergeant. He deposited her in an interrogation room, which looked more like a doctor's office than she would have expected. The table was in a corner, with two chairs facing each other on the exposed sides. She sat down facing the door and waited.

And she waited.

There wasn't a two-way mirror like she'd seen in the movies, but she spotted a video camera mounted in the corner of the ceiling aimed at her. She stared into the lens and wondered if Miriam was on the other side watching her from some separate room. She had expected a mirror, like the movies, but she supposed this was the modern version of the same thing.

She sighed and stood up when the door finally opened after forty-five minutes, but her relief was short-lived. It was just a young sergeant bringing her a cup of water and a sandwich from the breakroom. He smiled apologetically and handed her the meager lunch.

"Do you need anything else? We have chips or~"

"Where's Detective Balfour?"

"She's working on the case."

"I know! I should be helping her!"

He shrugged and backed out of the room. "Sorry. She told us to keep you in here. It shouldn't be too much longer." He closed the door behind her.

Jane slumped back into her chair.

She was halfway through the sandwich when the door opened again. She looked up, expecting the sergeant again. She was so surprised to see Miriam that she choked on her sandwich. She coughed, pressing the back of her hand against her mouth as she stood up. Miriam eyed her until the coughing fit ended, then pointed at the chair.

"Sit." Jane did as she was told. Miriam took the other seat. "Tell me everything the caller said to you."

"I already told the sergeant everything."

"And he wrote it down," Miriam said, "and now you're going to tell me the story again."

Jane groaned and put her elbow on the table. She pinched the bridge of her nose. "Why are we doing it like this? Why can't we just *talk?*"

"Because this is an ongoing case with six victims, and we're doing this by the book. I don't want any more surprises in the newspaper."

Jane slapped her palm down on the table. "You. Told. Me. To. Turn. It. In. How many times do I have to say it before you remember? Maybe publishing the story was a bad idea, which I still don't agree with, but you need to admit your own responsibility for it."

"Like you accept responsibility for what your editor did?"

"I had no control over that. Just like you have no control over what cases your captain assigns you. Maybe we both screwed up. But we worked well together, and if we can just~"

Miriam interrupted her by flipping open the case file. "We were able to trace the call," she said. "It came from a payphone not far from the newspaper's offices. We sent a uniform down to collect security footage to see if the bastard was caught on camera. It's a busy intersection so we're not especially hopeful. The intern at your office said that the guy called multiple times trying to reach you, so we're looking into those calls as well. If he used the same payphone for every call, we might get lucky. But if he used a different one for each attempt, well..."

Jane said, "You're really just going to go back to treating me like a stranger?"

Miriam looked up at her. For a second, Jane saw a flicker of something behind her eyes. It might have been disappointment, or regret, but whatever it was, Miriam looked away before Jane could get a handle on it.

"He said my name," Jane said. "He said my name, and the way he said it made my skin crawl. No matter how you feel about me, I'm part of this case. You can either treat me like a hostile outsider, or you can keep me on the inside and we can work together to track this guy down."

Miriam looked at her again. "He didn't say your name because you're part of this case. I'm not keeping you in here because I'm mad at you. Do you honestly not get what's happening here?"

"What do you mean? Why else~"

"You're not part of the case to him, Jane. You're a target."

CHAPTER NINE

"ALL OF the women he's killed have been prostitutes." Jane didn't like the tremor in her voice when she spoke, but when she tried to control it, the words came out barely audible. "I don't fit the profile."

"So far, that's been the case." Miriam's voice was softer now. She tapped the file with her pen. "But the profile is also women around your age, no real connections, who live alone. We don't know what will change now that he's been exposed. But he reached out to you for a reason. Until we have a better idea of what that reason is, we're going to take precautions."

Jane sat up straighter. "Wait. What kind of precautions?"

"You'll have a protective detail outside your apartment~"

"Absolutely not."

Miriam closed her eyes. She'd fought for the protective detail. Captain Webster didn't think it was necessary either. He thought the killer was just bragging, showing off, trying to get notoriety. He and Sergeant Babbitt both believed her was taunting her in the hopes of getting another story written about him. Miriam didn't want to take that chance. She believed what she'd said about Jane fitting the profile enough to potentially justify the killer taking action, and she wasn't going to be caught sitting on her hands when she could offer protection.

Jane pushed her chair back and stood up. Miriam's eyes snapped open.

"Where do you think you're going?"

"I'm going to talk to your captain. This is nonsense."

Miriam swore under her breath as she followed Jane out of the interrogation room. Webster was blocking the doorway of his office, talking to Detectives Clark and Patterson. All three men looked at Jane as she approached.

"I don't need babysitters."

"We're not going to have you killed on our watch, Miss Ross," Webster said. "In your statement, you said the caller made a point of identifying you by name. He may have only done that to scare you, but we have to take it as a threat until we know more. And the threat against you is the only lead we have about where he might strike next."

"So you're using me as bait?" Jane said.

"Not in so many words," Miriam said.

Webster shrugged. "You put yourself in the crosshairs with your article. We're not going to ignore the opportunity."

Her cheeks were red. "For how long?"

"I wish we could give you a timeline, but we're not sure. Until we're confident he's not going to try to make a move on you. So until further notice, you and Detective Balfour are going to be joined~"

Miriam blinked and furrowed her brow, holding up a hand to stop him. "Wait, what? Me? No one said anything about *me* being her protective detail."

"It was your idea," Webster said, fixing a cold stare on her. "You practically forced me to agree with this plan. Why wouldn't it be you?"

"Because this is *my case*. I can't sit around watching her all day. I need to be out there following leads to catch this asshole."

Webster said, "It *was* your case. And you did some real good work here, Detective. But going forward, it belongs to Clark and Patterson."

"You've got to be fucking jo~"

"We're bringing Patterson in because the killings cross into the Sixty-Second Precinct's territory," Webster interrupted. "And you've already got such a good rapport with Ross, it makes sense. Besides, Miss Ross, would you rather have Detective Dooling sleeping on your couch and following you around all day?"

"This is unbelievable," Miriam said.

Webster shrugged. "It's what's happening."

Miriam glared at him and then turned away before her fist could fly on its own. She wanted to smash something, wanted to cause damage, but she knew that would only deepen the hole she was already buried in. She started for the stairs but was stopped by Sergeant Babbitt's voice.

"Balfour! They're going to need your files."

She stopped and closed her eyes, grateful her back was turned. She took a deep breath, then pointed at her desk.

"Get them your fucking self."

Miriam didn't remember going downstairs, and she didn't remember leaving the building, but she only stopped walking when she reached the curb and had to wait for traffic to clear before she could go any further. She was breathing hard, as if she'd run to the ground floor, and her hands were clenched into fists so tight that her fingernails dug painfully into her palms.

Jane appeared next to her. Miriam considered pushing her into the street.

Thankfully her foul mood didn't extend to actual murder.

"We know one thing about the call for sure." Jane's voice was soft, cautious. Miriam kept her eyes forward. "It means he's getting sloppy. A-and he told me that he brings the slippers to the crime scene. That's a big piece of information, right? That's helpful. Potentially a smoking gun."

"Go tell it to the cops working the case."

She crossed the street and Jane followed her. "I don't know what to do here, Miriam. You tell me I can turn in the story. So I do, and it gets chopped up, beyond my control. And you completely cut me off. I get a call from the bastard you're chasing. Again, out of my control. I immediately come here to tell you about it. You lock me in a room, and then your boss takes you off the case. Once again, *nothing to do with me*, and completely out of my control, and yet you're *still* mad at me. I would apologize if I knew what part of what happened was my fault. I didn't have to get your permission to publish my story but I did. Out of respect for you. And it's frustrating to do that and all I get in return is this... this..." She gestured searching for the right words. "This fucking bitch."

Miriam stopped and turned to face her. "What did you just call me?"

Jane's eyes were wide with fear, but she didn't back down. "Admit it. You know I didn't do anything wrong. You're just scared that you let me in just a little, you showed me who you really are, and now you're retreating."

Miriam was finding it hard to keep her breath steady. She felt like she'd just finished running upstairs and her face was hot. Part of her anger came from the fact she knew Jane was right. Seeing the article that morning had almost felt like grabbing hold of a life preserver. There was relief in kicking Jane out of her apartment. She'd laid awake all night thinking of the woman sleeping out on the couch. A woman who had bonded with Sammy, who had been charming and funny. Jane had gotten under her skin in a way that so few people ever had, and it terrified her.

And now she was being called out over it, and that only stoked Miriam's anger to burn even hotter.

"I don't care if it gets me desk duty for the next six months," she said, her voice low. "I'm going back up there and I'm getting your protection detail reassigned. Enjoy having Abbamonte camped out in your living room for the next month."

"Don't bother," Jane said. "I don't need someone watching my front door day and night."

"Don't be an idiot," Miriam said.

Jane turned and walked away, flipping her hand in the air dismissively. "I reject police protection," she said without turning around. "Mail me whatever fucking forms I have to sign, just so long as I never have to see you again."

Miriam watched her go, grateful to be freed from the obligation of staking out her apartment. And it didn't matter if she was nice and charming. She was still the enemy. The paper that morning had been a painful reminder of the divide between their jobs. Knowing Jane went into it with the best of intentions only made it worse. Imagine if her intentions had been malevolent. Imagine if she had wanted to throw a grenade into the investigation. It could have been so much worse.

As Jane reached the corner, some sympathetic part of Miriam's brain took over. "Hey!"

Jane stopped, but it took her a moment to actually turn and look back.

"He called your work because he didn't know your home

number. Ross is a common name. There's no reason to believe he can actually find you."

She considered that, then nodded, and turned away again.

Then she rounded the corner and disappeared out of sight.

Jeremy came out of the kitchen as soon as Miriam unlocked the door. He had a pot of something that smelled delicious in one hand, stirring it with a spoon he held in the other. Miriam looked longingly at the pot, but he held it out of view and raised his eyebrows at her.

"Sammy said you yelled at Jane and threw her out this morning."

She glared at him. "That little girl has a big mouth."

He pulled back with surprise. "So it's true? What happened? When I left, you two were basically becoming best friends. Hell, she was the closest thing to an actual friend I've ever seen you make. What could possibly have happened~"

Miriam walked past him and took the trash basket out from under the sink. She fished out the paper and held it out to him. When she realized his hands were full, she unfolded it and held it up with the article facing him. He leaned forward to read it, but his eyebrows rose as soon as he saw the headline.

"Okay," he said slowly, dragging it out into a few syllables. "I thought you gave her permission to write about the murders."

"To *write* about them," she said, angrily stuffing the paper back into the trash. "Not this sensational bullshit. Not give the bastard a name and validating him. These guys either want to get caught or they want attention. They want to feel important and powerful. Giving him a name does that. Giving him a name makes him the boogieman."

Jeremy nodded slowly, but it was clear he still didn't understand. "It also lets women know he's out there. The sort of women he's targeting. The places where he's hunting them. Bars and nightclubs are going to be a little more aware of the people hanging around if they know someone might be prowling."

"That's *exactly* the argument *she* made." She slapped the paper down on the counter.

"So maybe she has a point?"

"Or maybe it could cause a panic. People calling in false leads. Pestering the cops because we're not moving fast enough for them."

Jeremy said, "It might make him more cautious."

"Or it might embolden him, since he knows we're aware of him. He called Jane at the newspaper today." Jeremy's eyes widened at that. "He took offense with the name they chose. Says he wants to be called the Goodnight Man or some shit."

"Wow," he said. "Well, okay then. That proves Jane's theory, right? He's gotten sloppy."

"Cocky."

Jeremy shrugged. "There's a fine line. He stuck his neck out. That was stupid of him."

Miriam shook her head. "Okay. Maybe. But the fact is, we don't know. I'll admit it could go either way. But now the ball is in *his* court. If he gets sloppy, if he gets scared, if he decides the heat is too much and just stops killing... we'll never find him. He could just pack up and move to a different city to start all over. The point is that we don't know for sure what he'll do next until another dead body shows up."

Jeremy placed the pot back on the stove. "Okay. I'll agree with you on that front." He tilted his head to one side like a confused dog. "I'm just not sure why that's any different than the situation you had last night. Sure, the article might change his behavior. But unless I'm mistaken, you didn't have a clue what he was going to do before this, either. So what does it matter if this makes him change course? Before, you had a good idea this guy was barreling down the highway, right? Well, now you definitely know he's there. The only thing that's changed is that she turned the lights on. If he turns left, if he turns right, it doesn't really matter because now you can move with him."

Miriam shook her head. She finally managed to snag his spoon and used it to fish a piece of pasta from the pot. She waited for it to cool, then popped it into her mouth.

"I think you're actually mad about something else."

"I thought I was supposed to be the detective in this relationship."

He took his spoon back. "You're too close to the case. Biased. They had to call in a consultant." He tapped the end of the spoon against his chest. "Anyway, it's not about the article. You wanted an excuse to be mad at Jane."

She scoffed.

"I'm dead serious. I saw you with her. You were relaxed. Chill. You two looked like you'd been best friends forever. It's why I was so shocked when Sammy said you went back to the angry screamy lady.

It's okay to have friends, Miriam. It's okay to be... vulnerable and open with people."

"The work I do~"

"Doesn't have to mean anything," he said. "You manage to separate work from me and Sammy. So why does it have to get in the way with your friends? You don't have to talk through all the gory details. You just have to let the people close to you know how it makes you feel. Jane doesn't seem like the kind of person who scares easily. Plus, working for the paper, I'm sure she's seen her own fair share of horrors. Don't push her away. Give her a chance to surprise you, and who knows what will happen?"

Miriam said, "I don't want to rely on someone who can just disappear one day."

"Who says she's going to disappear?"

"Everyone disappears eventually."

Jeremy gestured at himself.

"You're different. You're scared of paying rent in Brooklyn."

"That is true." He turned to face her. "You're right. Jane might disappear someday. But making her disappear *now* to save yourself from being hurt by it later... That's just crazy talk."

"Maybe," she murmured, looking down at the counter.

"Definitely. Besides, no matter what she'd written, there's a chance this guy would have called to give them his name anyway. I mean, wow, the 'Goodnight Man'? He's been workshopping that for a while. He wanted to make sure people knew that."

Miriam sighed and shook her head. "How long until dinner is ready?"

"Ten."

She untucked her blouse. "I'm going to say hi to Sammy, then get a quick shower."

He nodded and turned back to focus on the food again.

Before she left the kitchen, she turned back to look at him. "It matters because knowing *where* he is doesn't matter if he decides to come at us head-on. We still know nothing about this guy. And knowing he's out there isn't going to do us a damn bit of good if we can't get out of his way."

Chapter Ten

JANE SPENT the entire day expecting her anger to fade, to settle into some lesser emotion or become more manageable. It didn't.

She went back to work and spent the day writing the article she'd always intended to write. It was supposed to be a profile of all the detectives, the squad as a whole, but she had barely spent any time with the men. Truth be told, she thought centering the story on the sole female detective was a much better spin anyway.

So she wrote about working the investigation with Miriam, but the anger kept bubbling back up. It eventually got so strong that her hands were shaking too much to hit the keys. She got up and went to the stairwell, marching up to the next landing before she turned and went back down. She repeated the routine five times before she finally calmed down enough to get back to work.

Now the full article had been turned in. She didn't know if it was the story she'd hoped to write. The serial killer angle had overtaken the day-to-day things she'd hoped to illustrate. For a while she'd let herself believe that meeting Miriam, becoming friends with her, had made the week worthwhile. But even if that had been destroyed at the last minute, at least she could take comfort in the fact she'd shined a light on a murderer. That was something to be proud of no matter what else happened.

Jane dumped her things on the dinner table. She went down the hall to her bedroom so she could change out of her work clothes and settle in for the night. She needed something to take her mind off everything that had happened. Not just Miriam turning on her, not just the creepy phone call or her story being hacked to pieces, but the whole week. She needed to take a vacation. A nice long escape from the city and all the shitty, awful~

A pair of fuzzy slippers had been placed in the center of her bed.

The second it took her brain to register the sight felt like an hour. She backed up a step and bumped into something solid but soft and her already startled heart skipped another beat. The shape's arms wrapped around Jane before she could turn around, pulling her back against him. One hand pressed hard into her shoulder, the fingers like nails digging into the soft skin around the joint as his other hand pressed a balled-up towel against her face.

Jane flailed but he was too strong. She had been on the verge of hyperventilating when the towel went over her face, her heart had already been compromised, and now it felt like it was zigging side-to-side in her chest as her lungs burned. Fear and desperation took over everything else. She was a trapped animal fighting to survive, well aware that she didn't have a hope in hell of breaking free from him. She tried to scream though her voice was muffled, but she did it anyway, she screamed her throat raw until it felt like she was breathing out pieces of glass.

He wrestled her backward into the hallway. He was breathing hard from exertion. Jane tried to plant her feet on the floor but she'd taken her shoes off and her socks couldn't get any traction. She felt the cotton closing in on the edges of her vision, her eyes burning with tears as the man kept the towel locked firmly over her mouth and nose.

This is how I die.

Her mind filled with those five words. She was going to die in the next few minutes, and there was absolutely nothing she could do about it. Six other women had been in this exact situation and none of them had been able to stop him. What chance did she have? She twisted and pushed and pulled but his arm didn't give. His fingers dug harder into her shoulder and the pain it sent down her arm made her yelp.

The towel was too thick. She wasn't getting any air. The haze in her vision closed in further, further, and the things she could still see had grown fuzzy and weirdly flat.

She felt her limbs going limp as she was lowered onto the cold tile of her bathroom floor, angled so that she was propped up against the side of her tub. He had let go of her. She could fight now. She could get away from him. If only she could focus. If only she could find the strength to lift one of her arms. Her right shoulder, the one he'd been grabbing, felt like there were still nails embedded there. She couldn't open her eyes to check. She couldn't lift her head, which had fallen forward. She couldn't...

...her eyes opened.

Her shirt was unbuttoned. Her belt was undone. She saw her pajamas next to her on the bathroom floor. The fuzzy slippers had been brought in and were sitting on top of the pajamas. A man was kneeling next to her, fiddling with something in a black bag. He was dressed all in black. She had no idea how much time had passed since she lost consciousness but he didn't seem hurried. He took a syringe out of his bag, along with a small vial. He stuck the needle through the lid of the vial and drew the liquid up into the tube. Another shudder ran through Jane's body.

"Please don't."

Her words had to have come out slurred and unintelligible, but he still stopped and looked at her. His mask covered his entire face except for his eyes, which he'd obscured with a pair of dark goggles. All she could see was the white skin of his upper cheeks. He leaned forward and tapped her inner arm, just above the elbow, and positioned the syringe against it.

"Relax," he hissed, the only thing he'd said to her since this whole ordeal began.

"No..."

He injected her.

Jane screamed, but he had been prepared for that and clapped one hand over her mouth. He was wearing black rubber gloves. The smell of them was nauseating.

The syringe was withdrawn. Her whole arm burned. He kept his hand over her face to muffle her screams and shouts for help. She stared at him, seeing her panicked reflection in his bug-like goggles. She couldn't even tell the shape of his face under the mask, not that she would ever be able to tell anyone the details of her killer's appearance.

Her brain fog slowly rolled back in.

She slumped back against the tub.

He took his hand away from her mouth.

She could still hear herself screaming inside her head, but she could feel her lips hanging slack. The silence in the apartment was oppressive. He watched her for a moment, most likely seeing if she was playing possum, then turned his attention away from her.

He wasn't holding her down. He wasn't even looking at her. She could escape, get up and run, survive.

But she felt completely separate from her body.

The rest of the apartment seemed very far away.

And the rest of the world...

Jane was aware of being aware first. Not awake, but conscious of being somewhere soft, with strange smells and quiet voices. She drifted in and out of consciousness so much that she had no way of telling time. The voices were a jumble, waking her just enough to hear them before she was gone again. People were touching her, examining her, and she wondered if this was just part of being dead that no one could ever talk about. How terrible to be aware for so much of it.

She didn't know how much time had passed before she tried opening her eyes. To her surprise, it worked. She blinked down at her body, which was covered by a shroud. There was no room around her, just a waving curtain of fabric. She could hear voices and see light from the other side.

"Hello?"

One of the voices stopped. The curtain was pushed aside to reveal a police officer. He looked at her, then over his shoulder, then gripped his radio and twisted his mouth down toward it.

"She's awake."

Jane stared at him, confused. He offered an awkward smile that looked almost painful. "It's... uh, there's... someone's coming."

"Did I die?" she croaked.

"Uh." He looked over his shoulder again. "Someone's coming," he repeated. "They'll be here any second."

"I think..."

Her head felt so heavy, and the pillow was so soft. And it was much easier to close her eyes than explain to the policeman that she was dead.

"Jane?"

Her eyes flicked open, more reflex than anything. A blurry face was above her. She blinked until her vision focused enough to make out the features of Miriam's face.

"He got me," she whispered.

"You're in the hospital," Miriam said. "Do you understand what happened?"

Jane stared at her. "Wow." Miriam's face was pale, her eyes wild. An attempt had been made to pin back her hair, but one side had fallen free. "You're so beautiful. I never told you you're beautiful."

Miriam pressed her lips together. "Jane. Listen to me. You're coming down off a very strong sedative. I need to know you're~"

Jane's eyes widened. "Black mask. He was wearing a black mask. All black. And goggles. To cover his eyes. White! He's white! He's a white man. And he only... he said one thing. He said, um. He said." She closed her eyes and tried to remember. "Regrets? I think he said... regrets?"

"We don't need you to do that right now, Jane. We just need you to stay calm and let your body break down the drug, okay? You'll be fine. You just need to stop panicking, because it's making your heart work faster~"

"Relax!" Jane snapped. "He said to *relax*, not regrets. Then he killed me."

"No, Jane. He didn't kill you."

"Can you hear me? Am I a ghost? Can you hear ghosts?"

"Just rest. You're alive. You're safe. We have a police officer guarding your room right now. Do you understand? Jane?"

Jane felt herself slipping away again. "I'm sorry I died," she said, slurring her words, settling back into the softness of the bed again.

She was just grateful she'd been able to relay the important information before she finally succumbed and passed away.

Rest in peace.

CHAPTER ELEVEN

MIRIAM SPENT the rest of the night in Jane's room. There was nowhere else she could have been, because her mind would've been there anyway. She kept the two uniformed officers stationed outside as an extra level of security. She had been prepared to go to war with Webster to get a full crime lab team assigned to Jane's apartment, but he agreed without hesitation. They were there now, looking for the smallest fiber that might lead them to their man. And even though she knew the dying talk had just been Jane's confusion, she found herself constantly checking the machines to make sure she was breathing and her heart was beating normally.

She settled into the armchair next to the bed and watched Jane sleep. She didn't want to admit how much she was still shaken by the events of the previous evening.

At 10:18 that evening, the *Sentinel* switchboard received a call from a payphone. A man with a raspy voice whispered, "Your reporter isn't going to be writing any more stories about the Goodnight Man. He made sure of that." They contacted Jane's editor Simon Ludwin, who in turn called Lieutenant Webster, who woke up Miriam and sent her to check out Jane's apartment.

She'd been irritated by the assignment until she arrived to discover the front door was open a crack. The lights were on in every room. Miriam had entered cautiously, wary of a trap. When she reached the hallway she could see straight into the bathroom, directly to what she assumed was a corpse propped up against the bathtub like every other victim.

Jane was dressed in pajamas, fuzzy slippers on her feet. The only difference between her and the other victims was the strip of duct tape across her mouth.

Miriam remembered tears clouding her vision as she knelt next to Jane. She had cupped the other woman's head and lifted it carefully, tenderly. She felt guilt crowding her chest, clenching around her heart like a vice, making it hard to breathe.

Then Jane had made a quiet, croaking noise in her throat.

It was so shocking that Miriam had yelped, and then she tightened her hands on either side of Jane's head, forcing it to stay upright. She blinked away her tears and finally realized that Jane's chest was rising and falling. Two fingers pressed to her throat confirmed a pulse, weak but definitely there.

After that, it had been a panicked rush of phone calls and emergency vehicles. An ambulance arrived and the EMTs stabilized Jane enough to move her to a hospital.

Once all the pieces had been put into motion, Miriam went to the hospital and stationed herself in Jane's room. The guard had reported she'd woken up briefly and mumbled something, but he hadn't been able to make out the words. Miriam didn't want to risk missing another moment of wakefulness, and she was grateful she was there when Jane woke up again.

According to the doctor, she would make a full recovery once the drug worked its way out of her system. Miriam knew he was only talking about the physical toll. Mentally, she didn't know how anyone would be the same after experiencing something so horrifying.

She stared at Jane's sleeping face, so strangely plain against the white pillow. She wasn't wearing her glasses. Miriam remembered the night Jane had shown up at the crime scene without her glasses. She'd looked so young, so defenseless. The effect was even more pronounced now, with the life-saving equipment making quiet noises all around her.

He'd left her alive. Every other victim had been injected after he asphyxiated them. Had he screwed up? Maybe he'd been rushed and went through the motions without confirming she was actually dead? No, he'd used a sedative instead of any kind of narcotic. The injection had been meant to keep her unconscious long enough for someone to arrive and investigate.

She hated this bastard. It wasn't just about bringing a killer to justice anymore. She wanted him to pay, and she wanted to be the one who brought him down. She was surprised at the depth of her rage, but she had no interest in tempering it. She wanted to hurt him. She wanted to make him suffer.

"M'r'm."

Miriam was out of her chair before her sleep-deprived brain registered that Jane had spoken. She gripped Miriam's hand, squeezing gently, and rested her other hand on Jane's forehead.

"I'm here, Jane," she whispered. The words poured out of her as if she was afraid she wouldn't have another chance to say them. "I'm sorry. I'm sorry I didn't go home with you. I'm sorry I was angry and let it get in the way of my job. Let it keep me from being there when you needed me. But I'm here now, Jane. I'm not going anywhere."

Jane opened her eyes and looked at Miriam. The fog that had been in her eyes every other time they opened had almost completely cleared. For the first time since that awful moment in the bathroom, it seemed as if Jane was actually seeing her.

Jane smiled weakly.

"You're here," she whispered.

Miriam nodded and squeezed Jane's hand tighter.

"I'm here, Jane. And I'm not going anywhere."

Jane was kept at the hospital for a full twenty-four hours just to make sure there were no side effects from the sedative. She recovered quickly, though she admitted lingering drowsiness that didn't seem to concern the doctors. Miriam stayed at her side for the duration and, when Jane finally got the all-clear to leave, volunteered to take her home.

"A hotel, actually," she clarified. "The crime scene people aren't ready to let you back into your apartment just yet."

"Oh." Jane made a face. She was sitting on the edge of the hospital bed, buttoning her shirt. Miriam had bought her a whole new outfit, something the bastard couldn't possibly have touched. "That's weirdly disappointing."

"Would you *want* to go back?"

Jane shrugged. "It would make me feel like I'm not scared, or not letting him win. But honestly I don't know if I would've been able to relax at all. A hotel is probably for the best."

"You could also stay with me, if you want." The offer was out of her mouth before Miriam realized what she was saying. "I'm not going to claim the couch is better than a hotel bed, but the option is there if you want to take it. Either way, you'll have an armed officer watching over you."

Jane smiled and stood up. "I appreciate it. But I couldn't put you or your family out like that. I have no idea what my emotions will be like over the next few hours. Or days. And I don't want to freak Sammy out by having an episode."

"That's fair." Miriam opened the door for her. The officers outside snapped to attention. Miriam nodded to them. "Jane, this is Officer Cook and Officer Simpson. They're going to follow us to the hotel, and then they'll be keeping an eye on you until morning."

Jane looked at the two men, then at Miriam. "You... won't be..." She wrinkled her nose and closed her eyes. "No. Of course not. Never mind."

Miriam hesitated. "Would you prefer for it to be me?"

"No, you have you daughter, you have your work..."

Miriam put her hand on Jane's arm, then looked at the men. "You can go."

Officer Simpson looked skeptical. "Are you sure, ma'am?"

"Tell your sergeant I okayed it. Go on."

The men exchanged a look, then Simpson shrugged and they walked away.

"I'm sorry," Jane said. "I'm being difficult."

"Absolutely not," Miriam said. "You were attacked by a man in your apartment. A man who is responsible for killing six women, that we know of. I don't know anyone who would be okay with male guards after that. I don't know what we were thinking."

Jane nodded. "I appreciate you looking out for me."

Miriam said, "Sure."

She pressed the elevator button and stepped back to wait for it to arrive.

"You don't really have to–"

Miriam snapped. "If I had been there, none of this would have fucking happened. I let my emotions get the better of me, I took it out on you, and you could've died because I was being a stubborn asshole. I'm not going to give this guy a second chance to come after you. The only reason I didn't offer is because I didn't think you'd want me around. But since you asked, you're going to have a hell of a time getting rid of me. Is that clear, Miss Ross?"

Jane blinked behind her glasses, then nodded. "Yes, ma'am."

"Good."

The elevator doors parted and they stepped inside. A doctor joined them in the car, along with two nurses. Miriam stood awkwardly next to Jane once the doors closed. She hadn't realized there were other people waiting for the elevator with them. She wondered how much of her rant they heard but, judging by their silence, it had been a fair bit.

The doors opened at the lobby and Miriam escaped to freedom. She scanned the area for signs of anyone who seemed out of place. But it was a hospital. Everyone who wasn't wearing scrubs looked out of place. But none of them pinged her radar, so she placed her hand on Jane's arm and guided her forward to the revolving door.

"Do you really think he'll come after me?" Jane asked once they were outside.

"It's doubtful. He left you alive for a reason. To send a message, probably. 'Look how close I can get to you' or some bullshit. Mind games. There's no reason for him to do it again."

Jane said, "Well, what about you? What about, uh... y-your husband and Sammy? What if he wanted to prove he could get to me, but also he could get to *you?*"

"They're safe," Miriam said. "I called Jeremy once we got you to the hospital. His parents live in Perth Amboy so he took Sammy there to stay for a bit."

Jane breathed out a sigh of relief and got into the car. "Okay. Good. I'm glad she's safe." She waited until Miriam was buckled in behind the wheel before she spoke again. "They said you were the one who found me."

Miriam's hand froze on the ignition. She kept her face forward but looked at Jane from the corner of her eye.

"Who told you that?"

"Officer Cook. Or, um, maybe Simpson. And they didn't exactly tell me anything. I overheard them talking. They sounded like they were scared. Apparently you went on a bit of a rampage."

Miriam started the car. She cleared her throat. "Sometimes you need to be scary to get shit done. I had no idea how badly you were hurt. I just knew we didn't have time to fuck around."

Jane said, "Did you think I was dead?"

Miriam considered lying. She didn't see any benefit to admitting the truth.

"Yes," she said, surprising herself. "When I first got to your apartment. When I saw you lying there. I had no reason to think he'd..." Her mouth was dry. She wet her lips and looked out the window so Jane couldn't see her face.

"I guess that explains why you don't hate me anymore."

"I never hated you," Miriam said. "You were right. I gave you permission to publish what you'd written. And I know editors are fuckers who only care about selling papers. The bloodier the better. I just took it out on you because you were an easy target."

Jane nodded. "I understand."

"And because... I..." She put both her hands at twelve o'clock on the steering wheel. "I didn't like how close we were becoming. I didn't like how upset I was about not seeing you every day. So I made you an enemy. So that cutting you out would be my decision and not because you'd just left."

"Oh," Jane said.

Miriam gestured ahead. "So... are you ready to go?"

"Yeah. Let's get out of here."

Miriam pulled away from the curb and headed for the hotel.

Jane looked around the lobby as Miriam checked them in, then followed her to the elevator like a duckling or a puppy on a leash. She waited until they were in the room before she commented.

"This is a nice hotel."

"It should be, for what they charge."

"Does the department always put people up in a place like this?"

Miriam saw no reason to reveal the truth about who was picking up the tab. The department would've just sent her to a safe house, some random apartment in a neighborhood where she faced far more dangerous people than just the Goodnight Man. The room was fucking expensive, but she wasn't going to subject Jane to one of those hellholes after what she'd just been through. The hotel room was simple enough, with two double beds and a sitting area under the window.

"Yeah," she said. "Sometimes."

Jane sat on the edge of the bed, facing the window. "I don't know what I'm supposed to do. I don't know if I'm able to do anything right now. But it feels wrong to just sit here and... and do nothing." She pushed her hands through her hair and held it back out of her face.

Miriam walked over and sat next to her. "I don't think you're doing 'nothing.' You're coping with what you went through. Something like that, you need to just process. And you can do that while watching TV or listening to music, or... or, I don't know. I can bring you books or something. Do you like books?"

"Yeah," Jane chuckled, "I like books."

"Sure. Writer. Makes sense."

Jane stared out the window. They had a lovely view of the building next door.

"I don't know how close to death I actually got. The doctor never said, and I'm not sure I really want to know the actual... the real... percentages. I *did* die. There was a murderer kneeling over me. I was helpless. And I know I'm not stronger, or more clever, than the women he killed. So I accepted that was the end. And I faded out. And then. And then I came back. And none of this feels real. I keep waiting for the moment when I realize, oh right this is all just my brain throwing out some, some, some crazy fantasy before it finally gives in."

Miriam said, "The hotel room isn't *that* nice."

Jane laughed and looked at her. "But I'm here with you. And if my brain really was dying, this is what I think I'd want. To be with you. And to have you not hate me anymore."

"I never hated you," Miriam said quietly.

"I know."

The air conditioner hummed. Miriam could hear people talking in the hallway. She put her hand on the mattress between them. Jane looked down at it and, after a moment, covered it with her own.

"I thought you were dead, too," Miriam admitted. "When I first showed up. And I kept thinking that the last thing I said to you was calling you an idiot."

Jane said, "Actually you told me he probably didn't know where I lived."

Miriam flinched. "God. So *I* was the idiot."

"You were trying to put my mind at ease. I appreciated it. Or I would have, if I hadn't been so pissed off at you."

Miriam leaned to the side and pressed her lips to Jane's cheek. "I'm glad you're okay." She sat up straight again and faced forward, already embarrassed and hoping the kiss would be forgotten.

Jane leaned in and kissed Miriam's cheek. "Thank you for saving me."

Miriam looked at Jane, who hadn't retreated after the kiss. Their faces were very close to each other. Miriam could have leaned away, she knew that, and she knew Jane would read that message loud and clear. But she wasn't entirely sure that was a message she wanted to send.

Instead she turned her head slightly and kissed Jane's other cheek. She didn't pull back so she wouldn't have to see Jane's face. "I like you," she whispered. "Very much."

Jane didn't have to move her head to kiss Miriam's cheek. "I like you, too."

Miriam closed her eyes and leaned back ever so slightly. She moved blindly and pressed a kiss to what turned out to be the corner of Jane's mouth. Jane turned her head, and their lips touched. Miriam breathed in sharply but she didn't pull away.

"I don't do this," Miriam whispered, her lips moving against Jane's. "I'm not like this."

"It's okay," Jane said. "It can just be a kiss."

Miriam's tongue played against her bottom lip, then flicked out and touched Jane's. "But it doesn't feel like it's just a kiss."

"We don't have to decide what it is," Jane said. "It can just happen. And we can worry about it later. It can just be what it is."

Jane kissed her, and Miriam let her, eyes open so she could see herself reflected in Jane's glasses. The pressure against her lips changed slightly, became stronger and then relented, and Miriam found herself pulling back. Jane pulled back as well and opened her eyes. She seemed to read something in Miriam's face, because she turned away.

"I'm sorry," Jane said. "I know you're married, or, or you have a... You're straight." She finally settled on, "I'm sorry."

"Don't be sorry," Miriam said.

"No, I am. I pushed you further than you wanted to go. You were trying to comfort me. I took it too far." Jane finally pulled back. "Your husband..."

Miriam said, "My husband regularly fucks other women. We sleep in separate beds. Our marriage is essentially over and we're just parents together. So don't... don't use him as an excuse. And if you're worried about Sammy, she's a kid. She'll understand. Kids understand things adults don't. She likes you. I like you. That's why I kissed you first."

Jane looked at her. "I didn't want to bring it up."

Miriam returned her look. A lock of hair had fallen across her face, covering one lens of her glasses. She reached out and brushed it back, hooked it behind Jane's ear, and then leaned in.

"I like you, Jane."

"I like you, too." Her eyes were wide and scanning Miriam's face in a desperate search for something. "That's why I don't want to ruin what you have. Your life, your career, if it comes out that you... I can't let you throw all that away for me."

Miriam whispered Jane's name, then kissed her, and Jane kissed her back, and Miriam felt a jolt pass through her. She moved her hand to the back of Jane's neck and scooted closer, and Jane moved toward her. Miriam's other hand stroked Jane's arm, starting at her wrist and gliding up until it was under her sleeve, her fingers brushing against unseen skin. The bicep was hardly the sexiest thing for her to grope, but it was enough to intensify the electricity in Miriam's mind.

The kiss lasted longer than she expected it to, but shorter than she would have chosen. Jane was the one who ended it, turning her head with a gasp. She had put her hand on Miriam's shoulder during the kiss, and now she moved it to caress her cheek. She started to speak twice, but stopped herself both times. Finally she closed her eyes and rested her forehead against Miriam's.

"I'm alive."

"Yes, you are," Miriam said. "I've never kissed a woman before."

Jane smiled. "Well. You're good at it."

Miriam laughed. "Thanks." She moved her hand from Jane's neck into her hair. She stroked her hand down, and Jane closed her eyes like a cat being petted. "Would this have been part of your fantasy?"

"I couldn't have made it feel this good."

Miriam gently guided Jane down until she was resting against the pillows. She settled on top of her, both of them twisting to get their legs up onto the mattress without becoming tangled around each other. Jane looked up at her and Miriam held eye contact just long enough to convey her intentions before she leaned down and kissed Jane again.

She'd brought Jane a button-down sweater and a calf-length skirt, since they were similar to what she'd been wearing over the past week. Now she wished she'd gone for something with a bit easier access. Fewer buttons, less material... She reached down and grabbed a handful of Jane's dress, keeping up with the kiss as she pulled it higher, past her knee, over her thigh. She stroked the soft skin of Jane's leg and lifted her head.

"Are you sure about this?" she asked. "You went through something horrible and you might not be in the most~"

"Miriam," Jane said, "I need this. And I want it to be with you. Please."

Miriam licked her lips. "I don't know what I'm doing. But I want to figure it out."

"Take your time."

"Do I just use my hand?"

Jane nodded. "For now."

Miriam moved her hand under the shroud of Jane's dress. Jane moved her legs apart and Miriam rolled to the side to lay beside her instead of on top of her. She found a position that didn't hurt her wrist and moved her hand higher. Jane gasped and whispered, "Yes..." and Miriam used two fingers to rub against Jane's underwear.

"Do you want it faster or...?"

"I'll tell you." Jane's eyes were closed, her bottom lip shaking. "This is good for now. This is good... right there. Like that."

Miriam kissed Jane's cheek, then her neck.

"You're going to make me come," Jane whispered.

Miriam said, "Come for me."

Jane reached out her hand, landing on Miriam's hip. She dug her fingers in and moved her hips against Miriam's fingers.

"Harder," Jane whispered. "Please."

Miriam did as she was told. She sat up so she could see Jane's face, to watch her as it happened and mark the changes. Jane's eyelids fluttered, she pulled her top lip back against her teeth, and a wrinkle appeared between her eyebrows. She breathed out sharply once, twice, and then made a soft sighing moan. She settled back against the pillow and caught her breath before she opened her eyes and stared at the ceiling.

"Are you okay?"

Jane nodded. "Yeah." Suddenly there were tears in her eyes, and she turned her face away.

Miriam panicked. "Shit." She took her hand out from under Jane's dress and rested it on her knee. "Did I go too fast? We shouldn't have done that. I'm sorry."

"No!" Jane faced her again so quickly that her tears fell free. She wiped them away with the back of her hand. She took Jane's hand in hers and brought it to her lips, kissing the knuckles. "No, no, no. It's not... I'm just... I..." She sat up and used both hands to hold Miriam's against her chest. "None of this has felt real. Not since I woke up. But what just happened... what we just did. *That* was real. And that proved to me that all of this *is* real, and I *am* alive, and it all hit me at once. But it's good. They're happy tears."

Miriam let the tension out of her shoulders. "Oh. Okay. Good."

"Lay down with me."

"Okay."

They both lay back on the pillows. Jane rolled onto her side so they were facing each other.

"I've never done that before. I mean." She grinned. "With everyone's clothes still on."

Miriam laughed. "We did get a little ahead of ourselves, I think."

"It's okay." Jane wet her lips and looked at Miriam's mouth. "And it's okay if it doesn't happen again. If it was, um, you know, spur of the moment or... helping me get through something. I'm not expecting anything from you."

"Well, I'm expecting something from *you*," Miriam said.

Jane said, "What's that?"

"I believe you writer types would say 'reciprocity'." She smiled, then let it drop. "If you're... I don't want to rush you into anything or-or... I'm just saying I don't want it to be a one-time thing. God. That sounds so selfish after everything you've been through."

Jane laughed and put her fingers against Miriam's lips. Without saying anything, she sat up and got off the bed. She faced Miriam and patted the edge of the mattress in front of her. Miriam moved and sat where Jane indicated. Jane got down on her knees and looked into Miriam's eyes as she undid the buckle of Miriam's belt.

"I think," Jane said, "if I don't do this, then *I* would be the selfish one."

"Maybe." Miriam tucked her hair behind her ears as she watched Jane's fingers deftly undo her pants. "Understandably, given the circumstances. I'd be willing to wait."

Jane pulled her hands away. "Oh...?"

"Well..."

Jane laughed and leaned forward to kiss Miriam's lips.

Then she pulled Miriam's pants down and lowered her head.

Chapter Twelve

JANE LICKED her lips and felt another thrill at the taste there. Miriam was asleep, her arm against Jane's, spreading warmth where they touched. Jane didn't blame her for falling asleep, since she'd probably been awake ever since she got the call from the bastard killer. But she didn't know when she would ever be able to sleep again. Every time she closed her eyes, she was afraid she would drift off again and this time she would never wake up. She knew she was alive. She knew she'd survived. Miriam had proven that to her - twice, actually - but the fear was still there.

She licked her lips again and couldn't help but smile despite everything. She looked over at Miriam, who was lying on her back next to her. She was naked, such a distracting sight. The lamp on the other side of the bed was still on, and it cast golden shadows across her face and other parts of her anatomy that Jane couldn't believe she was allowed to look at. But considering she had touched and kissed most of those places in the past hour...

Jane didn't know how long she was staring, but apparently it was long enough for Miriam to sense she was being watched even in her sleep. Her eyelids fluttered open and she saw Jane, then she squeezed them shut and pressed the back of her hand against one of them.

When she dropped her hand, she looked at Jane again. "What's wrong?"

"Nothing," Jane said. "I'm sorry if I woke you."

Miriam shook her head. "No. I sleep light. You could have just breathed wrong and it would've been enough." She looked around for her watch or an alarm clock. "What time is it?"

"I don't know."

"You should try to sleep."

"I think I've slept enough for a little while."

Miriam looked at her, her eyes focused now. "Right. Sorry."

"It doesn't mean you have to stay awake. You stayed up watching over me. You deserve to rest, too."

"It still feels rude."

She sat up, realized she was still naked, and pulled her legs up against her chest. She wrapped her arms around them and faced forward. Jane sat up as well, taking her pillow with her and holding it against her chest.

"Do we need to talk about it?"

Miriam looked at her. "I don't know. I was kind of in a fugue state. You said nothing after waking up feels real because you accepted you were going to die. I think everything I've done tonight is because I felt the same way. I thought I'd lost you. And I didn't even have you. I don't even know if I want you..." She flinched. "I-I just mean~"

"I understand," Jane said.

"I don't know what happened tonight. I know I don't regret it. But for now..." She waved her hand. "I think that's all I can say for sure."

"Fair. I'm willing to leave it up to you, what happens next. You're the one with the family. If this is too much, or too weird, or if you're just not interested~"

"I *am* interested." Miriam was looking ahead again.

Jane didn't say anything. She just thought about earlier, when their clothes had first come off, and the way Miriam had looked at her body. She couldn't put it to words, couldn't quite assign an emotion to how her eyes had widened and then narrowed as they ran over her like she was reading a menu in another language. But what happened next had been undeniably enthusiastic.

"We don't have to decide anything tonight," Jane finally said. "We can just be grateful it happened and move forward."

"I'm fine with that."

Jane leaned in and kissed Miriam's cheek. "Should I move to the other bed?"

"It's probably the best choice if we're just going to sleep."

"Yeah."

The blanket had tangled around her legs, so she freed them and got up, moving to the other bed. She stretched out under the blankets while Miriam repositioned herself to be more centered. She stared up at the ceiling, her hands folded over her chest. That felt too funereal, so she rolled onto her side. Miriam was also on her side, facing her.

"How... I know you don't know how long it will be before you catch him. But how long do you think I'll have to hide here?"

"I don't know. A few days." Miriam rubbed the bridge of her nose. "The crime scene people will probably be done with your apartment by tomorrow. But the fact he knows where you live and was able to break in would scare anybody. I don't know when I would want to go back there if I was you."

Jane nodded. "I was thinking about that, too."

"We'll figure something out. For now, at least try to get some sleep. What you just went through, that wasn't real sleep. It wasn't rest. Your brain still needs time to refresh itself."

"I'll try."

"Good girl."

Jane shivered. "When you say that..."

"What?"

Jane bit her bottom lip. Considering what they had just done together, she supposed she didn't have to worry about crossing a line. "I like it when you call me a good girl. I don't know what it is. But even before tonight~"

"I've never said it before tonight."

"You have," Jane said. "At least twice. Believe me, I've noticed."

Miriam furrowed her brow. "I didn't notice. But I guess if you like it..."

"I do."

"Then I won't stop."

"Good." Jane smiled at her. "I'm going to need some clothes."

"We can go to your apartment tomorrow and pack a bag."

"Okay. Thank you. And thank you for bringing this outfit to the hospital. I know you didn't want to babysit me, and now you're being forced into becoming my roommate."

"No one is forcing me to be here. I may not be sure about a lot,

Jane, but I don't want there to be any doubt about that. Okay?"

Jane nodded. "Goodnight, Miriam."

"Goodnight, Jane."

The next morning, Miriam drove them to the station where she received the crime scene report on Jane's apartment. The killer had used the fire escape to break in. It hadn't been particularly hard for him to do since her windows didn't have bars on them. Miriam had glared at her for that, and Jane was sufficiently chastised for her lapse in judgement. "First thing I'll do when I get home," she promised.

"Good girl," Miriam said.

Jane snapped her head up and almost missed the smirk on Miriam's face that revealed she'd done it on purpose.

Unfortunately the rest of the report was much less useful. He hadn't left a single fingerprint or hair behind. Jane remembered he'd been wearing gloves and a full mask, but she couldn't imagine how he could have managed to get in and out so cleanly. The fuzzy slippers were a generic brand sold at dozens of shops in New York. They looked new, but with no way of knowing when or where he'd bought them, they couldn't find him through security footage or sales records.

"So in other words," Detective Patterson said once she'd finished reviewing the findings, "we're right back where we started."

Miriam tossed the file down onto the desk. "How can this guy be such a fucking ghost? He finds women who live alone, he never shows up on security cameras, and now he can get in and out of multiple apartments across the borough without leaving a *trace* behind. How is that possible?"

Patterson shrugged. "Maybe it would be better if he raped them."

Miriam and Jane both looked at him. Jane had to look away first, because she had to reach out and take the pencil from Miriam's hand before it ended up in Patterson's throat.

"What did you just fucking say?" she growled.

He held his hands up. "From a strictly investigative standpoint-"

"Walk away," Jane said.

He looked at her. "You shouldn't even be here right now. You're-"

"Walk away." This time she held his gaze so he knew it was a warning, not a threat.

Patterson held her stare, but he was the first to look away. Jane watched him until he disappeared into the break room, then closed her eyes with a shudder.

"Who says something like that?" she whispered.

"Men," Miriam said. "Especially these jackasses, who are a dangerous combination of male, jaded, and trained on gallows humor. Sometimes they don't know where the line is, and it turns out to be a tripwire." She took her pencil back from Jane. "Thanks for taking that away from me."

"Sure. It didn't look sharp enough to be satisfying anyway."

"I could've made it work."

Jane smiled. "I don't doubt it. So what do we do now?"

"Now we go back to the existing cases. We go over witness statements for something we might have missed."

"What if we didn't miss anything? You said he was a ghost. What if~"

Miriam settled back in her chair. "No. Don't go all woo-woo on me, Ross."

"He was in my apartment. I didn't even... I..." She hugged herself. "It didn't even feel wrong in there until I saw the slippers on my bed. And then he was just *there*. Behind me. I didn't hear anything. It was like he had just appeared out of thin air. I don't believe in~ what are you doing?"

Miriam had lunged forward while Jane was talking. Now she was flipping through the report on Jane's attack, and it was clear she'd stopped listening. Jane reached out and flicked the corner of the paper up to get Miriam's attention.

"What?"

"You were standing in your bedroom door, facing inside, when he appeared *behind* you?"

Jane nodded.

"Were you over the threshold?"

"Um. I don't know."

"Were you *in* the room when you saw the slippers?"

Jane had spent every waking hour trying not to think of that moment, but she forced herself to now. She imagined how she would normally enter her bedroom. Open the door, step inside, turn on the light. She couldn't have seen the slippers with the lights off.

"I was inside the room."

Miriam turned the paper around to show Jane a map of her apartment. Jane examined it carefully, brow furrowed, unsure what she was supposed to be seeing. Miriam brought her other hand up and tapped the square with BEDROOM written in it. She dragged her finger across the hallway to what appeared to be a solid wall.

"If he had come from the bathroom, you would've heard him. It's, what, three steps from one door to the other? Even if he was moving fast, you would've heard him. He'd have to go even farther if he came from the living room." She tapped the solid line. "What's directly across from your bedroom?"

Jane shook her head. "Nothing."

"No, something's there. I remember it. I ran past it on my way to your bathroom. Your bedroom was to my left, and there was a panel or something to my right, directly across from the bedroom."

"Oh," Jane said. "That's nothing."

Miriam looked hard at her. "I remember every second," she said quietly. "It's burned in my memory, Jane. I know what I saw. There's a panel there that isn't on this blueprint."

"I don't remember seeing a~"

Realization dawned on her and killed her voice. She'd stopped seeing it so long ago that she'd forgotten it was even there. When the building originally opened, each unit had its own washer/dryer units. At some point the manager or landlord or someone had decided it was cheaper to just install a single laundry room in the basement. Some tenants used the tiny, cramped space for extra storage, but Jane's had been covered over by a piece of plywood. She explained that to Miriam, who was almost shaking with excitement with each word.

"He could've been hiding in there." Miriam already had her phone in her hand, dialing a number with the other. "And when he left, he could have sealed it over again so the forensics team wouldn't have searched it. He might have left~" She looked away as someone answered her call. "This is Detective Balfour. I have a question for anyone who searched Jane Ross' apartment. There's a small room directly across from the bedroom. It's hidden behind a wooden panel. Did anyone..."

She closed her eyes. Jane made a 'well?' gesture, but Miriam obviously didn't see it.

"Let me know what you find. Thanks."

When she hung up, Jane said, "Did they search it?"

"The tech said they saw that panel, but it was sealed up tight. They didn't know it could be opened, or that there was a space behind it large enough for someone to hide."

Jane said, "Even if he hid there, it doesn't mean the other apartments had a space like that."

"They wouldn't have to," Miriam said. "He didn't intend to leave those women alive, so it didn't matter when they spotted him. He only had to worry about the element of surprise with you. I don't think he knew about the space when he showed up. He might have just gotten lucky. And if he thought he was lucky, then there's a very good chance that he also got sloppy."

"Fingers crossed," Jane said.

"In the meantime..." Miriam pulled a folder from her desk drawer and tossed it to Jane. "Help me go over everything again. Witness statements. Apartment floor plans. Anything. He got in because you don't have bars on the windows, and he found a place to hide once he was in. This guy is an opportunist and he thinks outside the box. Maybe we've been going at him too linearly."

Jane opened the file and saw a report on Sadie Wolf's crime scene. "I thought they took the case away from you."

"Anyone can make copies of a file."

"Isn't that—"

Miriam looked at her.

"Forward-thinking and helpful," Jane finished.

"Extremely," Miriam said, opening her own file.

Jane looked around to see if anyone was paying attention to them.

"People around here act like I'm invisible every day," Miriam said. "Sometimes I can use that to my advantage."

"Forward-thinking," Jane said again.

"Something like that." Miriam smiled at her and went back to reading her own file.

Jane had hoped - naively, it turned out - that they were right on the edge of cracking the whole case. When forensics called back about the hiding spot in her apartment, she physically crossed her fingers on both hands as she watched Miriam take the call. *We found him,* she imagined them saying, ignoring the look on Miriam's face that said otherwise. *He left behind a shoe print. It's only sold in one store in America, and they've only sold one pair in the last hundred years.*

Miriam hung up without saying anything. Jane raised her eyebrows. "Well?"

"They found a shoeprint."

"You're kidding me."

Miriam held up a hand to stop her from getting too excited. "Air Jordans."

Jane slumped back in her seat. "You're shitting me."

"Size ten." She shook her head. "And that's all they found. No fingerprints. No hairs, no fibers, not a goddamn thing but the most popular shoe in the most average size."

"He's still a ghost," Jane said softly.

Miriam leaned forward and put her elbows on the desk, linking her fists together and resting her forehead on them.

"So..." Jane mentally fumbled for something to say, a question to ask. "We keep going over the files, and look~"

"No." Miriam sat up quickly and grabbed the file Jane was holding. "No, we don't keep going over the files." She added it to the stack and then opened her drawer to toss them inside. "There's nothing new in those reports. Nothing we wouldn't have seen a hundred times before already."

"You *just* found out about the hiding spot in my apartment. Maybe there's something in there that won't make sense until we combine it with something else."

Miriam sighed. "This isn't my first case, Jane. I can feel when we're at a dead end. Patterson and Clark are going to hit the same wall. Maybe today, maybe tomorrow, but they'll hit it. And until this asshole kills another woman, we're not going to be able to make a move. All we can do is sit here and spin our wheels until he gives us something else to work with. And we have no way of knowing when that will be. Now, going by his pattern, he usually doesn't wait very long between victims. We have less than a week before we're at another scene. But depending on what he got out of threatening you, it could be much shorter than that or much longer."

Jane said, "I don't know how to feel about that."

Miriam checked the level of her coffee cup and stood up. "There's no way to feel about it, Jane. You're a reporter. You're used to hearing a full story, or digging up facts until you know what happened. Beginning, middle, and end. We don't always get that luxury. If we're lucky - and I'm using that word in the *loosest* possible sense - he'll kill someone else in the next few days and we'll have more to go on. We have to hope he'll give us more to work with."

"And if he stops right now?"

Miriam shrugged and walked away toward the break room. "Then he gets away with it."

"That's horrible."

"No, Jane," Miriam said over her shoulder. "That's just the way the story goes."

Six weeks later, when no new victim appeared, Patterson and Clark officially moved the Cozy Killer to the cold case files. All the leads had been followed, every angle tracked down, and it was decided the detectives would be better utilized on fresher cases.

Jane was horrified when she found out, but Miriam assured her they would reopen it immediately if any detective in any borough reported a murder that fit the MO. She said killers like that rarely just stopped for no reason, especially after getting so much attention from the police and the media.

"That's just it," Jane said. "What if he just wanted people to look at him and now that they have, he stops? And those women never get justice?"

They were in bed again, this time Jane's bed in her own apartment. She had been willing to risk going back, and Miriam had offered to stay with her instead of stationing guards outside. The blanket on the couch had never been unfolded, though Miriam had allegedly been sleeping there for the past week.

"It could have fed his appetite enough that he won't need to scratch the itch for a while. But it will wear off in time, and he'll have to go out hunting again. He's not a ghost, no matter how much it seems like he is right now. We'll catch him. It might be weeks. It might even be months. But he'll make a mistake, and we'll be ready."

Jane put her head on Miriam's shoulder and pulled her closer. "Weeks. Or months."

"Possibly," Miriam said. "More likely months."

Neither of them was brave enough to even float the possibility that it might be years.

II. ONE STONE
Brooklyn, New York
2024

Chapter Thirteen

"THIS IS the last time I'm having this argument, Sam."

Sam held up her hands in hallelujah. "Thank you! Pour the champagne, let's commemorate the death of this *fucking* argument."

Beau folded her arms over her chest. "I'm serious, Samantha. Either we make a decision tonight, or... or the decision gets made tonight."

"You're serious?"

They were standing with practically the entire apartment between them. Beau was in the doorway to the kitchen while Sam had stayed in the living room. She was still dressed for work in slacks and a pale yellow sweater, while Beau was wearing torn jeans and a black blouse that was unbuttoned just enough that Sam had mistakenly thought dinner would be preceded by a little mutual groping on the couch. Instead, she had been surprised to find Beau was scrolling real estate listings on her phone. Again.

"That's where we are right now?" Sam asked. "Move to the suburbs or we're over?"

Beau put her hands on her forehead and then pushed them into her thick black hair, which she grabbed and tugged with a growl.

"*No.* Of course not. But come *on*, Sam. We've been at this for a year. You keep saying when we find a house we like, or when the time is right, or... or..." She waved her hand helplessly out to one side. "You find a problem with every single place we look at."

"So I should just settle for a house that needs thousands of dollars' worth of work? Or in a bad neighborhood? Or~"

Beau crossed to her. "I'm not saying any of that, baby." She put her hands on Sam's cheeks. "I'm just saying that no place is going to be perfect. And you're looking for any and every reason to say no. There's always going to be a downside to any place we choose. If we use them as an excuse to stay here, we're never going to leave."

"Would that be so bad?"

Beau rolled her eyes and let go of Sam's face. She turned on the ball of her foot and slumped back toward the kitchen. Sam followed.

"Wait. Hold on. Look." She touched Beau's shoulder. "Turn around. Please."

Beau stopped retreating and, after a moment, turned to face her.

"I work in the city. The commute from the suburbs would be *brutal*." She stepped closer. "I like coming straight home to you." She brushed her thumb over Beau's cheek. "And if I can go straight from work to home, I still have energy to be your good wife."

Beau's eyes dropped to Sam's lips. "I know what you're doing."

"That's because you're a very smart woman." Sam leaned in and gave Beau's lips a fleeting kiss. "A very smart, beautiful woman."

"Sam," Beau moaned.

"Shh." She kissed Beau harder this time. "Let me show you."

Beau's shirt was already fairly open, so it only took undoing one button to see the lacy edge of her bra underneath. Sam bent her knees and pressed her face to the gap in the shirt, teasing with her lips and tongue until she heard her wife moan. Beau's fingers laced together on the back of Sam's head, catching threads of her hair between them. Sam kissed her way up the smooth stretch of Beau's chest, angling to the left and latching her lips onto the meaty part of Beau's throat like a vampire.

"I hate that this always works," Beau groaned.

Sam laughed. With her hands on Beau's hips, she guided her back until she could lean against the wall. She pinned Beau there and kept kissing, licking, sucking on her neck.

Her phone chose that moment to start ringing. She grunted and growled, keeping her mouth against Beau's skin. She could tell from the ringtone that it was work.

Beau could tell, too. She tightened her grip on Sam's hair. "Don't."

"Are you gonna make me late, baby?" Sam whispered against Beau's throat.

"You can't just manipulate me to get your way and then go running off."

Sam's right hand skimmed the line of Beau's pants until she was to the front. She slid her fingers inside as she lifted her head and kissed Beau's bottom lip.

"You want me?" Sam whispered.

"Always."

She nipped at Beau's lip with her teeth. "Say it."

Beau opened her eyes. "I want you, Samantha."

"That's right, baby."

Sam kissed Beau and pushed her hand into her jeans. The button was still done and the denim bit into her wrist, but she didn't care. She cupped her wife with her right hand, then reached into her back pocket and took out her phone with her left. Beau glanced at her, then opened her eyes wide when she realized what Sam was doing.

"What... no! Sam, *do not...*"

Sam answered the phone. "Balfour."

"Hey, Sam. Nelson Ainsworth, from the two-one. You got a second?"

"Yeah, I've got some time." She didn't take her eyes off Beau's, curling up her middle finger to press it against her folds. Her voice remained steady as she worked her fingertip back and forth. "What's up."

A look of irritation passed across Beau's face, but it was quickly overtaken by pleasure. Her eyes rolled back and she bit down hard on her bottom lip to keep from crying out.

"I've got a crime scene I'd like you to take a look at. I don't want to say too much and color your opinion on it before you see it yourself."

"Sure thing. Can you text me the address?"

"On it. Thanks, Balfour."

"No problem. See you in a few."

Beau opened her eyes to make sure the phone was closed, then said, "That was so fucking..."

Sam leaned close. "Fucking what, baby?"

Beau pulled her lips back in a snarl, then said, "Fucking hot."

Sam smiled and kissed her hard, moving her hand faster as Beau started grinding against the heel of her hand. Her tongue slipped into Beau's mouth and Beau started moving her hands over Sam's shoulders, down her back, tugging at her sweater.

"You can't undress me, Beau," Sam said against her mouth. "I've got to go to work."

"Fucking rude," Beau grunted.

"I can undress you, though." She licked her wife's mouth. "Would you like that?"

"Yes, Detective."

Sam stepped back and pulled her hand free. Beau released a small, unintentional moan and pressed her back against the wall as Sam unbuttoned her jeans and dragged them down. Once Beau had stepped out of them, Sam took her by the hips and turned her around so she had her face against the wall. She pressed against Beau from behind and reached between her legs.

"Maybe I won't let you come," she said into Beau's ear. "Maybe I'll leave you like this and go to work. Make you wait until I get home."

"Please," Beau whimpered.

"Please what?"

"Please let me come, Samantha." She turned her head to look at Sam from the corner of her eye. She lowered her voice. "Pull my hair."

Sam used her free hand to grab a handful of Beau's hair. She pulled, and Beau cried out her name. Sam kept her right hand busy until Beau grinded down against her and cried out her orgasm so loudly that Sam was sure their neighbors heard. She didn't care. Their neighbors had heard far louder noises in the past. So much so that they'd stopped knocking or leaving passive-aggressive notes on the community bulletin board.

Maybe living in the suburbs wouldn't be so bad, Sam thought. Lots more privacy, for one thing.

When Beau had stopped twitching and had caught her breath, Sam kissed her shoulder and brushed the hair away from her face.

"You okay, baby?"

"Mm-hmm." Beau turned her head and kissed Sam's lips.

Sam kept herself pressed against Beau, her arm still around her waist. "It's different when the rough stuff happens right after a real argument."

Beau lifted her shoulder. "Yeah. But it's still hot. And I like when you check to make sure I'm okay. *That's* the real turn-on."

"If you're sure." She kissed Beau's cheek. "I love you."

"I love you, too."

They pulled away from each other. Beau's shirt was almost long enough to work as a dress, but didn't quite manage to cover her completely.

"You really have to go to work, though?"

"Afraid so," Sam said. "Hopefully it'll be quick."

"I'll wait up for you."

Sam grinned.

"No. No smiling." Beau put a finger on Sam's lips. "I'm waiting up so we can keep talking about moving. You think you won because you made me come, but we didn't decide anything. We're going to keep talking about it when you get home."

Sam slumped and surrendered. "Fine. Fair enough."

Beau kissed her and pressed her hips against the rough denim of Sam's jeans. "And then when you've seen reason and admitted I was right all along... *then* I'll fuck you."

Sam's smile returned. "Deal."

Beau slapped Sam's ass and pulled away from her. "Go. Solve a crime. Be a hero."

"I'll do what I can."

Forty-five minutes later, Sam ducked under the tape across the crime scene's front door. Ainsworth was in the living room, next to a tall three-headed lamp, and made a show of his impatience as he crossed to meet her behind the couch.

"What's going on, Nelson?" she asked. "Need me to solve another case for you?"

"Ha," he said, motioning for her to follow him. "What the hell took you so long to get here? I called you like an hour ago."

"I was in the middle of something. I don't just drop everything when you call."

Nelson put a hand to his chest. "I'm hurt." He pointed at her head. "I don't think I've ever seen you at parade rest."

She self-consciously put a hand on top of her head. Her hair was cut short at the sides with the rest normally swept up in a half-hearted blonde pompadour. A few detectives had tried calling her Elvis and

Eraserhead when she debuted the look, but she'd ignored their mockery with enough aplomb that the fun had gone out of it for them. Tonight, she hadn't had a chance to do anything with it, so the hair hung limp over her left eyebrow.

She pushed it back and followed Nelson to the bathroom door.

"The coroner already took away the body, but I got a picture of it in situ."

He held his phone out at arm's length and lined it up right so it lined up with the actual scene. Sam stepped closer and examined the screen. A woman was on the bathroom floor, propped up against the side of the bathtub. She wore a white t-shirt and pair of blue pajama pants with clouds on them. She also appeared to be wearing fuzzy white slippers. She put her fingers on the screen and zoomed in to the item on the floor next to her left arm to confirm it was a syringe.

"Overdose," she said.

"That's what it looks like from here," Ainsworth said. "And if this was Homicide 101, you'd get a gold star. Notice anything else about the scene?"

She returned the picture to its original size and looked for anything that jumped out at her. Finally she shook her head.

"Is Waldo hiding behind the shampoo or something? What am I looking for? This is literally every overdose death I've investigated since I became a detective."

Ainsworth nodded. "You're right. It is very familiar. In fact, there are six cases exactly like this. Stop me when you hear a name that sounds familiar." He consulted a list on his phone. "Rosario Walker. Sadie Wolf. Kathy Drake. Leigh Hun—"

"Oh, shit." She'd recognized the first name, but it had taken hearing the others before she made the final connection. "You're bullshitting me."

He went back to his phone and held up the first photo for her again.

"Fuzzy white slippers."

Sam looked at the empty bathroom as if the killer was still kneeling there. "Shit."

"So, Detective Balfour." Ainsworth tried to sound casual, but he was smirking at her clear discomfort. "Have you talked to your mother lately?"

Sam spent the rest of the night going over the old files. The files were at Ainsworth's precinct, the Twenty-First, Sam's mother's old stomping grounds. She had called Beau from the car to let her know she could go to sleep.

"I didn't want you to think I'm just ducking the conversation."

"Well, it wouldn't be out of character if you were," Beau said, sounding sleepy. "You've spent a few nights sleeping on the couch in the break room to avoid uncomfortable talks."

Sam was stung, but it was a fair blow. Sam assumed Beau was already in bed, half-asleep. Even with the argument looming, she regretted not being there with her. "That was before we were married. I'm trying to be more responsible. Mature."

Beau made a settling-in sound. "So what was the case?"

"I can't say anything on the phone. But there's a reason they called me in. If what we're thinking turns out to be right, I may agree to move out of the city just to run away."

"Uh-oh. Not the win I want, but I'll take it."

"Get some sleep. We can fight in the morning when I get home." Beau snickered. "Okay. Be safe. I love you."

"I love you, too."

After she ended the call, she headed upstairs and signed the Goodnight Man's file out of the cold case storage room. Everything in the boxes would be digitized, but she wanted the actual photos and the physical reports. Thirty years wasn't terribly long in the grand scheme of things, but going through the old cases felt like slipping into another era. Back in the day, the Twenty-First Precinct hadn't yet made the jump to computers, so the majority of information on the killings was either hand- or typewritten. The pages had coffee stains, and the air inside the boxes was stale with what she swore was ancient cigarette smoke. She had to put the box on a different table just to escape the cloud of it.

She took the boxes upstairs and took over what looked to be an empty desk. She pulled a whiteboard over and lined up the six known victims along the top border. She wrote their names underneath with a black marker and then tacked up crime scene photos. They were all eerily similar, to the point where it looked almost like a macabre "Find the Hidden Differences" game.

A dead woman propped up against her bathtub, dressed in pajamas, drug rig on the floor next to her. White fuzzy slippers on all their feet. Sam looked for any kind of pattern that might be a message. Sometimes their heads lolled to the left, sometimes to the right, and one had fallen forward with her chin on her chest. Some of their hands were palm-up, some palm-down. All had their arms at their sides. Sam couldn't bring herself to believe any of these variations were important, but she made a note of them regardless. She examined the hands carefully and decided there was no hidden message in how their fingers were positioned.

Of course, there was a seventh crime scene she was ignoring.

She looked at the second box. After a moment of consideration, she lifted the lid and looked inside. This was the only crime scene photo without a body in it. It was the only case where the victim had survived.

Sam dug around until she found the victim's photograph, taken in the hospital. She drew a line between Victim Six, Angeline DiFabio, and wrote "JANE ROSS" underneath the picture of the woman who had gotten away.

Detective Ainsworth arrived while she was scouring the original crime scene reports. "Find anything interesting?" he asked, holding out a cup of coffee.

"Yes, I just found the one good man in New York." She accepted the coffee like it was a holy object. "Bless you."

"Don't deify me until you taste it." He sat down across from her and looked at the crime board. "Greasy spoon was the only place open. I think they've been brewing the same beans all week."

Sam sipped and shook her head. "Greasy spoons are godsends, too. And to answer your original question, no. There were only six bodies, and they didn't even know it was the same guy until Victim 5, Kimmy Bremer. Did you ever do that exercise in English class where everyone got the same prompt, and you wrote stories, and then you shared so the teacher could demonstrate how the same idea can be told in multiple ways?"

Ainsworth said, "No, we never did that."

"Oh. Well, these reports read like the opposite of that. The first five cases, they got all the same information, and since cops are trained to write up reports in a specific way, it just sounds like they all plagiarized each other. Then, when the dots were finally lined up, the sixth victim is the only one that takes the others into account."

"You said six." Ainsworth pointed at the board. "There are

seven."

"Seven survived," Sam said. "She's irrelevant."

Ainsworth raised his eyebrows. "Doesn't sound irrelevant to me."

Sam sighed. "Victim Seven. Jane Ross. Reporter for the–"

"Yeah, I know the case. She wrote the story that revealed this guy to the world. Spooked him into disappearing, but he went after her first. To prove a point." He rubbed a finger along his upper lip. "That's always bugged me about the case."

"Always?" she said.

He shrugged. "It's an unsolved serial killer case from my precinct. Every detective who has been through here has tried to solve the Goodnight Man at one point or another." He looked at her. "I assume you at some point…"

Sam rolled her eyes. "No."

"Really? That's surprising."

She glared at him. "Why."

"It's… I would have assumed, with the family history… your mother was the one who…" He finally read the expression on her face and let his words die. He cleared his throat and looked at the board. "So anyway, he called the paper to tell them about his name. Goodnight Man is infinitely better than Cozy Killer, I've gotta admit. And then he goes after the reporter to scare her. And then he just stops? Really? All that sounds like he was ready to step into the spotlight."

"Maybe he got scared. He thought he wanted the attention, but when it happened, he was too worried about being caught."

Ainsworth made a considering noise, but she could tell he didn't buy it. Sam stood up and went to the board.

"I don't care about his reasons for going away, and I don't care about how many of your detectives have tried to track this guy down. He's back now. And I'm going to be the one to get him. He'll get his time in the spotlight if I have to drag him there by his ears."

Chapter Fourteen

TWO DAYS later, Sam was sitting in her car outside her mother's house in Weehawken. Ainsworth had offered to make the trip for her. While she appreciated him for it, she knew that would just be postponing the inevitable. She would have to cross this bridge eventually, and she'd always been more of a 'take the Band-Aid off quick' type.

She was parked so she could watch the house in her side and rearview mirrors. She'd been there for about an hour when a Jeep pulled up to the curb. Sam tensed as the driver got out and walked to the back, unloading several reusable grocery bags. Even from a distance, even with more than a decade since laying eyes on her, Sam recognized her mother immediately.

"Okay," Sam muttered. "Band-Aid time."

She got out of her car and started across the street. Miriam Balfour closed the back of the Jeep and gripped the handles of the bags. She started to head for the house but stopped when she saw Sam's approach in her periphery. *Once a cop*, Sam thought wryly. She turned her head and Sam saw the recognition in her eyes. Miriam straightened and turned to face her fully.

Miriam had always been a bit stocky. Broad in the shoulders and leading with her hips when she walked. The decades since Sam had last seen her had added a bit more bulk, but it only served to make her more intimidating. Her hair was cut short at the sides but long enough that it could hang over her eyebrows, which were currently furrowed in Sam's direction.

Sam stopped just outside of arm's reach of her. "Hey, Mom."

Miriam narrowed her eyes. "How'd it happen?"

The question threw Sam. "What?"

"My guess would be cancer." Miriam looked toward the sky as she scanned her memory. "I think that's how his father went, but I can't remember for sure right now."

Sam finally realized what she meant. "Are you talking about Dad? He's not dead."

"Really?" Now it was time for Miriam to look confused. "Why else would you have come here after all this time?"

Sam took a deep breath and let it out slowly. "The Goodnight Man is back."

Miriam's whole face changed. For a moment, Sam could see her as she'd been in the early nineties. Young, ferocious, determined. Something lit up in her eyes, something like anger, but it flickered out just as quickly as it had appeared. She'd clenched her teeth and worked her jaw from side to side until it relaxed.

"No," she said.

Sam blinked. "What do you mean 'no'?"

"It's a very self-explanatory word." Miriam turned and started up the front walk of her house. "First, that's not his fucking name. That's what he wanted to be called, it doesn't mean you have to actually use it. Secondly, it's been thirty-three years. If he was going to show his face again, it would have happened a long time before now."

Sam followed her mother up the walk. "Maybe he was in prison."

"And then just got right back into the swing of killing when he got out? Picked up where he left off?" Miriam laughed. "No. The killer is not back, because he moved away, or got hit by a bus, or... these guys don't just lay low for three decades and jump back in like they're picking up an old hobby."

On the porch, Miriam had to put down her groceries to get the keys from her pocket. Sam joined her at the door.

"We've looked into the possibility that he branched out. Other cases in the state, New Jersey, Pennsylvania, the entire eastern seaboard. Hell, last night I got a call from Sacramento. No staged killings with fuzzy slippers. But two nights ago, a woman was found in her bathroom with the same damn slippers." She turned on her phone and opened the crime scene photo. She held it up. "You think that's a coincidence?"

Miriam glanced at the phone. "They showed those damn photos ten thousand times on *Dateline*. It's not hard to copycat." She opened the door. "If you're going to stay, make yourself useful and carry some of these bags."

Sam picked up two of the bags and followed Miriam inside. They passed through a dark living room to the kitchen. Sam kept her eyes on the back of her mother's head, not interested in seeing any details of the life she'd been living. She didn't want to see mementos, framed photos, no evidence of the home that had been built from the ashes of the one left behind.

"Why did you come to me anyway?" Miriam asked, lining the bags up on the kitchen counter. "What help could I possibly provide?"

"You were there when this guy first showed his face," Sam said. "You're the one who figured out he even existed."

Miriam said, "Jane figured out he existed. I was just the first cop to fail at finding him. So I guess now that every other cop in New York has had a shot it finally circled back around to start over?"

Sam added her bags to the row and stepped back, crossing her arms. "You've been thinking about him for longer than anyone else. You've got the biggest bone to pick with him. You may not be a cop anymore, but I know he's been eating away at your mind all this time. It's what happens to me when there's a case I can't solve. You know these murders like the back of your hand. If there's anything to be found, you're going to be the one to find it."

"That's a lot of confidence in me," Miriam said. "I'd be surprised if I thought it was coming from you." She turned to face her. "Who ordered you to come talk to me?"

Sam shook her head. "This was my choice."

Miriam held the stare. "When did the latest murder happen?"

"Two nights ago."

"You expect me to believe you got desperate enough to show up here after *two days?*" She laughed. "No, someone higher up wanted my input and your name put you on the chopping block. Anyone I might know?"

"Commissioner Dooling."

Miriam looked like she was going to throw up. "*Commissioner...?* Christ on a cracker, that is just..." She put her hand to her forehead. "That is just depressingly believable. God almighty."

"Look, even if it's *not* the same guy who killed the first six women, he's clearly someone connected to the original killer. The scenes are too identical. It's more than just copying what they saw on *Dateline* or the internet. If we find whoever killed the latest victim, it could finally answer the question of who was doing it back then. I know you don't want to get dragged back into this, and you've got to know I don't want to be here asking you for help."

Miriam rested her hands on the counter. "Damn it."

Sam put her phone on the counter next to Miriam's hand. Miriam stared ahead for a long moment, then turned to look at the displayed picture.

"Her name was Julia Ramsey. She lived alone, in Red Hook, she worked as an escort. The night she was killed, she spent a few hours at a local bar but didn't leave with anyone. Security cameras at the bar didn't pick up anything suspicious. Same with cameras around her apartment."

"*None* of the cameras picked up anything?" Miriam said, finally showing signs of life. "That made a little more sense back in '91, but now? These days I thought everyone had a damn camera filming every corner of the city."

"Yeah, so did I. But somehow the bastard got around it."

Miriam was still staring at the crime scene photo. "Maybe he really is a ghost after all."

"A time-traveling ghost."

"The perfect crime."

Sam smiled despite herself. She took her phone back and slipped it into her pocket. "Dooling doesn't want this case going cold again, and he doesn't want to give the guy a chance to add more bodies to his tally. That's why he agreed to bring you in as a consultant."

"Nothing has changed since the first time we worked the case. It's been three decades of cops going over the exact same information over and over again, and no one is coming up with anything new. How many times was Rosario Walker's boss from New Jerrk brought in for a conversation? That asshole spent the last decade of his life being everyone's prime suspect." She tapped the phone screen and then pushed it back toward Sam. "Well, it looks like he's in the clear now. Who else do we like? No one. Thirty years and we had *one* suspect who ended up having an airtight alibi. Great track record."

"Dennis Jones could still be responsible for the first murders. If he had a protégé or someone he entrusted with his legacy—"

"Who then waited twenty years to follow through?"

Sam said, "Whoever is doing this, he's *not* a ghost or a time-traveler. He's just a man. He's not smarter than other killers, he's just been getting lucky. So fucking lucky he should buy a lottery ticket. But nobody's luck lasts forever. Like you said, there are cameras everywhere. People are always watching these days. I don't know what made him crawl out of the shadows after all this time, but I guarantee you he won't get a chance to go back. Now are you going to help or are you going to sit here and let someone else kill your white whale?"

Miriam looked at Sam, examining her face. Sam didn't know what she was trying to find, but she kept her eyes steady and her lips set in a firm line.

Finally Miriam surrendered. "Fuck it." She pushed away from the counter and went into the living room. "How much does this consulting thing pay?"

"I, um, I think Dooling was going to figure that out after we knew if you'd agree."

"Excellent. I can negotiate." She started up the stairs. "Wait here."

Sam stopped at the base of the stairs. "I... what are..."

"I'm coming with you." She didn't look back when she said it, and her tone made it clear she wasn't asking for an invitation.

Sam decided not to question it. "Okay. Fine. No rush."

She looked into the living room, considered moving to the plush armchair next to the couch, but she didn't want to get too comfortable. Instead, she took a seat on the bottom stair and rested her elbows on her knees as she waited for her mother to finish whatever needed doing upstairs.

She'd been there for a minute or so when the door knob rattled. Sam sat up straighter. Her heart skipped a beat, then restarted double-time. She started to stand but she knew there was nowhere she could flee before she was spotted. The door swung open and an older woman ushered a dog inside. The woman untangled the leash from around her wrist, leaning forward to say something to the animal as they crossed the threshold. The dog saw Sam first and went rigid, eyes locked on the intruder.

Jane Ross followed the dog's gaze and straightened. She was still tall, but her hair had gone silver. Her octagonal glasses that seemed slightly too big for her face. She was dressed in greys and beiges, a flowing sweater over a matching blouse and pants. She looked like the kind of literary figure who was interviewed on *60 Minutes*.

Sam recognized her immediately. She flashed back to being a child, sitting at the dinner table while some woman smiled at her through glasses that looked just like these. Sam had been too young to understand what was happening back then. She just thought her mom had a friend, she didn't know what it meant for that friend to be there, after dark, having dinner with them like she was part of their family.

It took a moment for recognition to dawn in Jane's eyes. "Sammy?" she said.

Sam offered a pinched smile. "I go by Sam now, whore."

Miriam stopped halfway down the stairs when she saw they weren't alone anymore. Jane looked away from Sam and seemed to deduce the entire situation from Miriam's expression. Jane's face had been neutral as she tried to figure out how to react to Sam's presence, but it hardened when she read whatever was on Miriam's face.

"You're not going back to help them with something, are you?"

"It's him, Jane."

Jane muttered under her breath and ushered the dog away from the door. Miriam hurried down the stairs to follow her.

"Another woman was killed. I have to–"

Jane didn't turn to look at her. "After *everything*–"

"I can't just–"

"Unbelievable. If they wanted your help, they could have had it *easy*."

Miriam pursued her into the kitchen. "So I'm just supposed to let this guy keep killing women? If I can help catch him–"

Their voices would have faded as they entered the other room, but they both grew louder the further away they got. Sam, still seated on the bottom step, dropped her head and laughed without humor.

In a way it was nice to know some things never fucking changed.

Sam eventually got up and went outside to wait for whatever was happening in the house to finish. She was close to just getting up to leave when the door opened. Miriam came out and breezed past her.

"Come on."

Sam eased herself up and followed at a casual pace. Miriam was moving quickly for her age, but Sam was younger and in better shape, so it wasn't hard to keep up.

"Trouble in paradise?"

Miriam ignored her. She stopped next to the passenger door of Sam's car and waited, arms folded, until Sam got in and unlocked it for her. Sam had no intention of being the one to start the conversation, and Miriam seemed to have become a statue the second her seatbelt was fastened, so Sam pulled away from the curb and headed back to Brooklyn.

Her phone was mounted on the dashboard next to the steering wheel, showing her route. They had just emerged from the Lincoln Tunnel when the map disappeared and was replaced with Beau's face combined with her ringtone: a recording of her singing the chorus 'Mr. Brightside.'

"Shit." Sam jabbed the screen with her finger until it answered. She kept her eyes hard ahead so she wouldn't see her mother's reaction to anything that had just happened, or was about to happen. "Hey. Hi. You're on speakerphone."

"Okay," Beau said. "Why is that important? Never mind. I'm just calling to let you know I'll be late tonight."

"All right. I probably will be, too. Everything okay?"

"Everything's fine." She gave a weary sigh. "If you were free, I'd talk your ear off for an hour, but I won't do that to whoever you're with. I'm planning to get dinner while I'm out. I'll text if I'm later than nine, okay?"

"Sounds good."

"I love you."

"Love you, too."

The call ended and the map returned. Sam kept her eyes straight ahead, willing the stony wall of silence to continue. Maybe Miriam had fallen asleep, or maybe–

"So that *is* a wedding ring."

Sam looked down at her left hand. "Always a detective, huh."

"That's why you came all the way to Jersey to find me, right? So. What's her name?"

"Beau."

"Beau?" Miriam said. "That's a girl's name?"

"Unlike *Sam?*"

"Fair enough, I guess," Miriam muttered, turning to look out the window. "Beau. Jesus."

Sam took a steadying breath. She flexed her fingers on the steering wheel. "We got married about a year and a half ago. The wedding... well, if you can even call it a wedding, it was more of a~"

"You don't have to explain why I wasn't invited," Miriam snapped. "I assume it was the same reason you weren't at my wedding to Jane. Right?"

Sam didn't answer.

"Right. I guess that explains the hair."

"What, I have gay hair?"

Miriam said, "Honey, the *dog* knew."

Despite the tension between them, Sam couldn't stop herself from laughing.

CHAPTER FIFTEEN

MIRIAM'S EYES were closed when the elevator doors opened. She just needed the extra second before she faced the reality.

"You coming?" Sam asked.

Miriam nodded and let the past back in. The room looked mostly the same. The desks had been rearranged, obviously, and the walls had been painted a lighter color. There were more women - three, by a quick headcount - and more color, and the room didn't reek of a dozen ashtrays. Sam seemed to realize Miriam needed a moment and stepped to one side of the elevator doors to wait for her to be ready to move on.

"You got computers," Miriam finally said.

"Uh." Sam looked at the desks as if to confirm, then nodded. "Yeah. Those came in a few years ago. They're pretty useful."

"I'll bet."

Sam pointed. "I'm set up over here."

"This isn't your precinct?"

"I'm with the Two-Eight," Sam said. "My captain is loaning me out for the time being so I can work with the lead detective on the new killing."

Miriam said, "Oh. I just assumed..."

Sam shook her head sharply. "Things may have changed around here. But after all this time, when people hear 'Detective Balfour of the Two-One,' they only think about one thing."

Miriam flinched and dipped her chin. People were slowly becoming aware of her arrival, lifting their eyes from paperwork or turning their heads to follow her progress through the bullpen. Sam ignored them and stopped next to a whiteboard with a row of photographs stuck along the top. Miriam didn't need the labels to identify them; she'd had every name, address, and vital detail memorized for most of her daughter's life.

She looked up at Jane's photo, a headshot from the *Sentinel*, then moved to the newest victim. Julia Ramsey.

"Something has to be different about her," Miriam said.

"Do you still think it's a copycat?"

"Either it is a copycat and they got something wrong," Miriam said, "or it's the same guy and he's thirty years older. Things change in that amount of time. I know I can't do everything I did back in the day. It's just a fact of life. He'd be weaker, he'd make more mistakes."

"Maybe." Sam pulled a chair away from the desk, then took one for herself. "So the, ah, main reason we wanted you involved. There isn't a whole lot of information about what happened with..." She gestured at the board. "When he decided to make his statement."

Miriam took the offered seat. "Can you not even say her name?"

Sam held her stare for a beat. "Jane. We don't have a full report on what happened to Jane."

"She went over it countless times. Both after she recovered, and whenever someone else decided to take a crack at the case. Over and over again, like it was some kind of game. We finally unlisted ourselves so they'd stop showing up on our doorstep."

"And she always just repeated what was in the official report."

Miriam narrowed her eyes. "That's what happens with the truth. If she changed things, it would mean she was making shit up."

Sam leaned forward. "There has to be more. The woman was attacked by a serial killer, who left her alive, but went through all the motions of his other murders. He changed her into pajamas and slippers, he injected her, he posed her. He did *all* that, and the best description she can come up with is..." She checked the folder. "Average height and build. Goggles. Mask."

"I've told her time and time again to pay better attention when she's being traumatized and thinks she's about to die, but you know, she's stubborn."

Sam sighed. "We're grasping at straws here, okay? Anything she remembers could be useful. Could help us actually bring this guy down. He's not a ghost. He's not psychic or a time-traveler or anything supernatural. He's a person, and he is bound to make a mistake eventually."

"He already has," Miriam said quietly.

Sam looked at her. "What do you mean?"

Miriam shook her head, arms crossed. "Nothing."

Sam moved closer. "This is why you're here. If you see something, if you've noticed something, you have to tell us. We have to stop this guy. What was the mistake? Because I'm not seeing it."

"It's staring you right in the face. The same way it was back then." She stood up and walked to the board, placing a finger on Jane's picture. "He left her alive."

Sam frowned. "And that was a... mistake?"

"Technically speaking, yes. The fact he targeted her at all was a mistake. He didn't have a specific hunting ground. He chose victims from Red Hook, Carroll Gardens, Gowanus. There was no way to narrow it down beyond that. The women were ages 24 to 38. Statistically meaningless given their profession. Jane is where he screwed up. He finally got recognized for his 'work,' and they gave him the wrong name. So he reached out to her. He exposed himself for the first time. Maybe that scared him enough that he went into hiding. Maybe attacking someone he had a personal vendetta against finally scratched his itch. Whatever happened, I think that's why we haven't heard from him in all this time. He knew he'd taken a huge risk that could have ended everything."

Sam blinked, surprised. "You've thought about that a lot over the past thirty years, haven't you."

"Thirty-three."

Sam flipped her hands in frustration. "Why do you keep doing that? Thirty years, thirty-three, it's the same thing."

"Not when you've been counting every day."

Sam didn't know what to say to that. She cleared her throat and tried to get back on track. "You said he reached out because Jane gave him the wrong name. What does that mean?"

Miriam rolled her eyes. "The editor came up with the name Cozy Killer when he printed Jane's article. He wanted to be called the Goodnight Man."

Sam looked at the board. They had written Goodnight Man at

one corner. All the files used that name. But she *did* remember the original name in the files, and there'd been a record of where the new moniker came from. She assumed Goodnight Man caught on because Cozy Killer was objectively terrible. But if he'd chosen his own name, if it had been important enough for him to step out of the shadows to make the correction...

"This is how we get him," Sam said.

"Maybe thirty-three years ago we could've exploited it," Miriam said, "but it's useless now. That was *my* mistake. I was so distracted by taking care of Jane... which I don't regret, just to be clear... that I didn't see it for the opportunity it was."

Sam turned to look at her. "You don't regret it."

Miriam realized what she'd said and, more importantly, how her daughter would take it. "That's not what I meant. I would change a lot of things about what happened back then~"

Sam cut her off with a wave of her hand. "Save it. Not important now."

She walked away, heading for the captain's office. Miriam rose from her seat and followed. Sam knocked on the door and waited for the captain to respond before she went in.

"How much does the press know about the case Ainsworth and I are working?"

"The new Goodnight Man murder?" Captain Morris clarified. "The bare minimum for the moment. We don't want to cause a panic. Or worse, a media circus."

Sam considered that, then nodded. "With all due respect, Captain, I think it's time to send in the clowns."

Forty-five minutes later, the briefing room had been transformed into a press room. Miriam stood off to one side with a squad of uniformed officers and detectives who seemed impossibly young for the job. Meanwhile the rows of plastic chairs were quickly filled by representatives from newspapers and television news agencies. She was surprised to see there was also room for podcasters, bloggers, and other various online sources that she couldn't begin to understand.

Once the room was full, Captain Morris took his position at the podium. He got everyone's attention by clearing his throat.

"Good afternoon. Thank you all for coming out on such short notice. I'm Captain Charles Morris of the Twenty-First Precinct.

We've asked you here today to make a public safety announcement. For details, I'd like to turn it over to Detective Samantha Balfour of the Twenty-Eight Precinct." He stepped aside and let Sam approach the microphone.

"Thank you, Captain." She cleared her throat. "Two days ago, it was reported that a woman named Julia Ramsey was found dead in her apartment. What was not revealed at the time was that elements of the crime scene resembled key features of an infamous serial killer from thirty years ago. The scene was identical to those credited to the so-called Cozy Killer."

Miriam tensed and scanned the crowd of journalists. They whispered amongst themselves, a few of them already taking out their phones and starting to text. She couldn't help but imagine Jane among their number, furiously scribbling follow-up questions in her notepad.

"You may remember," Sam said, raising her voice above their murmurs, "that the Cozy Killer was never identified. He went silent after his sixth attack, in which the victim survived. That would make Julia Ramsey the seventh victim of the Cozy Killer. Technology has come a long way since the last time he was terrorizing our streets. You can be assured we're doing everything in our power to identify this man and ensure that there won't be an eighth victim. In the meantime, we ask that women stay alert and aware of their surroundings at all times." She lifted her hands in a gesture of surrender. "If it's actually possible to be *more* aware..."

A few of the women in the crowd chuckled nervously. Hands started to go up.

"We won't be taking questions at this time," Sam said. "We simply wanted to inform the press that the Cozy Killer *does* seem to be active again and precautions should be taken. We'll keep you updated as the case progresses. We reached out to the original..." Her eyes cut across the room to Miriam and, after a pause, tried speaking again. "We've reached out to the original detective on the case, who also happens to be my mother. Detective Miriam Balfour. She's agreed to join us as a consultant until the Cozy Killer is officially brought to justice. Thank you."

She stepped away from the microphone.

One of the reporters rose. "Just so we're clear," he said, confusion written all over his face, "you *are* talking about the serial murderer commonly known as the Goodnight Man?"

"While that's the name he seems to have chosen for himself," Sam said, "we see no reason to use it in an official capacity. I don't give a shit what this asshole *wants* to be called."

With that, she turned and left the room. Miriam followed, ignoring the journalists shouting her name and asking for 'just one question!' She caught up with Sam at her desk.

Sam looked past Miriam into the briefing room, where Captain Morris was wrapping things up. "Do you think it will work?"

"I think you said 'Cozy Killer' enough that, if it *is* a trigger, he won't be able to resist."

"I hope so. I'd much rather this psycho target me than some random woman."

Captain Morris approached and heard Sam's comment. "Hopefully you'll be prepared for him, Detective Balfour." He looked at Miriam. "And I hope you and your wife have arranged for a safe place to stay for the duration."

Miriam frowned. "What do you mean?"

"Detective Balfour mentioned you during the press conference," Morris said. "There's just as much reason for him to come after you. And your wife, if he decides she counts as unfinished business. I thought that was part of the plan here. Poking the bear with the name, and with the fact the woman who uncovered his crimes in the first place was back on the case."

"I... guess so, yes," Sam said.

"Then Miriam and Jane Ross are both in danger."

"We don't need babysitters," Miriam said. "We're fine. Our address is unlisted, he won't even be able to find us–"

Morris held up his hand, shook his head. "This isn't up for debate. I'm sorry. Thirty years ago, Jane Ross went home by herself and was confronted by the killer. This all could have ended back then if she'd had someone watching her back."

Miriam worked her jaw. The comment had been casual, he couldn't know the guilt she carried for that decision, but it still cut deep.

"Detective Balfour, I expect you to arrange protective custody for your mother and her wife. If you don't, I will. Understood?"

"Yes, Captain."

He nodded and left them.

"You don't have to do that," Miriam said. "We'll be just fine~"

"He's right," Sam snapped. "About all of it. If you go home and the fucker is waiting there... And he was right about thirty years ago. *You* decided Jane didn't need someone watching her. I won't let you screw up the case again."

Miriam took a deep breath to steady herself. "So. What's the plan?"

Sam sighed. "I guess you're going to meet my wife after all."

Chapter Sixteen

SAM HATED every second of the making the call to have someone pick up Jane Ross and bring her into the city. She knew that her mother would refuse a hotel, and she would absolutely fight a protective detail tooth and nail. The only way to ensure their safety would be to watch them herself. She hated the idea, and the fact it put Beau in the line of fire was only one item on a very long list of why it was going to be a disaster. But she called the Weehawken Police and they agreed to escort Jane to Brooklyn.

Miriam's attempt to argue was nipped in the bud when Sam pointed out Jane was also in danger. "If I left you to twist in the wind, I'd have to leave her out there, too. Do you want to give this motherfucker a second chance to take her out?"

On the drive home, Sam kept her phone in her lap and texted Beau at each stoplight. "*do u want to spend a few nights in a hotel?*"

"*Sure. What's the game? Touring rock star and stalker?*"

Sam couldn't resist smiling. "*No game. And just u.*"

"*Boring. I'm home btw. Dinner will be on the table when you get here. What a good wifey, huh?*" This was followed by a dancing lady and a pair of bright red lips.

"*I love you,*" Sam texted back. "*I'm bringing home a surprise.*" She couldn't drop the bombshell in a text message.

"*R we going to play? I hope it's a redhead*"

"*Not that kind of surprise. Behave urself*"

"*Boring again,*" Beau texted. "*But okay. ETA?*"

"*About 15.*"

"*Perfect. ilu.*"

When Sam returned the phone to its dash mount, Miriam said, "Preparing the wife for my arrival?"

"I wasn't typing long enough to cover all that," Sam said. "She knows I'm bringing *someone* home. I'll save the details until we're in person."

"How much does she know about me? I can't imagine you've told her the whole story."

Sam said, "Just my side of it."

Miriam snorted and looked out the window. "In that case, are you sure your apartment is the safest place for me?"

"Is your version really that different from mine?" Sam asked.

"Considering how much of it probably came from your father, I bet we could have quite an interesting time comparing notes."

"I don't need Dad to tell me what happened in my own life."

"You were *four.*"

"I was old enough to know who wasn't fucking there," Sam snapped. She gripped the steering wheel with both hands and let out a primal growl.

Miriam let the silence hang for a block. "I wanted to be," she said softly. "You know that, right? You have to know I *wanted~*"

"Yeah, because no one has ever crossed Manhattan to visit their kid."

Miriam sighed. "And going from Brooklyn to Jersey is just as impossible."

Sam stared straight ahead, jaw tight. "I had no fucking reason to go."

After that, the rest of the car ride passed in silence. Sam parked in the garage of her building and led Miriam to the elevator. Stuck inside the cramped car, Sam knew she should've been planning what to say to Beau, how to explain their current situation to her, but instead she simply spent the entire silent ride dreading the moment she had to introduce their new houseguest.

Sam still didn't have a plan when she opened the door and ushered Miriam inside. Beau was sitting on the couch, computer perched on her lap. "Hey, babe. I was just~" She had twisted her head mid-sentence and sat up straighter. "Oh! Is this the surprise?"

"Yeah." Sam closed the door. "Beau Martin, this is Miriam Balfour. My mother. Mom, this is Beau. My wife."

Beau's eyes went wide. She nearly dropped the laptop moving it to the table, unfolding her legs as she moved to stand up.

"Oh my god," she said. "Sam's mom? Are you kidding me? Hi! It's so lovely to finally meet you." She came around the couch and pulled Miriam into a hug.

Sam stepped back, arms crossed, and waited for the hug to end. Miriam, stiff as a board, eventually patted Beau on the shoulders before gently pushing her off.

"Sorry," Beau said. "It's just that I've been *so curious* about you, and Sam always says the two of you have a really awkward~"

"Ah," Sam said. "Beau, can I talk to you in the bedroom?"

"Um. Sure. Uh..." She looked at the computer, then pointed at the door. To Miriam, she said, "I've got some food coming. I wasn't sure what or who to expect, so I just ordered Chinese. I figured we could do a buffet type thing. If the buzzer buzzes before we come back, just let them in. I already paid on the app."

"I think I can handle that," Miriam said.

Sam took Beau's hand. "We'll be right back."

She dragged Beau down the hall to their bedroom and shut the door behind her. Beau covered her mouth and laughed.

"Your mom? Oh my god, Sam."

"I know." Sam exhaled sharply. She went to the closet and started unbuttoning her shirt. "I didn't know how to tell you on the phone with her sitting right there. I wasn't sure how you'd react. The hug was kind of unexpected, to be honest."

Beau sat on the foot of the bed. "Well, I'm excited! It means one way or another, I'm finally going to get the full story about what happened with your family."

Sam shrugged out of her shirt and looked back at her. "What are you talking about? I told you the full story. Mom worked with a reporter, fell in love with her, then decided to completely restart her life as a lesbian. Having a kid wasn't part of the new version of her, so I got dumped as much as Dad did. And when her coworkers found out she was living with a woman, they made her life such hell that she eventually gave up her whole career and moved to the suburbs." She pulled a sweater on and faced Beau. "It's a pathetic history of a woman who keeps burning all her bridges behind her because she expects to find something better on the other side."

Beau got off the bed. She went to Sam and smoothed the static from her hair. "She stayed with your dad after their divorce so you would have both parents. You don't think it's a *little* strange she decided to completely abandon you when she met someone else?"

"I don't know," Sam said. "All I know is that one day she was just gone. And she wasn't in California or London, she was in New fucking Jersey."

"I can see how that would sting." She rested her hands on Sam's hips and pulled her close. "So what's she doing here now?"

Sam rolled her eyes. "Oh god. That's a whole other mess. The woman she ended up running away with? They were working together on the Goodnight Man case back in the day."

"Oh, I heard a podcast about that. But didn't he stop killing, like, when we were in pre-school?"

"He's back."

Beau's eyes widened. "You're shitting me. Oh god. Is that the call you got the other night?"

Sam nodded. "That's why Ainsworth called me. Because of Mom's connection to the original investigation. And that's why she's here. Last time, he reached out because Jane Ross used the wrong name in the newspaper and he got vain about it. So we're hoping the same thing will happen now. We had a press conference where we referred to him as the Cozy Killer to see if it triggers him to reach out again."

Beau blinked and leaned back. "Damn, honey. That's risky."

"Risky and stupid," Sam agreed. "But this guy has been getting away with it for thirty years. Getting under his skin worked once before, and they didn't take advantage of it." The buzzer sounded and Sam sighed. "Okay. There's our dinner."

"Ready to face her?"

Sam laughed. "No. Not even a little bit." She cupped Beau's face. "You have my back, right?"

"Always. And if you're a good girl and behave yourself, I'll give you a treat when this is all over."

"Ooh, now that might be a reward worth suffering for." She kissed Beau, then kissed her again and let it linger.

Beau finally chuckled and pulled away. "Not while your mom is here."

"I thought that made it hotter," Sam said. "All those teens sneaking their girlfriends in. I never got to experience that."

"It's overrated, believe me."

Sam raised an eyebrow. "How many bedroom windows did you climb through?"

"Only about half the ones I was invited to."

"At least you have standards."

They headed back out into the main room. Instead of a delivery person, Sam was startled to see Jane Ross standing in the doorway. Again she flashed back to being four, to sitting at the dinner table while Mommy had a date with the woman she would eventually destroy their lives for.

"Looks like the gang's all here," Miriam said.

Sam said, "Beau, this is Jane. Jane. Beau."

Jane stepped forward and offered her hand. "Pleasure to meet you. I'm sorry it's under such horrible circumstances."

Beau shrugged and shook Jane's hand. "Honestly, I was worried I'd have to settle for just meeting one of you at the other's funeral. So this is... uh, preferable." She took her hand back. "Sorry. That was darker than I intended."

Jane smiled. "Well, we're hiding out from a serial killer. A certain amount of gallows humor is to be expected, I think."

Sam cleared her throat. "Okay. So. I guess I'll set the table..."

Beau put a hand on her arm. "Wait, no, sweetie, I can do that. You can catch up with-"

"I'd rather set the table," Sam said. "Thanks."

She retreated into the kitchen before Beau could put up further argument. She heard Beau tell Miriam and Jane to have a seat at the table. She followed her into the kitchen and put a hand on her shoulder.

"Hey, I know you've been through a lot with her. And I'm not asking you to forgive and move on. I'm just asking you to... maybe... while we're being forced to share a space with her... don't make it a war. Or at least keep it at cold war. I'm not trying to undermine your feelings. I'm just being a buffer. If she talks to me, it'll be less awkward that you're not talking to each other. I want you to know I'm on your side, even if I'm acting like the gracious hostess."

Sam cupped Beau's cheek. "I love you."

Beau kissed the inside of her wrist. "And if you need to spend an hour before bed ranting about something she said, I'll be prepared for that."

"You better be."

When they returned to the dinner table, Jane was leaning close to Miriam. "~officers sitting outside seems like a bit of overkill, especially since they're just watching an empty house."

"I would've thought you'd welcome overkill," Sam said. "Considering you were the one that was actually targeted by this maniac last time."

Jane sat up straighter. "I suppose it's better than the opposite. I just can't help feeling like it's a waste of resources. Our address isn't listed anywhere publicly. We've made certain of that."

"And back in the day, you thought 'Jane Ross' was generic enough of a name that he'd never be able to find you," Sam said. "Look how that turned out."

Miriam started to say something, but a look from Jane stopped her. Beau offered Jane the container of fried rice, and they settled into the silent routine of filling their plates.

Just before the quiet became oppressive, Jane said, "So... Beau. How did you and Sam meet?"

Beau glanced at Sam, who gave her permission with a slight flick of two fingers.

"There was a break-in at the gym where I work," Beau said. "Sam was assigned the case and came around to question everyone on the morning shift. The guy turned out to be a former manager, and she needed someone to identify him on the security tape. When she escorted me out of the station, she asked if it would be more awkward to ask me out then, or if she would have to get a membership at the gym and stalk me for a few weeks before she made her move."

Jane smiled. "That's kind of cute."

"Stalking isn't really a joke," Miriam muttered.

"Well, no," Beau said. "But it was... flirtation..."

Miriam shrugged.

Sam caught Beau's eye and gave her a quick smile. The story wasn't a lie, but it had been heavily edited. When she first arrived to the crime scene, Beau was the first employee she'd interviewed. The pinkie and ring finger of her right hand had been splinted. Sam casually asked her what had happened.

"I jammed them on a machine last night," Beau explained, then seemed to realize the question was more than idle curiosity when it came from a cop. "Am I a suspect?"

Sam had smiled. "Everyone is a suspect right now."

A visible shiver had gone through Beau when she said that, but Sam had discounted it as a random reaction. She didn't think about it at all until they saw each other again, at the station, where Beau identified her former manager as the man on the security camera from the yogurt shop next door. They were alone in the stairwell when Beau turned to her. She was one step lower, so she had to tilt her head up to meet Sam's gaze.

"Does this mean I'm not a suspect anymore?"

Sam smiled. "Yeah, I think you're in the clear."

Beau moved up a step, forcing Sam to shift her weight. Her back was to the wall and Beau crowded her just enough to be on the verge of uncomfortable.

"What if I did something else?" Beau whispered.

"Like what?" Sam asked, unsure if this was still playful banter or a true confession.

Beau shrugged, her eyes shining. She leaned in, her lips right next to Sam's ear. "Maybe not every bad thing I've done is illegal, detective..."

"Maybe I should take you to an interrogation room," Sam said. "We can figure it out together."

"I think that might be a lot of fun for both of us."

Beau lightly kissed Sam's cheek and then stepped back. She took out a folded piece of paper and slipped it into the chest pocket of Sam's blouse. The back of her fingers brushed the curve of Sam's breast, deliberate or happy accident, Sam couldn't tell, and then stepped back.

"Come pick me up sometime, Detective Balfour. Take me in. Don't let me go until you're satisfied with my answers."

"I'll... be sure to do that, Miss Martin."

Beau gave her a wide smile, a wink, and then turned and headed down the steps. Sam was so flustered that she forgot she was supposed to be escorting her.

It had taken Sam four days to get up the courage to show up at Beau's apartment. They were both still dressed for work - Sam in a blazer over a T-shirt, Beau in Lycra. Sam had said she 'just had a few more questions' and grabbed Beau's arm to lead her down to the car.

She put her in the backseat and got behind the wheel, saying nothing until the first stoplight.

She looked at Beau in the rearview. "So far?"

"Very good," Beau said with a wicked smile.

They didn't say anything else until they were outside Sam's apartment. Sam moved her lips to Beau's ear and whispered, "Are we going through the whole scene…?"

Beau said, "Yes, please."

Sam had nodded and gripped Beau's upper arm tightly. "You're not leaving here until I'm satisfied. Is that clear?"

"Crystal, Detective."

Again, Sam had heard a tremble of excitement in Beau's voice. She unlocked her apartment door, which was about to become a very private interrogation room, and kicked the door shut behind them. Beau tried to escape, Sam wrestled her back to the wall, there was a struggle, clothes were torn…

She snapped back to the present when a takeout container full of beef and broccoli was placed in front of her. She looked at the faces around her to see if she'd been missed during her reverie, but Beau was talking to Jane, and Miriam seemed focused on her meal to acknowledge the fact anyone else was in the room.

Beau cleared her throat. "Sam has never really told me the story about how *you* met," she said to Jane. "I've heard some of the, um, speculation and the official sources have mentioned it, of course. But I'm sure there's more to the story."

"I'm sure Sam doesn't want to dig up those old bones," Jane said.

"I'm sure no one does," Miriam said.

Sam leaned back in her chair. "No, why don't we dig them all up? Get it out in the open."

Miriam looked at Sam. Her expression seemed almost like a dare.

Sam didn't look away. "Jane was assigned to follow Mom around for a week. For some article she was writing for the paper. They happened to uncover a serial killer. They never actually caught the guy, but a few months later Mom had moved out of the apartment and I never heard from her again."

Jane said, "That's not exactly~"

"How dare you," Miriam snapped. "You know it wasn't that

simple."

"Sure as hell seemed that way," Sam said.

"You were *four years old*," Miriam said.

Sam said, "Convenient for you to acknowledge that *now*. Did it ever occur to you that I might have needed you growing up?"

"I tried," Miriam said. "I reached out. Letters. Phone calls. Birthdays, Christmases, Thanksgiving. You never replied. You never wanted to talk."

"You never sent me any goddamn letters," Sam said.

"Constantly."

Everyone turned to look at Jane, whose single word had cut through the angry shouting. She was looking down at the napkin in her lap, twisting it with both hands. She looked at Miriam, then to Sam.

"She sent you letters constantly, Sammy. At least one per week. I watched her write them. I mailed a couple for her, too, when she ran out of stamps. She mailed you presents. Christmas and birthday. Every year. Until you were twelve, when I guess... I guess she finally got the message."

Sam wanted to keep up her rage, wanted to stoke her anger, but she could tell Jane wasn't lying. She tried to remember a single letter, a single present... maybe something with the tag changed to "From Santa" to conceal its real origin. She didn't remember anything. Maybe there had been phone calls, her dad asking from the other room if she wanted to talk to mama.

"You didn't get... *any* of them?" Miriam's voice was small and fragile. Despite a lifetime of anger at her, Sam couldn't help but feel her heart twist a little.

Sam cleared her throat. She stared at the food. "No."

Miriam closed her eyes. After a long moment filled with deep, steady breaths, she finally said, "Fucking Jeremy."

Sam tried to remember her father in the immediate aftermath of Miriam leaving. She hadn't understood exactly why her mother was suddenly gone, she only knew that she missed her. She sort of knew her parents weren't like her friends' parents. They were "separated" even though they lived in the same house. Her other friends knew what divorce was, and they said that was when the daddy or mommy usually went away. But she thought separated was different because they both stayed.

Until Mommy left.

Sometimes they walking to the library and she would ask if they could go see Mommy on the way home. Or if he splurged on taking her out to a restaurant, she said they should call Mommy and invite her.

She distinctly remembered one afternoon on the subway. She didn't remember where they'd been going or what had brought up the subject, but she remembered her father taking her hand between both of his and gently telling her that they probably wouldn't be seeing her mother again for a very long time.

"She decided she doesn't want to be part of this family," he said. "She has someone else for that now, and we're... we're the past for her. Do you understand that?"

Sam remembered crying in bed that night. The idea that her mother could just get a new family, start over, and not want her anymore was devastating.

"What did he tell *you?*" Sam asked.

Miriam cleared her throat and furrowed her brow. "He said..." She looked at Jane. "He said you didn't understand. And when he tried to explain that I was with Jane now, you said it was gross."

Sam clenched her jaw. "I was just a little kid. I wouldn't have cared."

"And what was I supposed to do?" Miriam said. "Hang around outside your school and wait for you to come out so I could hear it directly from you? Bust my way into the apartment to tell you my side of the story? I tried. I wrote down my side of the story so many times I could probably recite it for you now. But I... I... eventually... thought you'd made your decision."

Sam shook her head. "I should have realized when Dad found out I was gay."

Miriam raised an eyebrow. "Not supportive?"

"I was fifteen. He threatened to send me to a conversion camp. Luckily my stepmom was human enough to talk him out of that. And then he started blaming himself. He thought it happened because he always took me to baseball games instead of ballet or whatever. I guess it was like he thought you had a disease and he could've prevented me from inheriting it if he'd tried harder."

"As much as I want to say that's unbelievable," Miriam said, "that does sound like something he would say. He was such a good guy, otherwise." She looked at Sam and said, "I'm glad you had a good stepmom, anyway."

Sam nodded. "She was good."

Silence fell across the table again, but this time it felt more relaxed, calmer. It was Jane who finally broke it, taking a deep breath and holding her hands out in front of her.

"Well, we tackled the hard part of this reunion," she said. "Now all we have to do is catch a serial killer."

Sam laughed despite herself.

CHAPTER SEVENTEEN

AFTER DINNER, Jane offered to wash the dishes in a way that allowed no argument. Beau went to the bedroom for a blanket and pillows to make up the couch. "Should we offer our bed?" she asked when Sam joined her. "They're kind of... old." She whispered the last word.

"They're not that old. Anyway, it's pointless to try. They'd just say no, we'd insist, they would refuse..." Sam waved her off. "It's not worth doing the dance."

"Probably." Beau closed the closet and walked over to Sam, holding the blanket and pillows against her chest like a shield. "Hey. You did good tonight."

"I lost my temper."

Beau shrugged. "A little bit. But you were under a lot of stress and you didn't let it explode. You had a real talk. You found out you'd both been lied to and maybe cracked the wall a little bit." She leaned in and kissed Sam's cheek. "I'm proud of you."

Sam felt herself melt at that. She put her arms around Beau and pulled her close, squeezing the bedding between them.

"Thank you, baby."

"You're welcome." She kissed Sam's lips softly. "Are you sure you don't want to fool around while your mom is here?"

Sam grinned and closed one eye, feigning thought. "Kinky if it's just when Mom is in the apartment. But when there's also a chance of a serial killer stopping by…"

"Yeah, that makes sense." She kissed Sam again, more firmly this time. When she pulled back, she offered Sam the blanket and pillows. "Want to take this out to them?"

"Shirking your hostess duties?"

"Well, she *is* your mother."

"Yeah, yeah." Sam took the bedding. "I'll be right back."

She went back out into the living room. Jane was lying on the couch, propped up on the throw pillows that had already been present. Miriam was in the process of moving the armchair so it would be in front of the door.

"What are you doing?"

"I'm going to stand guard." Miriam saw the pillows and took one of them. "That couch is too narrow for both of us anyway."

Sam said, "You don't have to literally sit in front of the door. There's a cruiser downstairs."

"And this guy has gotten past cruisers and security cameras for thirty-three years."

"Yeah, three decades ago," Sam agreed, "back before this city was wired like *The Truman Show*. He's not going to be so lucky this time."

"He already has once." Miriam put the pillow in the chair longways, stuffing it into one corner to act as an extra cushion. "I'm not going to take the risk."

Sam rolled her eyes and went to the couch. "Fine. Whatever. Have it your way."

Jane took the other pillow and blanket. "Thank Beau for letting us stay over. I'm sure it's not the most ideal evening for her."

"Oh, trust me, she's *thrilled* with this whole thing. She's a little insane." She looked around the living room. "Bathroom is down the hall. Towels are in the cabinet under the sink if you want to take a shower or whatever. Knock on our door if you need anything."

Jane said, "Do you really think there's a chance he'll come after us?"

Sam stopped. "Tonight or at all?"

Jane shrugged.

Sam said, "I have no idea what this guy is going to do. I don't know why he disappeared or why he's back. I just think it's safer to cover our bases since he made it personal once. Maybe he's dying and wants to finish old business. The new killing might have been a trick to draw you both out again. I'm not taking any chances."

Miriam nodded. "It's sensible."

"Thanks," Sam muttered. "I'll see you in the morning."

"Goodnight," Jane said.

Sam was luckily far enough down the hall that she could pretend she hadn't heard her. She turned on the hallway light, then went into the bedroom and shut the door behind her.

Beau was sitting up in bed, her legs crossed in front of her under the blankets. The diamond-shaped hollow formed by her position was filled with a tablet, the screen currently showing the pastel colors of a computer game.

"Hey, hey," Beau said, not looking up from the game. "Come help me."

Sam unbuttoned her blouse and shrugged out of it. "You're not supposed to have help."

"So call the cops on me."

Sam took off her slacks and climbed into bed next to Beau. "Okay, but if the people you play ever find out, I'm not going to perjure myself for you."

"Coward."

Sam took the tablet from her. "Let me see what mess you've gotten yourself into this time…"

"That went about a thousand times better than I ever imagined it would."

Miriam smiled a bit at that, then turned to look at Jane over her shoulder. "I saw you brace yourself a couple of times. Like you were afraid you'd have to jump across the table to stop us from going after each other."

"No, no," Jane said. "I trusted you could behave yourself. Beau was a bit of a wild card, but I had faith in her, too. She seems really great. She balances Sam well." She smiled. "Little Sammy. I can see the little girl in her still. It's so strange, seeing someone with a three decade gap. She probably thinks I turned into an old crone."

"You're not even sixty."

Jane looked at her. "Yes, I am."

"No, you're…" She thought for a second, doing the math. "Hm." Miriam let it drop and faced the door again. "Fucking Jeremy. I never should have taken his word for it. I never should have given up on my daughter so easily."

"You thought you were respecting her wishes," Jane said. "The important thing is that you both know the truth now. The healing can start."

Miriam said, "You don't think there's been too much…" She held her hands out and gestured vaguely. "It just feels like there's a brick wall here, and even though we know the truth now, I don't know if we'll ever be able to see past it."

"I think you'll manage," Jane said. "Now that you know there's something to fight for."

"Maybe." She settled back against her pillow. "I couldn't believe it when she said she was married to a woman. I spent all these years thinking my daughter was homophobic and here she is, an openly gay detective with a wonderful wife. I know we want things to be better for our kids, but I was forced out of the job just for *dating* you. I can't help but be jealous of her."

"That's understandable. It's a long history of anger on both sides. I don't expect you to start going to brunch every Sunday. But this is a start. It's a very hopeful start."

"Hm," Miriam said again. "A lot of years missed. And it's all my fault. Like she said, she was a child. I should've fought harder. Even if it meant hearing her say she hated me to my face. I was a coward. I couldn't face that, so I stayed away and ruined everything." She sighed and closed her eyes. "I'm going to kill that motherfucker the next time I see him."

"I'll help you hold him down."

Miriam grinned. "Thank you, sweetheart."

After a few seconds of silence, Jane said, "There's actually plenty of room for two on this couch now that I'm actually on it."

"You know it's not about the space," Miriam said. "I'm fine here."

"You're going to mess up your back sleeping in that chair."

"I'm not going to sleep."

"You're not *planning* to sleep. When you need to wake me up in two hours—"

Miriam said, "I'm not going to do shifts."

"—or if you want to wake up Sam so she can take over," Jane continued, "just nudge me and I'll scoot to the back."

"I am not going to sleep."

"It's very comfortable."

Miriam sighed and shook her head, grateful it was too dark for Jane to see her scowl. Thirty-three years together and she still had a hard time admitting when Jane one-upped her. But that time had also given Jane a sixth sense to know when she'd won an argument whether Miriam gave in or not. It was horribly frustrating, annoying as hell, and it was something she'd never known she craved until she had it. To be known by someone so completely that they could have an entire conversation under the words they were saying. *I'm concerned about you,* Jane had been saying. *You get hyper focused. You get distracted from taking care of yourself. You don't have to do this alone anymore. Let Sammy take some of the weight.*

And Miriam, in turn, had said, *This is my case, it's my problem to solve. I'm not going to toss it off to Sammy. I'll clean up my own mess.*

There was also, of course, the third layer where Jane was trying to make Miriam acknowledge they weren't in their thirties anymore. Miriam was sixty-seven, but she was no old lady. She ran four miles every day. She had perfect posture. Her hair had changed color, sure, but that was just aesthetics. She could handle the cosmetic changes of growing older but she refused to surrender to the preventable aspects of aging.

She felt the same way about the Goodnight Man. She wasn't obsessed with him. If Sam caught him, or if one of the other cops made the connection that led to an identification, she would be more than happy to let them have the collar. She just needed to be here for it. She needed to see the dots being connected, had to know what she had missed all those years ago. Maybe then she could finally put that horrible time behind her for good and move on.

Jane was guilty that she'd been spared most of the fallout, though she knew Miriam was grateful for the same thing. Miriam had taken the brunt of the consequences of everything that happened. Her entire life had been destroyed by the Goodnight Man case. First, when he went silent, rumors floated that she'd fumbled the ball. Implications were made that any male detective could've solved it in a heartbeat, completely ignoring the fact she'd worked with Kenneth Patterson, a male detective, for the majority of the investigation. He'd gotten away scot-free as well, naturally. A captain now, last they'd heard.

"Good for him," Miriam had said when they heard the news.

Then, a few seconds later, she'd added a muttered, "Good for fucking him."

Jane knew there was no use arguing for Miriam to take it easy or let someone else help. To her, sitting up all night in front of the door was her penance for her perceived failures back in the day. All Jane could do was give in and sleep so she'd be strong enough to deal with whatever consequences they had to deal with in the morning.

Miriam didn't know how long she'd been staring at the door, or how long she'd been resting her eyes, when she heard the bedroom door open. She sat up straighter and opened her eyes wide, forcing her expression into one of wakefulness before Sam emerged from the shadows. She was in a long T-shirt that stopped just above the legs of shorts that were either pink or gray. It was hard to tell in the dim light coming in through the living room window.

"Go back to bed," Miriam said.

Sam ignored her and went to the dinner table. She picked up one of the chairs and brought it over, sitting it next to her mother's but facing the other direction. She sat down with a quiet sigh.

"Kitchen window," Sam explained. "Leads to the fire escape. It would be embarrassing if the guy snuck in behind your back."

Miriam confirmed the window was there, and saw the grating of the fire escape outside. "Oh," she said, facing the door again. "Okay."

"Should we keep it down?" Sam nodded toward the couch.

"No. Once she's out, she tends to stay out."

Sam nodded and settled into the chair. Miriam noted the chair had padding on the seat and back, but there was no way it would be comfortable enough for Sam to stay there all night.

"So I guess if you're taking a shift, I can sleep for a few minutes."

"Sure. Do whatever you want." Sam kept her eyes on the window. "I couldn't sleep anyway, so I decided I might as well make myself useful."

Miriam said, "Makes sense."

"Mm."

"Yeah."

Another long silence stretched out between them. Sam finally ended it. "So how'd it feel to be back after all these years?"

"Back?"

"At the station," Sam said. "Doing the work."

Miriam scoffed. "I'm not back there. Physically, sure, doing the work, maybe. But I'm not 'back.' They just pulled me out of storage on the off chance I might end up being useful. I'm Rudolph the red-nosed reindeer."

"People like Rudolph, I thought."

"Rudolph is bullshit. The message is that bullying is fine until you're useful to the bullies."

Sam laughed. "Wow. Okay. I guess that's one way to interpret the song."

"It's the entire story of the song. He was ridiculed and ostracized until he was helpful, and then boom. Come help us out, please, forget about how we treated you. Do you think they kept him around after the fog cleared? Hell no."

"Oh, I'm starting to regret all the Christmas shows we didn't get to watch together."

Miriam flinched and looked down at her feet. Sam cleared her throat, indicating she also realized she'd crossed a sensitive line.

"I'm sure you had plenty of Christmas memories with your stepmom," Miriam said.

"Oh. Sure." Sam shifted in her seat. "Yeah, she... she was... pretty great. Really supportive with the whole coming out thing. I think if I'd had to rely on Dad, I'd have just stayed in the closet until... whenever. Probably still been in denial."

Miriam rubbed her finger along her bottom lip. "I'm sorry I left you with him."

"I—" Sam stopped herself from saying anything else. "I believed him because I had no other version of events to work with. I guess I accept the fact you tried, but you have to understand I never even got a hint of those letters existing. I thought you'd just gone away one day. You chose her—" She nodded toward the couch again. "—over me, and I just... I was a kid. You know? Looking back now, yeah, that's cruel and unthinkable, but when someone tells you a story as a kid, it settles in deep. It puts in roots. That can be really fucking hard to overcome. He wasn't the best father, but he's what I had."

"I get it," Miriam said.

"Did you ever... Did it ever cross your mind to take me when you left?"

Miriam waited so long to answer that Sam started to speak again, probably to withdraw the question, but Miriam cut her off.

"It's all I thought about, Sammy. I spent... pretty much all of the first few weeks thinking I was crazy to throw everything away for-for some woman. I almost ended things with her so many times so I could go home. Go back to normal. It would've been so easy, and so less scary, and I would've had you back. But the longer I waited, the more I realized what I felt for Jane was more than just... fleeting. And by that time, I knew... well, I *thought* I knew where you stood."

"I can't believe he's lied to both of us for so long." Sam scoffed. "Actually, you know what, no. I completely believe he'd do this shit. I just can't believe I fell for it. Especially after how he reacted when I came out. I should have put those two dots together and realized he was lying about you and Jane. Some detective."

"Even the best detective has blind spots." Miriam turned to look at Sam's profile. "How much do you remember from back then? You met Jane, you know."

Sam nodded. "I remember her being in the apartment. I was mostly confused back then, because for some reason neither of you wanted to talk details about a serial killer in front of a toddler."

Miriam chuckled. "She pushed me, you know. She said, 'that girl is growing up every day, growing wiser, and one day you might actually reach her.' She tried. She didn't realize how much it hurt. I would send a letter and spend a full week checking the mail for a reply. And then another week. And then I'd spend a month accepting the fact I wasn't going to get one. It was heartbreaking. Eventually I just couldn't do it anymore."

Sam sniffled. Miriam realized she was crying and did her a favor, turning away to look at the opposite wall.

"We'll make up for it when this is all over," Miriam promised.

"Yeah." Sam sniffed and chuckled. "Beau would force us to, even if we fought her tooth and nail."

Miriam laughed. "Jane would do the same. It sounds like you got a good one."

"The best one," Sam said.

"Make sure she knows that. I don't tell Jane enough. I hope she knows after all the time we've been together, but sometimes I feel like..."

"I think she knows," Sam said.

"To be fair, you've only seen us together for one meal."

Sam said, "True. But also, I'm facing the couch, and I can see that she's not as sound a sleeper as you claimed."

Miriam twisted to look. She could only see the top of Jane's head from her position.

Jane, without moving, said, "Shit. TV reflection?"

"TV reflection," Sam confirmed.

Miriam saw that the streetlight shining into the room hit the couch and created a blurred image on the TV screen. Sam must have seen Jane sit up, roll over, or do something else to indicate she was actually awake and eavesdropping on their conversation.

"What are you, some kind of detective?" Miriam asked.

"Some kind," Sam said. "Yeah."

From the couch, Jane said, "It would be smarter if you took shifts. But I'm going back to sleep if you want to keep saying nice things about me behind my back."

Miriam said, "I was wrong. I'm sick of her. She's insufferable."

Sam chuckled and pushed herself up out of the chair. "All the worthwhile ones are. I'm going to go try and sleep a little. I'll be back at three for my shift." She padded down the hall. "Don't fall asleep again."

"I wasn't asleep."

"You're an unreliable witness."

Miriam sighed and shook her head. When the bedroom door shut, she looked back at the couch. "How dare you embarrass me in front of my kid like that."

Jane only chuckled in the darkness.

CHAPTER EIGHTEEN

AT BREAKFAST the next morning, Sam tried to ignore how strange it was to see Miriam and Jane seated at the kitchen island with bowls of oatmeal in front of them. She was still in her pajamas, but tradition meant that she woke up first and made breakfast while Beau slept in a few extra minutes. Then Sam went to shower and Beau ate her breakfast and cooked for Sam while she got dressed for work. Having two more people in the apartment threw off the rhythm but she tried to ignore them as she went through the paces and started on Beau's eggs.

"Miriam tells me nothing happened last night," Jane said.

"Yeah," Sam agreed. "Pretty quiet."

Jane said, "So how long is this going to go on? Are you two going to stand guard every single night until he's caught? Or until he disappears again? We have to get back to our lives eventually."

Sam said, "I don't know. We still have no idea if our press conference triggered him the way it did last time. If we don't get a response from that~"

Beau came in from her shower still wearing her pajamas, her hair wet and combed back from her face. Miriam, Jane, and Sam all looked at her, and she waved her fingers nervously.

"Morning, everyone," she said. "Not used to the place being so packed this early."

"Morning," Sam said, sliding the plate of eggs across the counter to her wife. "Are you off today?"

"Afternoon shift." Beau took a seat on the stool next to Miriam.

Sam said, "Would you mind spending the morning with Miriam and Jane? I would feel a lot better if the three of you are together instead of~"

Beau held up a hand to stop her. "Spend the morning unsupervised with my wife's mother?" She looked at Miriam and grinned evilly. "I would pay for that opportunity."

"Fine. Give me twenty bucks."

"It's a figure of speech," Beau said.

Sam held out her hand, made a 'give it' motion with her fingers.

"I'm in my jammies!"

Sam grunted and took her hand back. "You'll owe me."

Beau said, "Actually, I might be able to pay you in a breakthrough on the case. Now, I know I haven't studied the case the way you all have. And this might be a really dumb question. But did anyone ever try to figure out *why* the bunny slippers? Sam told me the killer provided them himself, so there has to be some significance."

Miriam started shaking her head halfway through Beau's question. "Without a suspect, any profile we tried to make was just guesswork. We brought in experts from the FBI to analyze the crime scenes, and I'm sure other detectives have done the same thing in the decades since. And when shows like *Dateline* or *Cold Case Files* cover it, they always have some retired asshole or, god forbid, a *psychic* who claims to know why the slippers are so important."

"Childhood trauma, memory of his mother's death, hooker his dad hired," Sam said. "We know they're important to whatever narrative he has in his head. He's gone out of his way to recreate the scene every time. And it's why he was so upset when the papers gave him the wrong name. The crime scenes are a story, and he's desperate to have it told properly."

Miriam took a sip of her coffee and carefully placed the mug down on the counter. "Not that you bothered to ask my opinion... Samantha... but your wife won't be required to babysit me. I'm going to work with you."

"No," Sam said. "You're a consultant, and we will consult you when and *if* there's a break in the case. We're not reinstating you or giving you a desk~"

Miriam cut her off. "I need to be involved in this investigation.

That means every part of it."

"You're here to help us as we see fit." She placed her hands flat on the counter and met her mother's gaze. "You're fucking Rudolph."

Beau frowned and looked at Jane. "Did she just call her a reindeer...?"

Jane shook her head. "Long story."

Miriam pushed her bowl and coffee away. "Come on, Jane. We're leaving."

"Wait." Jane looked at Beau and Sam. "Let's be reasonable about this."

"If the bastard decides to come after us, I can protect us both just fine." She looked at Sam. "You don't have to worry about us anymore, Detective Balfour."

Beau stood up. "Wait, you... i-it was going so well..."

Miriam was already at the front door. Jane was at the couch, gathering her bag and the things she'd brought from their home. Beau watched her reluctantly pack everything, then looked at Sam.

"Stop them."

"If she's going to be stubborn..."

Beau stood up and pointed a finger at Jane. "You! Stop." She swung her hand around to Miriam. "And you, stay right where you are. And *you*." She pivoted to aim her finger at Sam. "You know *exactly* what you're fucking doing and you know you're going to fucking regret it when the feeling passes. You're being a stubborn brat who knows it's so much easier to just fall back into your old routine with your mom because fixing it means doing hard work and letting go of a whole lifetime of disappointment."

Sam grimaced and looked away.

"And you." She jabbed her finger at Miriam. "You *know* Sam can't just take you into work and let you sit in on an active investigation. Were you just waiting for something to not go your way so you could throw a tantrum and storm out? First sign of trouble and poof, Mom's a ghost again."

Jane cleared her throat and looked pointedly at Miriam. "It wouldn't be unprecedented. Kicking me out over the article~"

Miriam said, "Don't *help* her."

Jane put down her bag and crossed her arms over her chest, clearly choosing her side. "She's making a lot of good points."

Beau continued. "Sam is trying to take care of you. Protect you. She *wants* your input but maybe the brass isn't interested in having you lurking over their shoulders. Maybe she's *also* trying to protect you from a world that turned against you for being gay. I know *I* wouldn't want to go back to a place that treated me like shit just because I was suddenly useful to them. Oh!" She looked at Sam. "Rudolph! I get it now."

Jane crossed her arms and looked at Miriam. "What that young lady just said. Saved me the trouble of figuring out how to say it on the way home."

Sam sighed heavily.

Jane said, "We sit tight with Beau. Sam goes to work, and she keeps in touch with us throughout the day. She shares whatever information we need, as we need it—"

Miriam glowered. "So we only know what she chooses to tell us."

"Would you have done *any* different in her shoes?" Jane asked.

Miriam grunted and crossed her arms defensively. "Fine."

"Sam?" Beau said.

"It was my plan in the first place," Sam muttered. "So sure, yeah. Whatever. But you're going to have a police escort." Miriam started to argue but Sam stopped it with a look. "That part is absolutely non-negotiable. We'll take the detail off the house. They'll be completely invisible unless they become necessary."

Beau said, "Are they ninjas?"

"They can be," Sam and Miriam said together. Sam looked uncomfortable with the harmony, but pushed on. "Part of their job is to blend in and be incognito. You'll never know they're there."

Jane said, "That's a little more creepy than it is comforting."

"Just think of them as guardian angels."

Miriam shrugged. "Fine."

"Fantastic," Sam said.

Beau held her hands up, palms out. "So everyone is settled, yeah? Miriam, Jane. You two and I are going to get to know each other today. Sam's going to go to work. And then we'll all meet up back here tonight. And if we need to adjust the arrangement, we'll talk about it over dinner. Sound good for everyone?"

Miriam and Sam both mumbled their agreements. Jane, fighting a smile, nodded.

"Fine," Sam said. "I'm going to go get ready for work. Beau? Can

I see you in the bedroom?"

Beau nodded and followed her down the hall. Sam held the door for her, closing it once she was inside.

"Don't be mad," Beau said. "I went a little overboard, but you~"

Sam held up a hand. "No, no. You were right. I was being stubborn, she was being stubborn, we were both just brick-walling each other. You put us in our places."

Beau relaxed. "Okay. Good."

Sam slipped her thumbs under the waistband of her pajama pants and moved closer. "So I was wrong and you were right. And that means..."

Realization dawned on Beau's face, then was quickly replaced with confusion. "Oh. You want to... I mean, I'm game. But your mom is..." She gestured at the door.

"So we'll have to be quiet and quick." She pushed her pants down and let them pool around her feet. "How many, do you reckon?"

"Um. Two?"

Sam frowned. "You think that was only worth two?"

"Well," Beau said, "I'm worried the sound will travel. And also, if I do more than two, I might get too into it and get carried away and~"

"Right. Smart. So two."

Beau said, "Okay. If you're sure."

Sam shrugged and went to the bed. "Rules are rules." She bent forward and rested her hands on the mattress. "I'm not going to slip by on a technicality."

Beau stepped up behind her. She rested a hand on the small of her back. "I think you get credit for following the rules even when it's awkward."

Sam looked over her shoulder. "Keep that in mind for the next time I really screw up."

"You know we don't rollover credits in this house, babe." She cupped one cheek of Sam's ass with her right hand. "Ready?"

"Mm-hmm." She faced forward and closed her eyes.

A second later, Beau's hand smacked down hard. Sam grunted and grabbed with blanket with both hands. She bit her lip in anticipation of the next spank. She'd never anticipated this kink. Hell, the first time a girlfriend had swatted her ass as a joke, she spun around and slapped her back. But with Beau, it felt right. It felt more collaborative, like it was something they did together instead of one partner doing it to the other. They had rules, they talked about it, and that level of trust and understanding meant that Sam had no problem bending over when it was called for.

The second smack made her whimper, and she hung her head low. Beau had been right; if they'd risked three, things would've gotten out of hand very quickly. She pushed herself up and twisted to sit on the edge of the bed. Two spanks wasn't really enough to make it hard to sit, but she could definitely feel the sting. Beau cupped her face and kissed her softly.

"You good?"

"Mm-hmm. It would've felt weird going to work without sorting that out."

Beau smiled. "Love you."

Sam kissed the inside of Beau's wrist. "I love you too. Let me up. I need to get ready for work or I'm going to be late."

Beau backed up. "I'll try not to get too comfortable with your mother. But I won't stop her if she starts telling me juicy details about you."

"Keep in mind, the woman only knew me until I was four."

"Oh, I'm sure there are still plenty of embarrassing stories just waiting to be unearthed."

Sam undressed and went to the bathroom. "Hey. That was a good thought about the 'why' of the posing. The slippers and all that."

Beau shrugged. "Apparently not very helpful, if everyone else has already explored the angle."

"That doesn't matter," Sam said. "Sometimes going back over old ground is exactly what we need to crack the case. There might be something unique to the new crime scene that puts the originals in perspective, and I wouldn't have thought to compare them because the ground is so well-covered. So thank you."

"My pleasure." Beau opened the bedroom door. "Have a good time at work. Catch a killer. Be home in time for dinner."

"I'll do my best," Sam promised.

Beau blew her a kiss and then left her to finish getting ready.

Sam threw her coat over a chair and scanned the room until she found Ainsworth. She whistled to get his attention. "We have someone looking into the fuzzy slippers, right?"

"The generic slippers that could've been bought at any CVS, Walgreens, or a thousand internet shops? Yeah, we're crossing our fingers something will crop up. Why?"

"My wife brought them up this morning."

"You talk to your wife about your cases?"

She shrugged. "Some of them."

"That's not–"

"Yeah, I don't care," she interrupted. "The point is, what's the point? Why the pose? Why are the slippers the only thing he cares enough about to provide himself? Look." She went to the board and pointed at the pictures in turn. "All the pajamas are different designs. They're similar, but they all came from the victims' wardrobes. Plaid pants, cotton, T-shirts with cartoon characters on them, a Yankees tee. He doesn't care about that. What he cares about are the fucking slippers. Why."

Ainsworth examined the pictures. "Maybe they're his calling card. Everything else is different, but the slippers are the same, so we know it's him. The guy obviously cares about notoriety. He wanted to choose his own name, after all, so. Maybe he needed one thing to be uniform and slippers were the easiest to come up with. Pajamas, you have to worry about body size. Slippers can be a little too big and no one notices."

Sam considered that possibility. "Maybe," she said under her breath. "Have we gotten any reaction to the press conference yet?"

"Nope," Ainsworth said. "The tip line has been a wonderful assortment of helpful members of humanity, though. Just the cream of the crop."

"I'll bet."

"We also checked recent parolees," he said. "No recent releases have the right timeline to match up with this guy's hiatus."

"Of course not," Sam said. "That would be too easy."

Ainsworth sighed. "It's so frustrating waiting for the guy to screw up just so we can have another piece of the puzzle."

She shook her head. "That's not the frustrating thing. It's the fact that I can feel we have enough here to catch him." She indicated the whole board. "I feel like they had enough to catch him back in the day, and that's why he stopped. I don't know why he started again,

I don't know why he's comfortable now, but I have no doubt that he stopped killing back in the nineties because he realized how close they were. He was retreating."

"So the answer is up there," Ainsworth said.

"We just have to find it."

Chapter Nineteen

NOTHING.

Sam spent the entire day reading case files, watching security footage, scanning crime scene photos. And the grand total of her efforts when the day ended was nothing. To be exactly where she had started. Nothing leapt out at her. Nothing triggered an insight. She rested her elbows on the desk and pressed her fingers against her eyelids, rubbing in slow circles. Technically she was back where her mother had been in the nineties. She couldn't imagine thirty years of this frustration, of not knowing for so long.

"Look at the bright side, Balfour," Ainsworth said as he passed her on his way out. "The guy is probably close to retirement age. So if we don't get him, he'll probably die soon anyway."

"That's very comforting, thank you."

"I try." He patted her shoulder. "Get some sleep. Fresh eyes in the morning."

She sighed. "Fat lot of good fresh eyes have done so far. Hold the elevator."

She turned off her computer, grabbed her bag and coat, and hurried to catch up with him. He pressed the button for the lobby and leaned against the wall.

"So how are things with your mother? I'm surprised she wasn't here today."

"I figured no one would want her underfoot, getting in the way." He made a noise, so she rolled her eyes. "Okay, *I* didn't want her getting in the way. I want to solve this case. And I don't want her second-guessing me or telling me I'm going down a path she already dismissed, or... or any of a hundred other annoying things she might have done."

He laughed. "Fair. God, I have no idea what I'd do if one of my parents was also a cop. I wouldn't want them within a thousand miles of a case I was working, that's for damn sure. You're braver than I am, Balfour."

"Well, we've always known that."

They parted ways in the lobby. When she got to her car, she placed her phone on the dash mount and dialed Beau's number.

"Hey!" Beau's voice was hushed. "On your way home already?"

"Yeah. Only so many times I could bang my head against a brick wall here." She ran her hand through her hair and grunted. "How about you? Productive?"

Beau said, "Uh. Well, Jane is a delight. Really like her a lot. Your mom..."

Sam smiled. "Hopefully she wasn't too difficult."

"No, no, not difficult at all. But it was obvious she spent the entire day thinking about the case and brooding about not being at the office with you."

"Maybe I should rethink that." Sam sighed. "All hands on deck sounds pretty good right now. If we let this guy kill someone else..."

"You have time," Beau said.

"We've *had* plenty of time," Sam said. "Thirty years. I wouldn't be surprised if he came back just to taunt us."

"But you *are* coming home, right? Because you have to put give that big crime-stopper brain a chance to rest if you're going to have any hope of catching him."

"Yes, ma'am." Sam started the car as if to prove her intention. "Do you want me to pick up something for dinner on my way home?"

Beau said, "Yeah, I'll poll the ladies and text you with the verdict. Be safe out there."

"Will do. See you soon. Love you."

"Love you."

She hung up and looked at herself in the rearview mirror. There were always a few days between killings back in the nineties. She couldn't imagine he'd speed up now, but any predictions they made about him was pure guesswork. And, in this case, wishful thinking.

All they could do was work the case as quickly as possible and hope they moved faster than he did.

She gave herself a determined nod and pulled out of the spot, hoping she wasn't setting herself up for disappointment.

Dinner ended up being from a sandwich shop called Tommy's down the street from their apartment. The text had only indicated Jane wanted 'veggie' and Miriam wanted 'turkey,' so Sam got them with the works. They could just pick off anything they didn't want. She and Beau ate there frequently, so she got their usuals. When her order was ready she sighed and headed upstairs, already dreading the long night ahead of her. She and her mother had made some leeway on chipping away at the wall between them, but it had been a long, angry time, and she couldn't flip off the hate switch just because she had a better understanding of what her father had done.

To be fair, she wasn't just angry at Miriam anymore. Hell, *most* of her anger was no longer directed at her mother. It was solely aimed at her father and herself. Him for coming up with the lie. Her for believing it. She was a child, yes, but certainly over the years there'd been doubts. There had been times, even before he revealed himself to be a fucking homophobe, when she doubted his true beliefs.

But to tell a little girl her mother had just walked away... She still couldn't fathom how anyone could come up with that lie. He'd sold it so well. She remembered being with him at a Yankees game, grabbing his sleeve, begging to let Mom come to the next one. She even remembered the way his eyes shined with tears when he said Miriam wouldn't accept the ticket. The motherfucker managed *tears* when he said Miriam didn't want her anymore. And she'd bought it. Why wouldn't she? He was her dad, and her mother was nowhere to be seen. Without a chance to defend herself, the lie became reality in Sam's eyes.

She let herself into the apartment. Miriam was on the couch, already pushing herself up to her feet when she heard the key in the lock.

"Anything?" she asked before the door was closed.

Sam held up the bag. "Sandwiches."

"I meant with the case," Miriam said.

Jane had also come to greet her, and she took the bag from Sam. "Don't mind her," she said, taking the sandwiches to the kitchen.

"She's been pestering poor Beau like crazy to text you for updates all day. I'll get plates and drinks and everything."

"Luckily Beau knows better than to ask," Sam said. "Where is she?"

"Bedroom," Miriam said. "I think she needed a little space from us. And to be honest, we needed some space, too. Not that she's..." She held up her hands. "It's just... a whole day is a lot for anybody."

"Understood." She headed down the hall. "Stay here."

Miriam said, "The case~"

Sam aimed a finger at her. "Stay. Here."

Miriam stopped, crossed her arms over her chest, and sighed.

Sam went to the bedroom. Beau was stretched across the bed with her phone in hand, scrolling through some app or another.

"Hiding?" Sam asked.

"No, no, your Moms are great. They're just..." She sighed and put her phone down. "Text Sam, see what she's doing on the case! So how did you and Sam really meet? Text Sam about the case. Who proposed, you or her? Text Sam about the case. What was the wedding like? *Text Sam about the case.*"

Sam chuckled and walked around the foot of the bed so she could climb on the mattress behind Beau. "I think I have a good idea who was asking what." She put her hands on Beau's shoulders and began massaging. "I owe you one for babysitting them."

"Mm. Lady of the house comes home... babysitter has done a good job..."

Sam laughed and shook her head. "Everything is a potential game for you, isn't it?"

"I should've been a writer."

"I would read all your books." She bent down and kissed Beau's hair. "I love you, Beau-zo."

Beau leaned back against her. "Truth. Before we go back out there. How was today?"

"Frustrating as fuck," Sam said. "Demoralizing. I'm starting to lose faith. Mom and I worked the same case, maybe the next thing we have in common is we both fail to solve it. But we have to take this guy down. We can't let him win. If he's as old as we think he is, this might be our last chance to make him pay for what he's done. What he's doing."

Beau twisted away from her massage and sat up. She kissed

Sam's lips. "You'll do your job, and you'll do it well, 'cause you never do anything less. Whether you catch him or not, you'll still have done everything in your power. Understood, Samantha?"

"Yes, ma'am."

"Good." She kissed Sam again. "Did you get my turkey club?"

"Yes ma'am."

"Such a good wifey."

"I try." She got off the bed and held her hand out for Beau to help her up. "I might take Mom off your hands tomorrow."

Beau winced. "Really...? Because honestly... she might have been a broken record, but at least I was able to tune that out eventually. Jane, though."

Sam laughed. "She has that mom energy combined with a journalist's nosiness."

Beau put her head on Sam's shoulder and faked a sob. "Save me."

Sam patted her back, holding her for a little longer than necessary to delay going back out into the main room.

Over dinner, Miriam reluctantly agreed to stay another night. "But if the bastard didn't get in touch today, we might be in the clear. He might not give a shit about his name anymore. If tomorrow goes by without a call, I think we can just go home and be content with a squad car parked at the curb." Sam didn't have an argument against that plan, so she agreed. She was already looking forward to having her home back.

Miriam volunteered to take the first watch again. Sam was exhausted enough to not fight her. She was in bed skimming the notes she'd taken on the case when Beau got out of the shower. She opened the bathroom door but didn't come into the bedroom. The light was still on behind her, and the shower had been hot enough that steam was still swirling around her bare legs like fog in a music video. Sam looked up at her, admiring her black briefs and matching tank top. After a minute of appreciating the view, she put her phone down on her chest and raised her eyebrow questioningly.

"Not that I mind the display," Sam said, "but is there a reason...?"

"I have to tell you something, but I'm worried you'll freak out. Or feel embarrassed."

Sam frowned. "Embarrassed?"

"Yeah. I solved your case."

"My...? The Goodnight Man case?"

"Yeah."

"You solved it."

"Mm-hmm."

Sam put her phone aside and pushed herself up, resting against the headboard. "Well, this should be good. I promise I won't feel bad. So hit me with it. Who's the Goodnight Man?"

Beau took a deep breath and finally came into the room. "Me."

Sam lifted her chin. "Pardon?"

"It's me," Beau said. "I'm the Goodnight Man."

"Okay." Despite how ridiculous it was, Sam couldn't deny that her heartrate had ticked up a little. She struggled to keep her breathing steady. "Why don't you run me through that?"

Beau climbed onto the bed and sat on her knees. "So obviously, it wasn't me back in the nineties. I was just a little girl."

"Right."

"But the same way you're picking up the case from your mother, I picked up the case from my father. He was the original killer."

Sam nodded. "Okay. You lived in Montreal until you were fifteen, right?"

"Yeah."

"So. Your dad... the Goodnight Man... traveled back and forth across the border multiple times. Six hundred miles here and another six hundred back. Just to kill women."

Beau bit her lip and nodded solemnly.

"Do you remember introducing me to your dad?"

"Sure."

"The economics professor."

"Mm-hmm."

"Okay. So he was secretly killing women down here in Brooklyn when you were a kid. So now you're taking up his mantle."

Beau nodded. "Yeah."

"Why?"

"Because... uh." She scanned the room for inspiration. "To, um, make sure he's not forgotten?"

Sam sat up and pushed the blankets away. She suddenly didn't care about her mother and Jane being in the apartment. There were only so many times she could rebuff this beautiful woman's advances. She opened the bottom drawer of her nightstand, retrieved a pair of play handcuffs, and turned to face Beau.

"Good enough for me. Beau Martin, you're under arrest."

Beau stuck out her arms. Sam closed the cuffs around her wrists with a loud snap, then pushed her down onto the mattress. She threw a leg over Beau's hip and settled her weight on her.

"You realize this is more than a little twisted, right?" she said. "We play a lot of borderline offensive games, but you're talking about real victims, and you're accusing your father of truly horrific things."

Beau nodded. "I know. Really poor taste all around. But I thought of it in the shower and I couldn't resist. Don't hold it against me."

"I'll hold *something* against you," Sam said, leaning down to kiss Beau's neck. She kissed until Beau was squirming, and she ran her hands down her flanks, teasing the spots she knew were the most sensitive. "And," she said as she moved down to kiss Beau's chest, "the long-distance theory isn't the craziest thing people have come up with. There are people who sincerely believe he's a ghost."

Beau sighed. She lifted her cuffed hands over her head and arched her back to offer her breasts to Sam. "Or he can turn invisible."

Sam kissed Beau through her tank top. "Or he's using magic to get in and out."

Beau laughed. She bent her knees and squeezed Sam's hips, trying to pull her lower. "Well. You know what Penn Jillette says about magic."

"Oh, you are the mistress of dirty talk." She hovered her lips over Beau's stomach. "What does he say?"

"The only secret to doing a magic trick is putting in more work than any reasonable person would ever think is worthwhile."

"Work harder, not smarter."

Beau shrugged. "Basically." She moved her legs apart. "But you, work *lower*."

Sam scooted down on the bed and settled between Beau's legs. Beau sighed happily and settled back against the pillows.

A minute or so later, Sam's head popped back up. "Holy shit."

Beau grinned. "Yeah, baby, still blowing you away with how good I taste?" She tried to push Sam's head back down with her hands. "Keep going, I'm almost there."

"No, wait, stop."

Sam pulled away from her and got out of bed. She started to pace, drawing a line between the nightstand and the bathroom door turning around and walking back. Beau sat up and watched her, the disappointment on her face transitioning to concern.

"What's wrong? What happened?"

"Nothing," Sam muttered. "I don't know. Maybe nothing. Maybe...maybe not." She stopped pacing and looked at Beau. "I have to go back to work."

Beau said, "Now? It's ten o'clock."

"I know, babe." Sam was already gathering her clothes. "I'm sorry. For running out and for getting things started and not finishing. But I think... I'm thinking of something. And it might be big. But I have to check the case files." She cupped Beau's face and kissed her long and hard. "I'll make up for it later. I promise."

Beau held up her hands, revealing she was still cuffed.

"Oh right. Shit." Sam went to her nightstand, retrieved the keys, and let her out. "That could've been embarrassing."

"Good luck," Beau said.

"Thanks, baby." She kissed her again, then fled.

Miriam was at her station in front of the door. She looked up as Sam came out of the bedroom, sitting up straighter when she saw she was fully dressed.

"What happened?"

"Nothing. I have to go into the station."

Miriam stood. "Don't give me the bullshit about staying put. If something is breaking, I want to be there."

Sam started to argue. But if she was right, then Jane and Beau weren't likely to be in any immediate danger. And it would be nice to have her mother's eyes on the files when she tried to put the theory into words.

"Fine," she said. "You can come."

Miriam went to the couch to get her shoes. She bent down, whispered something to Jane, and then hurried to the door where Sam was waiting.

"So what is it?" Miriam asked. "New body?"

"No," Sam said. "If I'm right, we may be making sure the last one actually *is* the last one."

"Sorry, I still don't understand what Penn and Teller have to do with any of this."

Sam sighed. "It's not really *them*, it's just a quote about how magic works." They were walking up the stairs at the station. The elevators apparently shut down every night at nine, something Sam vaguely remembered from her days on the night shift and burning the midnight oil. "Penn said that the actual secret of being a magician is putting in more work than any reasonable person would think was worthwhile. They aren't really magic, they're just willing to spend three thousand hours practicing how to shuffle cards in a certain way."

Miriam said, "I suppose."

"Back in the day, you had a joke theory that the Goodnight Man was a ghost. What if he just spends an unreasonable amount of time preparing so it looks like he's invisible?"

Only half the desks in the bullpen were occupied by night shift detectives. Miriam ignore them and went to the desk she'd commandeered and turned on the computer. The whiteboard still displayed the victims and listed their information.

"What exactly are you looking for?" Miriam asked.

"Hiding places," Sam said. "Thirty years ago, you confirmed he found a place to hide in Jane's apartment. A nook that even she didn't even know existed. But somehow the killer did? And he left behind a shoeprint. It was the only physical evidence he *ever* left behind. Why? Because he only had one day to prepare. And because he was only there for a few hours. Every other victim, he had more time. He designed it that way. He's a rat. He would take what he needed and then just sit in the dark and wait. For days, if he had to."

"You think he hunted the others?"

"It would explain why he was never on security cameras the night the women were killed. Do me a favor and put together a timeline?" She pointed at Ainsworth's desk. "How many days or weeks were between all the original murders? We might be able to figure out how long he was hiding before he made his move."

Miriam took Ainsworth's seat and turned on the computer. "So your theory is that he chose his victim, then found a place to hide in her building—"

"Or right in her apartment, like with Jane."

"—and when he struck, he cleaned up his nest and snuck out when no one was looking."

"It's a lead no one has followed yet. We've spent thirty years looking all over Brooklyn for this son of a bitch. We never considered he was right under our noses the whole time. The shitty part is, even if we somehow confirm this, it won't help us find him. Unless he's still holed up in Julia Ramsey's apartment waiting to clean up after himself, he might already be hiding out in the building of his next victim."

Miriam suddenly stood up. Sam looked over at her.

"He's not still in Ramsey's building," Sam said. "I called to have some uniforms sent over when I first came up with the theory. They texted me, he's not there."

"No, no," Miriam said. "He would have already moved on to the next victim."

Sam said, "Well, fat lot of good that does us."

"It's me."

"What?"

"Well I mean, it's, me and Jane." Miriam said, "That's why he didn't call. He wanted to catch us off-guard. Is the security detail still watching our house?"

"I pulled them to follow you around with Beau. The captain decided there was no reason to send them back." Sam stood up so quickly she nearly knocked over her chair. "The son of a bitch is at your house."

"To finish the job he started thirty-three years ago."

Sam was already moving toward the elevator. "Let's go make sure he doesn't get the chance."

CHAPTER TWENTY

"BY THE time we get there," Sam said, "I want to know every hiding place he could possibly be using. Every closet, every crawlspace, any cupboards that might be big enough to hold a full-grown man."

Miriam was hanging onto the grab handle over her window as Sam sped through traffic. A strobing red light on her dashboard alerted other drivers to make way for her, but she was still forced to weave between lanes to avoided rear-ending people who had nowhere to go. Sam had called dispatch about the officers who were supposed to be watching Miriam and Jane's house, but they hadn't reported any suspicious behavior.

"Maybe he got there before they were in place," Sam said.

"He would have to be a patient motherfucker."

"I think we've prove that," Sam said. "However long he's been hiding in your walls, I'm just glad we got you and Jane out of there before he could do anything."

Miriam didn't react to Sam using Jane's name so casually. Instead, she said, "You're not planning to ambush the guy on your own."

"We'll never have a better idea where he is. The only reason there's not a fleet of squad cars behind me is because I don't want to spook him."

Miriam said, "If you go in there like a one-woman SWAT team, he'll just escape out the back door or the garage or the window. There are only two of us. We can't cover every possible exit. And if anyone is going to get lucky, it's this bastard."

"So what do you suggest?"

"You're going to dismiss it."

"Probably." Sam looked at her warily. It clicked as soon as she saw the look in her mother's eyes. "I am not going to use you as—"

"You use me as bait."

"Damn it, Mom," Sam muttered. "Out of the question."

Miriam said, "We let him think he has the upper hand. Let him get cocky. When he creeps out of his hidey-hole, you pounce."

"You really think he'll attack you while I'm there?"

"You'll pretend to leave."

Sam sighed and shook her head. "This is absolutely out of the question."

"You wanted my help with the case," Miriam said, "but you wouldn't let me actually go to the station to help. Well, this is the other way I can be of service."

"If he's too quick or too strong, if I'm too late—"

Miriam snapped, "*I was too late.*"

The silence hung between them. Miriam was breathing hard and seemed to be on the verge of either tears or screaming. Sam kept her eyes straight ahead and listened to each sharp inhale, the following ragged exhale, and waited for her mother to compose herself. Finally, Miriam took one last deep breath and let it out calmly.

"I decided not to protect Jane. And my punishment for that was walking into her apartment and seeing her splayed out like a corpse. For a... f-for a minute... just one minute, at most, I thought she was dead. And it was my fault. I didn't even love her yet, I don't think. Not the way I would come to love her. But the thought of living in a world without her in it was... so... dark. You think it was easy walking away from our life? I shared a bedroom with my ex-husband to make life easy for you, damn it. But that minute. That one minute when I thought Jane was gone forever, part of me wanted to die, too. I never felt that for your father. I'd only ever come close to feeling that way about you. So when I finally accepted I had to make a choice, I... I may have made the wrong one. I should have fought harder for a compromise. But I don't regret staying with Jane."

She was quiet again for a long time. Sam imagined herself in the same situation, walking into a room and seeing Beau displayed like a serial killer's victim. Her brain crashed the image before it could fully form, her arms going stiff and her fingers tightening on the steering wheel so tightly she was afraid she wouldn't be able to let go.

"God, that was a long minute," Miriam finally said.

"I get it," Sam said quietly.

Miriam sniffed and swiped quickly at her eyes. "I need to do this. I need to face this fucker down. For Jane."

"You think she wants you putting your life at risk to prove a point?" Sam said.

"Absolutely not. This isn't about her. It's about me. About what I need."

Sam chewed the inside of her cheek. She had to admit that she felt the same way. It was part of her reasoning for not calling backup. She blamed the Cozy Killer or the Goodnight Man, whatever the fuck he wanted to be called, for destroying her family. She didn't want to just sit on the sidelines while a bunch of Weehawken uniforms took down the man who had taken her mother from her.

"I know the danger," Miriam said. "I used to be you, remember. I'm sixty-seven, not some grandma. I know what position I'm putting myself in."

Sam surrendered. "Fine. We'll do it your way. But if you die, I'm telling Jane it was your stupid-ass idea."

Miriam chuckled. "Oh, she'll know. She won't blame you."

"I might," Sam muttered.

They used the rest of the drive to work out the finer details of the plan. Sam fought back a wave of anxiety as she pulled onto her mother's street. She parked five houses away so the car wouldn't be directly in front of the curb. If the killer was there, if he had been monitoring the parked cars, he would notice if she was that obvious. They eyed the dark windows on either side of the front door, looking for signs of disturbance that would prove their theory. Sam unfastened her seatbelt and looked at her mother.

"Last chance to back out."

"No." Miriam opened the door. "This ends tonight."

They went up the front walk together. Miriam fished out her keys, fumbling with them on the dark porch.

"Jane always insists on leaving the porch light on all night," she said. "But when the bulb burns out, who is the one climbing up the damn ladder to change it, hm?"

Sam ignored the complaining and scanned the neighborhood. Nice. Quiet. Calm. She tried to imagine herself living in a place like this. Car at the curb. Neighbors far enough away they couldn't be heard through the walls. A backyard for grilling. She'd have to mow, or hire someone to mow, and both options seemed like a huge pain. But Beau seemed to have her heart set on it. Would it really be such a bad tradeoff, a life here to make Beau happy...?

Miriam opened the door and reached inside to turn on the hallway light. She looked back at Sam, who gave her a nod. Miriam stepped into the house. Sam followed.

"This is fucking reckless," Sam said.

"I'm not going to spend my life hiding like a mouse, Samantha," Miriam snapped. "I'm letting you keep Jane in custody~"

"*Protective* custody!"

"~but I'm not going to be babysat like some civilian. I've had enough of that. I'm spending the night in my own house, in my own bed."

Sam said, "You're being ridiculous. It's only until we catch the son of a bitch~"

"Oh please, you haven't been able to catch him in thirty-three years. You *really* think that's going to change now?" She tossed her jacket across the back of the couch. "Go home, Sammy. Your services are no longer required."

Sam held her hands up. "Fine. You know what, *fine*. Have it your way. Get fucking murdered, see if I give a shit."

She turned around and stormed from the house, slamming the door behind her. She drew her gun as soon as she was outside, jumping the porch railing to land on the grass next to the walkway. According to the original case file, the killer had attacked Jane immediately after she got home. In this case, she thought he might wait a few minutes to be sure that Sam had gone before making his move. She still had to behave as if seconds counted.

Miriam had told her to go around the east side of the house, quietly through the fence gate, into the backyard. Sam stayed low, making sure to duck below any windows she passed. She tried not to think about what was going on inside. The plan was for Miriam to act like everything was normal. She would check the fridge for any leftovers that needed to be thrown out. She would set the automatic coffeemaker in the kitchen so she'd have fresh brew in the morning. The dog was staying with friends, but she was going to empty and wash the food and water dishes so they'd be fresh when he got home.

Then she would go upstairs.

Sam believed that would be where the killer was waiting. Convenient, easy access to the main bathroom, and more hiding places. Miriam had listed four possibilities off the top of her head. Coat closet. Jane's office. Main bedroom closet. Attic access. Sam didn't think he would risk hiding out on the ground floor and risk being heard on the stairs. He would be upstairs, as close to the bedroom as possible. That meant the coat closet.

Sam pressed her shoulder to the wall next to the back door. Miriam had been tasked with making sure it was unlocked for her. When the kitchen light went off, it would be Sam's signal to come in. She flexed her grip on the gun, wet her lips, and waited. She refused to check her watch, refused to count the seconds. It would make sense if Miriam didn't rush. Her routine was supposed to look normal, unhurried, casual. Rushing would look suspicious.

The light stayed on. Sam worked her jaw, twisting her neck to look up toward the window for signs of movement. She tapped her foot on the grass, flexed her grip on her gun. She finally moved toward the door and tried the knob. It remained firm. She squeezed harder, put more strength into the twist, but it remained steadfastly locked.

Her heart skipped a handful of beats, then made up for it by going triple-time. She jiggled the knob but it was now very clear that it was locked.

"Oh, you stupid stubborn bitch."

Miriam had no interest in being bait, in playing the damsel in distress. She went along with the part of Sam's plan that she agreed with. The part that got her into the house on her own. But that was where the game ended. She wasn't going to go through the motions of getting ready for bed. She wouldn't give the bastard the satisfaction of thinking he'd outsmarted her. As soon as Sam was outside, Miriam locked and bolstered the front door.

She went to the foot of the stairs and looked up at the dark second floor landing. She put her hand on the railing and started up. She didn't have long before Sam realized the plan had changed. She climbed carefully. She wasn't an old woman, but her knees hadn't gotten the memo. She wasn't going to gain anything by rushing just to have the dumb joints give out on her when she needed them to work right. When she reached the top, she looked toward the hall coat closet. She turned to face it fully.

"You must think you're pretty goddamn clever," she said, raising her voice to be heard through the wall. "We gave you so much fucking credit. Time travel. Ghost. Invisible. But you were just a pathetic little boy playing hide and seek the whole time. Cowering like a rat in the shadows. How long have you been squatting here in my house? Pissing and shitting in plastic bags. Might as well give it up now. You've waited thirty-three years for this. Let's get it over with."

She waited. A second later, the closet door slowly swung out. Miriam was surprised by the jolt of fear that went through her. It looked like something straight out of a horror movie. The space beyond the door was solid black, and a piece of the darkness peeled off and unfolded itself into the shape of a man. Black turtleneck, black jeans, a ski mask, and goggles that covered his eyes. Exactly like what Jane had reported.

"Well," Miriam said under her breath. "There you are."

His shoulders rose and fell with his breathing.

"You just gonna stand there, Cozy Killer?"

He grunted and lunged forward. Miriam braced herself and brought both fists up. Something smashed against the front door downstairs. She ignored it, keeping her focus on the masked man coming toward her. He'd kept his right hand near his hip since he'd emerged from the closet but now he brought it up to reveal a syringe. Miriam had anticipated that. He brandished it like a knife, swinging his arm out in a wide arc. Miriam stepped to her left, grabbed his wrist, and stomped her foot down on his ankle. He crumpled and let out a yelp, falling so hard and fast that he didn't have a chance to brace himself. His head smacked against the drywall and rebounded, and then he was on his knees.

"Gotta admit," Miriam said, annoyed at how out of breath she was, "I'm a little disappointed."

He put his free hand against the wall and, with a howl, shoved backward. Miriam was caught off-balance, his shoulder pushing into the center of her chest. They both tumbled, hitting the ground hard enough that the wind was knocked out of her. He pulled his arm free, rolled away, and got to his feet. Miriam didn't have time to formulate a plan so she just did the first stupid thing that came to mind.

She rolled at him, bowling into his legs. He fell forward and grabbed for the banister, but his fingers slipped off the wood and he hit the stairs at just the right angle to let gravity take over. He tumbled headfirst down, grasping at the railing in a useless attempt to slow his fall.

The front door exploded open just as he hit the ground. Sam came into the house, gun already drawn. She aimed it at the man laying sprawled at her feet.

"Mom?" Sam shouted, keeping her eye on the killer.

"Up here." Miriam had found the strength to rise to her knees, but she doubted she could get much further. She slumped against the railing. "I changed the plan a little."

"I noticed," Sam said. "You okay?"

"I'll live."

Sam nudged the man with her foot. "Hands open. Arms out to the sides. Now."

He complied slowly. Sam crouched, keeping her gun trained on him with one hand as the other pinched his mask and pulled it up to reveal his face.

"Uh. Mom..."

Sam's body was blocking her from seeing what the man looked like. "What's wrong?"

Sam stood up and stepped out of the way so Miriam could see for herself. The man had a bloody nose, and he was still wearing the goggles, but enough of his face was revealed that they could clearly see he couldn't have been more than mid-twenties.

"You've got to be fucking kidding me," Miriam grunted. "He's a fucking copycat."

On the floor, arms spread wide in surrender, the second Goodnight Man started to laugh.

EMTs determined Miriam was fine save for bruised knees and a contusion on the back of her head. The man they arrested had fared much worse: a broken collarbone and a fracture above his eye socket. He was treated at the scene before he was allowed to be taken into custody. Sam rode in the squad car that took him back to Brooklyn, to the 21st Precinct, where he was officially booked. Miriam was allowed to follow in Sam's car, mostly because Sam knew it would be pointless to try stopping her.

It was almost two in the morning when Sam and Nelson Ainsworth walked into the interrogation room where the killer had been handcuffed to the table.

"Hi, Richard Beswick," Sam said as she sat down across from him. "Do you go by Richard? Rick? Dick? What do you like?"

He lifted his chin defiantly. "I like the Goodnight Man."

"That's adorable, Dicky." She opened the file and scanned the printout she'd gotten when they ran his prints. "Petty larceny, vandalism. Stole a car. Quite an escalation from that to killing someone."

"Olympic-level leaping," Ainsworth agreed.

"Did you make that leap all by yourself, Dicky? Or did someone give you a push? Like a little shove from the nest from a bigger bird."

He kept staring at her. "I told you that's not my name. I'm the Goodnight Man."

"No." Sam shook her head. "The Goodnight Man killed six women and then found a rock to hide under for thirty years. You, on the other hand, killed *one* person and got caught immediately because he couldn't handle a woman who is almost seventy. My mom kicked your ass, bro."

He worked his jaw and finally looked away from her.

"I've never regretted not having kids," Sam said, "but it would almost have been worth it just so we could tell the press you were taken out by a grandmother. That would've been a nice little touch, don't you think, Nelson?"

"Kind of poetic."

"I *am* the Goodnight Man."

Sam clucked her tongue and shook her head. "No, man. You're not even worthy of the name Cozy Killer."

He smiled. "I am the true successor to the title. It's my destiny."

"Why don't you tell us who passed down the title and we'll go confirm that with him?"

Beswick closed his eyes and hummed softly. "It doesn't matter. I'll plead guilty. The date of my death will be scheduled and carried out by the justice system."

Ainsworth said, "New York doesn't have the death penalty."

Beswick opened his eyes and looked at him, confused. "Of

course it does."

"Abolished in..." He looked at Sam.

"Oh, it's been at least twenty years," she said.

Beswick looked legitimately confused, but he shook it off. "It doesn't matter. Prison is a dangerous place. I will die quickly enough. And when that happens, the Goodnight Man will be passed to the next vessel." He laughed and met Sam's eye. "You'll never catch him because *he* cannot be caught."

Dread settled in Sam's mind, but not the kind he intended. "So. You're saying the person who committed the other murders, back in the nineties. He's dead."

"That person was merely a tool. Like I am. Unimportant in the grand scheme of things."

"Fuck," Sam whispered. She leaned forward. "Did you murder Julia Ramsey?"

"I was the tool with which the Goodnight Man killed her, yes."

She pushed away from the table. "Good enough for me. Save the rest of the mythology for the psych evaluation."

Ainsworth followed her out of the room. "You're just going to leave it at that?"

"We're going to have to hand him over to psych sooner or later. No sense in wasting our time with him. We've already got the only piece of information that matters from him."

"We did?" He looked back at the door. "Was I there for it?"

Sam said, "He claims he inherited this killer... demon or spirit or whatever."

"You don't believe he's actually possessed."

"Of course not," Sam snapped. "But that's just the narrative his delusion whipped up for him. Whatever the real story, there's just one kernel of truth in it. The original killer is dead. Whether that happened recently or thirty years ago, it doesn't matter. He's dead. And that means the six women he killed will never get justice."

She slapped Beswick's file against Ainsworth's chest and walked off.

"The case is closed, Nelson. The motherfucker got away with it after all."

"It can't just end like that," he shouted after her.

Sam shook her head and held her hands out to the side, symbolically letting go. "Just the way the story goes."

CHAPTER TWENTY-ONE

RICHARD JAMES Beswick, 38, lived in a single bedroom apartment over a pizza parlor on Coffey Street. He was currently employed as a barback at a dive nearby. Both addresses were less than half a mile from where Julia Ramsey worked. Dawn was just breaking when Sam joined a crime scene unit at the apartment to go through Beswick's things to lock up their case against him. Miriam had politely requested to come along, but gave up quickly when Sam said no. It was a small apartment, and they didn't want too many people tramping around inside until it had been cleared.

The main item of interest they uncovered in the apartment was a stack of journals written by someone named Charles Beswick. A uniformed officer handed her the black composition book when he found it. The empty space on the cover had been labeled "Early 1991-199_." She flipped to the first page and gave her eyes a few seconds to adjust to the jagged combination of print and cursive writing that was crammed into every line.

"I felt HIM again today," the journal began. "Whispering in my head coming out of the cracks and the shadows and saying things and telling me to do things. I just want HIM to be quiet. I know how I can make HIM quiet. It would be easy. But I don't want to. But when I see them, I know why HE wants it. The lost souls, the forgotten and ignored, the pained ones. Life is their Hell and HE grants them peace. I can see the pain in their faces. Every day. Worse and worse and it's never going to get better. It's a KINDNESS what HE wants me to do to them, even if they don't understand it and even if the police don't understand it. Sleep and rest. IS A GIFT. I wish I could receive. But I give it to them. HIS LOST SOULS. Poor left behind children. HE wants to take away the pain and let them sleep and I will be HIS tool. I wish I could keep the gift for myself. I wish I could have the PEACE but HE tells me no no no no NO no NO no. It's not for me. I can't sleep. The sleep is for those who have earned it. For those precious souls~"

Sam closed the book. "Jesus H. Christ..."

A nearby officer glanced over at her. "*Silence of the Lambs* or *Se7en?*"

"Hard to say," she said. "This guy might be his own unique brand of scary." She closed the notebook and slipped it into an evidence bag. "I'll let someone else read that and take the nightmares off my hands. Do you have everything under control here?"

"Yeah. Officer Schoeneman has some more information for you. He's in the living room."

"I'll grab it on my way out."

"Where are you going?"

She sighed. "I have to deal with next of kin."

"I didn't think they'd found anyone yet."

"Not his," she said.

He was dead. Miriam heard the words, and part of her had always known the possibility existed, but she was still stunned by the confirmation. She finally knew his name. She could finally look at a picture of the bastard. But it didn't matter. None of their investigations or their digging had ever mattered because he'd been gone. Wiped off the face of the planet. According to Sam, he had been hit by a delivery truck while crossing the street six days after breaking into Jane's apartment. The man she'd spent thirty-three years obsessing over, who had occupied every spare thought, the man who had inadvertently destroyed her entire life and forced her to rebuild.

He was gone.

She was aware that her hand was being squeezed. She looked down and saw Jane was holding it between both of hers. While Sam had been at work, Miriam had gone back to Sam's apartment. She needed to confess to Jane about what she'd done, the risk she'd taken. Jane was furious, horrified, grateful, relieved, and then simply angry when she heard about what had happened at their house. But her wave of emotion ended with her clutching Miriam in a tight, tearful hug and then giving her a long, lingering kiss. Miriam knew the anger would take a while to fade completely, but the kiss was proof they would make it through all right given time.

Sam was standing in front of them, having reported everything they knew so far about Richard Beswick and his father, Charles.

"The father kept an exhaustive journal detailing his possession by an entity called 'the Goodnight Man,'" Sam explained. "He claimed he was giving his victims a peaceful escape from a bad world. All that time we thought he was just sensitive about not getting to use the name he chose. He really just hated the idea of being called a killer. That's what set him off and made him break his silence. He thought he was just putting them to bed. I assume that's also why he didn't follow through with killing Jane. She wasn't one of his, whatever, 'lost souls.'"

Miriam looked at Jane, who was looking down at her fidgeting fingers as she processed that information.

"And then one day when he was crossing the street..." Sam shrugged and shook her head. "He left behind a wife and kid, and a safe in the back of his closet that contained all his writings. The wife died earlier this year, and the son found it while he was cleaning out the house. He started reading the journals and I guess... I guess he suffered from the same delusions his father had."

"So this is it?" Jane asked. "Those original files are just marked as closed?"

"They *are* closed," Sam said with sympathy. "We know who killed those women. Even if we can't bring him to justice."

Miriam said, "And it's not like he's been running around scot-free laughing behind our backs. That's something, I suppose."

"Not much, but yeah."

Jane said, "So what happens now?"

Sam ran her hands through her hair. "Now? He gets a psych evaluation, talks about how he's possessed by a demon, and probably gets declared unfit to stand trial. He'll be admitted to a state hospital for treatment."

"Treatment," Miriam said under her breath, then shook her

head.

"The important thing," Sam said, "is that we stopped him from killing anyone else. That's what we need to be focused on. This is a win."

Jane nodded. "That is true."

"I suppose," Miriam agreed.

"Does this mean we're free to actually go home now?" Jane asked.

"Actually, your home is still a crime scene. You're more than welcome to stay here as long~"

Miriam shook her head. "We've imposed long enough." She stood up and offered Jane her hand. "We agreed to stay here because there was a chance a killer would hunt us down. Now that the threat has been dealt with, we can stay with friends."

Jane allowed herself to be helped up. "What friends?"

"Katherine and Hillary."

"You can't stand them."

"It'll just be for a night or two," Miriam said. "Besides, they have a full-on guest room. With a bed and its own bathroom."

Sam added, "And anywhere would be less awkward than staying here longer than necessary."

Miriam said, "I wasn't~"

"It's okay." Sam held up a hand to stop her. "Awkward isn't bad. Awkward just means we have a lot of work left to do. It's fine."

Miriam nodded. She stepped forward and, after a brief hesitation, held out her hand. "Thank you, Samantha. It took a lot of strength to come to me with this. I don't know if I would've been able to reach out to you if our positions had been reversed."

Sam took her mother's hand. "I appreciate that."

She helped them pack their belongings, then spent the entire walk down to the garage arguing about whether Sam would drive them to their friends' house. They eventually settled on Sam paying for the Lyft, and she waited with them on the sidewalk until it arrived and took them away. She watched until the car rounded the corner and finally went back upstairs.

Beau was in the bedroom, sitting in the armchair next to the closet. "How'd it go?"

Sam shrugged. "I don't know. I think interactions with my mother require several hours of therapy before I can assess how they went. But good, I think. We shook hands. We were grown-ups about it."

"Good. I'm proud of you." She stood and went to Sam. She hugged her, then kissed her softly on the lips. "Sorry if it seemed like I was hiding back here..."

"You were giving us space. I appreciate it."

Beau nodded. "I'm glad it worked out. Are they staying here tonight?"

"With friends."

"Good." She flinched. "I mean. Not 'good,' but~ you know what I mean."

Sam grinned. "Yeah, I understand completely. Just you and me, kid."

"Just the way I like it."

"Mm-hmm." She kissed Beau's cheek. "I love you."

"Love you too." She stepped back. "I know your clock is all messed up because you've been awake for, what, two days straight at this point? What meal is next on your food clock?"

Sam grunted. "God, I don't even know." She hadn't even been hungry until Beau brought it up. Now her stomach had been reminded that food existed, and it was demanding satisfaction. "Let's just go out somewhere. Whatever sounds good to you, I'll find something that appeals."

Beau nodded and went to the closet so she could change. "We'll go to Mara's. They've got a breakfast and lunch menu."

Sam watched as Beau traded her nightshirt for a button-down.

"I'll move to the suburbs."

Beau stopped buttoning half-way and turned to look at her. "What?"

Sam shrugged. "It's... nothing. I don't know. I love the city. But you don't, and if you would feel more comfortable living somewhere else, that's all I need to know. We can find a place out of the city."

Beau walked to her. "I shouldn't have threatened to leave you. That was shitty of me. And I didn't mean it. And if that's in any way affecting your change of heart, please know~"

"Sh," Sam said. "I know. We were pissed off and fighting. I know you didn't mean it." Beau's eyes had filled with tears, so Sam leaned in and kissed her cheek. "My mother fought a serial killer. Well, attempted serial killer. And she told me about... the night she found

Jane thirty years ago. I couldn't help thinking about how it would feel to walk into our apartment and see you like that. And I kept thinking... it's just a fucking apartment. It's just a fucking *house*. I want you to live somewhere that makes you happy."

"Wherever I live with you makes me happy," Beau said.

"Same. Even if it means mowing lawns and mortgages."

Beau put her hands on Sam's shoulders. "And kids with lemonade stands in the summer."

"Sorry, is that a pro or con?"

"You'll love it." She kissed Sam. "Thank you."

Sam nodded. "It doesn't matter how much time we have together. It won't feel like enough. I'm not going to spend it fighting if I can compromise instead."

"I like that plan."

Sam slipped her hand under Beau's half-buttoned shirt, stroking her hip. Beau looked down as she was guided toward the bed.

"I thought you were hungry," she said.

"I can still work up more of an appetite."

Beau grinned and ran her hands down Sam's chest. "So who are we? Teacher and parent of a problem student?"

Sam said, "How about... you're Beau, gym manager, and I'm her wife, Samantha."

"A brilliant and beautiful cop?" Beau said.

"Something like that."

Beau nodded and leaned in. "I think this will be my favorite," she said against Sam's lips, pulling her down onto their bed.

Sam's prediction about Richard Beswick's fate turned out to be extremely accurate. He was declared non compos mentis and transferred to the custody of a state facility where he could get the help he required. Miriam told Sam that it was still justice, that she was satisfied, but Sam could tell she was still frustrated with the way the case had resolved. They'd started meeting up twice a week - Tuesdays and Thursdays - to talk over coffee or dinner. Some days they barely said anything of consequence, other days they nearly caused a scene by crying or making an outburst.

It was during one of their dinners that Sam realized there *was* a way they could still get the closure they needed.

"Beswick might be getting treatment," she said, "and his father may have died before he paid for any of his crimes. But there's still one asshole in the middle of all this we can take our anger out on."

So that weekend, they took a trip to see Sam's father, Miriam's ex-husband, and the man whose lies had kept them apart for almost Sam's entire life.

Sam kept in vague contact with her father through birthday dinners and the occasional holiday get-together neither of them were particularly interested in. Sam's stepmother, Tracy, insisted on inviting her to anything that felt vaguely mandatory. "Come on, it's Father's Day!" or "It's Christmas, you have to at least drop by and pick up your presents!" It was an unspoken rule that Beau was *not* invited to these meetings, not that Sam would have subjected her to them anyway. So she suffered through them, getting out as quickly as possible, and prayed an asteroid would hit the city before the next one rolled around.

She drove to his apartment and led her mother to the elevator. "Any idea what you're going to say when you see him again?" Sam asked.

"You would've thought I'd come up with something on the drive over," Miriam said. "Or in the past thirty-three years. But honestly, the idea of wasting any thought on that man... And that was *before* I found out the shit he was pulling to keep us apart. Consider us all lucky if I don't just punch him and walk away."

"Hell, you do that and I get to see it, I'll call it a best case scenario. Let's just play it by ear."

They rode up to the fourth floor. Sam told Miriam the apartment number and let her lead the way. As much as Jeremy had hurt her, she felt her mother's grievance was much greater. They stopped in front of the door and Miriam shook her shoulders as if she was really about to throw a punch.

"You're not really going to hit him, aren't you?" Sam said.

"No. Maybe. I haven't thought it through yet."

She brought her hand up, knocked, and then took a step back. Out of punching distance. After a few seconds, they heard a man cough inside the apartment. Then the door swung open and Jeremy stepped out. Sam had seen him over the years, so he'd aged gradually. She tried to see him as Miriam would, with three decades of age happening all at once. A new beard, hair receding, then both going gray, the cheeks becoming a bit more sunken.

He saw Miriam first, and it was clear he didn't immediately recognize her. Only when his gaze shifted to Sam did he seem to make the connection, and he looked quickly back to Miriam. His eyes widened and he clenched his jaw. Sam saw his hand tighten on the door.

"Hi, Dad," Sam said. "Remember her?"

"Miriam," he said.

She raised an eyebrow. "Wow, first try. I would've bet money you'd fumble that."

He looked between them. "So you two are talking again?"

"Yeah," Sam said. "A little pissed off it took this long for us to compare notes. But better late than never, I guess."

"Did you keep the letters?" Miriam asked, surprising both Miriam and Jeremy.

"What?" he asked.

"The letters I sent my daughter," she said. "Did you keep them? Or did you just throw them in the garbage?"

He sighed. "I..." His hand dropped from the door and he stepped back. "Stay there."

When he was gone, Sam looked at Miriam. Miriam looked back at her and shrugged. "Better late than never," she said.

"Right."

A woman appeared in the doorway. Sam recognized her as Tracy, Jeremy's new wife, but Miriam was able to connect the dots even though they'd never met.

"Hi," she said meekly, folding her hands in front of her. "I'm so sorry for everything--"

"It's his behavior, not yours," Miriam interrupted. "It's not your fault he's a bastard. If you want to make it up to me, keep this in mind. That he was willing to do this shit to his wife and daughter. Think about if that's someone you really want to be tied to until death do you part."

Tracy pressed her lips together in a line, still wringing her hands. The three of them stood together in awkward silence until Jeremy returned with a metal lockbox. He flipped open the lid and took out a stack of envelopes tied together with a piece of twine.

"Unbelievable." Miriam took the stack. "All of them."

"Most, I think." Jeremy at least had the presence of mind to sound sheepish, as if he was fully aware he was in the wrong. "I've...

I've had a lot of time to think over the last few years. And I know what I did was shitty. I wish there was something I could do to make up for it. I hope the letters are a good first step."

"It's true," Tracy said. "He's been talking about how much he regrets lying to you both."

Sam said, "Thanks, Dad. That means literally jack-shit. You could've taken the 'first step' at any point during the last few years but you chose not to. That's years you kept me and Mom apart. Nothing can make up for that. You can earn more money, you can get back trust, but time…? You can't get that back, and I'm not forgiving you for keeping us apart because it would've been an uncomfortable conversation. You did something fucking awful. We're not here to grant you absolution for that."

Jeremy sighed. "At the time… Look, i-it wasn't as accepted at the time. Being that way. A-and I wanted to protect you—"

"Don't bother," Miriam said. "Thank you for the letters. And fuck you for everything else."

She turned and walked away. Sam watched her go, then looked at Jeremy again. "Might as well go ahead and cancel any birthday or Christmas plans you might've had with me. I'm going to have other plans for the next few years."

She turned her back and joined Miriam at the elevator. The apartment door closed quietly just before the elevator arrived and they stepped into the car together.

"I can't believe you didn't punch him," Sam said.

"Did you see those cheeks?" She looked down at her hands. "Probably would've done more damage to my knuckles than I did to him."

Sam chuckled. "True. That's probably true."

In the lobby, Miriam held up the stack of letters. "These are officially yours. I admit, I have no idea what I wrote in them. Most were just random thoughts I happened to have and then sent off. But they're sincere. And they give you an idea of what I was going through back then." She held them out. "I know this doesn't absolve me for not fighting harder, but I'd like it to be a start."

Sam took the letters. There had to be at least sixty of them. "You thought you were respecting my wishes when you gave up," she said. "It might take my brain time to accept that and fully shift to the idea that you weren't at fault, but—"

"Thirty-three years of bad feelings are hard to erase overnight."

"Yeah." Sam tapped the envelopes against her fingers. "But it'll be worth the effort."

Miriam smiled. She put her hands in her pockets. They walked out of the building together. Sam checked the time on her phone.

"Do you want a ride home? I don't have to be at work for another hour."

"No, I'll take a Lyft. I need some time to myself to process seeing him again."

Sam nodded. "I understand."

"Give my love to Beau? Jane's, too?"

"I will." She hesitated, then closed the distance between them and hugged her mother. "I'm sorry I didn't fight harder for us, Mom."

"You were four, as you keep reminding me." Miriam tentatively returned the hug. "We'll be okay. It'll just take time. We can't change the story up to now, so... we just have to change where it goes from here. That will have to be enough."

"I can live with that." Sam stepped back from the hug. "I look forward to reading these."

"Yeah," Miriam said. "Me too. I'll see you soon, Sam."

"See you soon, Mom."

Miriam lifted her hand in an awkward wave, then turned and walked away. Sam watched her go, then took out her phone and started toward her car.

"Floating Rock Fitness, my name is Beau, how may I help you?"

"I'd like to cancel my membership. Your trainer keeps walking in on me in the locker room."

"We take those allegations very seriously, ma'am. We'll need you to come down here so I can handle your complaint personally and we'll fire the trainer immediately."

"No, I'm not complaining. I just wanted to know if next time you could send in the perky blonde with the tattoos instead."

Beau made a horrified sound.

Sam smiled. "I did it. We saw my dad."

"How'd it go?" Beau asked, immediately dropping her teasing tone.

"No one got punched."

"I'm weirdly disappointed."

"Same. But I managed to get the letters my mom sent me when

I was a kid."

Beau whistled. "That's going to be some interesting reading."

"Yeah. Will you be there to hold my hand tonight?"

"Absolutely, love. We'll make a ceremony out of it."

"That sounds perfect."

Beau said, "So what happens now?"

Sam stopped and looked around as if the answer was hidden in the storefronts around her.

"I honestly don't know," she said. "But we've made a lot of progress, Mom and I. I think if we keep it up, we might have a chance of being... some kind of family again."

"I'm so happy for you, babe."

Sam beamed. "Nothing's written in stone yet. But I'm hopeful."

"Then I am, too."

"We'll just have to see where the story goes from here.

ABOUT THE AUTHOR

Geonn Cannon is the author of over sixty novels, including the Riley Parra series which was adapted into an Emmy-nominated webseries by Tello Films. His novel *Can You Hear Me* was adapted into *Static Space*, an award-winning short film. He's also written two tie-in novels for the television series *Stargate SG-1*. He was the first male author to win a Golden Crown Literary Society Award for his novel *Gemini*, and he won a second for *Dogs of War*.

www.ingramcontent.com/pod-product-compliance
Lightning Source LLC
Chambersburg PA
CBHW061305210726
48293CB00003B/1116